I0741976

REFORMING HARRIET
Copyright © 2024 Eileen Putman

This is a work of fiction. Names, characters, places, and incidents are products of the author's imagination or used fictitiously and are not to be construed as real. Any resemblance to actual events, locales, organizations, or persons, living or dead, is entirely coincidental.

All rights reserved. This book or any portion thereof may not be reproduced or used in any manner whatsoever without the express written permission of the publisher except for the use of brief quotations in a book review. For permission requests, please contact the publisher.

Cover Design & Interior Format:
The Killion Group, Inc.

First Edition, 1998
Second Edition, 2014
Third Edition, 2016

Reforming HARRIET

Love IN DISGUISE

EILEEN PUTMAN

Love in Disguise Series

Daring masquerades, with love as the prize

In these tales of Regency intrigue, nothing is as it seems: A street wench masquerades as a debutante to fulfill a rake's wager; an actress pretends to be a vengeful lord's mistress to catch a killer. A noble war hero disguises himself as a much older man to woo an on-the-shelf spinster. An independent widow forces her disapproving business partner to pretend to be her fiancé — and teach her about passion.

All are daring masquerades, with love as the prize.

THE BOOKS:

The Perfect Bride
The Dastardly Duke
A Passionate Performance
Reforming Harriet

www.eileenputman.com

CHAPTER ONE

Spring, 1817

*L*OAF OF LIFE. Elias squinted at the name spelled out in cheerfully crooked letters on a sign above the village bakery. From behind a cracked green door in grave need of paint wafted the odor of spirits — odd for a bakery on a Sunday morning.

Elias trusted his nose. It, more than the lofty title he'd inherited, had made him rich. His nose had an unerring ability to sniff out distinctions among pepper berries, detect the subtle aroma of his favorite cassia plant, and judge which coffee beans would appeal to pallid English tastes. He had parlayed the gift of his nose into an uncanny ability to predict and inspire the culinary tastes of his countrymen.

But while Elias had no difficulty detecting the fumes behind the door, he could not imagine why a bakery smelled like a brewery. Perhaps it was simply of a piece with this ramshackle village. The military had taught him that home was wherever a man could spread a pallet, but Elias certainly had no desire to linger in this dilapidated place. With any luck, his time here would be short.

It was irksome enough that the trip to Worthington — a full two hours from London, even with his coach and four — had been necessary. That his business partner, the late Lord Frederick Worthington, had had the poor judgment to bequeath his share of their business to his spendthrift widow was the one nasty surprise of an otherwise fortuitous partnership.

Elias tried the bakery's door handle, but it did not give. Through the window, Elias could see someone moving about. He knocked firmly.

He could not imagine why Freddy had given his widow his shares, or why the woman's trustees were so rash as to permit her to control her own finances. Speculation had it that the crusty but shrewd Duke of Sidenham — a reputed hermit who preferred his castle on the cliffs of Cornwall to the refinements of town — had dictated the terms of Freddy's will as a condition for betrothing his only daughter to a penniless viscount. Now Freddy's merry widow was fast ruining Elias's carefully constructed enterprise.

Elias had called at Worthington Hall and been informed by a painfully withholding butler that her ladyship was not expected for some hours. Hoping to find someone more helpful, he had walked down the hill toward the village. It was mostly deserted, though he'd spied quite a throng of folk milling about the little church on the hill. Elias had no intention of venturing there. Churches made him uncomfortable — no, that was too mild a word. Indeed, he hoped never to set foot in one again.

And so, he had strolled through the village amid empty shops and shuttered windows until his nose unerringly guided him to this ridiculously named bakery and its pronounced odor.

Elias tapped his foot impatiently. No one had responded to his knock, so he rapped once more. He had no intention of being put off by a tipsy baker. As he weighed whether to give the door a decisive shove, it suddenly swung open — seemingly of its own accord, for no one stood at the threshold. For an uneasy moment Elias imagined himself back on the Peninsula, every sense alert for ambush. He quickly banished that thought, but was nevertheless wary as he bent slightly to clear the top door frame and entered the shop.

"No need to pound," admonished a cheerful voice. "Everyone knows I am here on Sundays. My, you are tall — not that you can help it, of course. Have a petty-patty. Minced veal and cinnamon, though the crust is a bit tough. I fear I worked the dough too long."

Smiling, the woman behind the long, wooden worktable indicated a platter of pastries on a small table by the door.

Elias eyed her suspiciously. The odor of spirits was even more pronounced. The woman must be sheets to the wind.

A red kerchief covered her hair, peasant-like, though some flour-dusted tendrils had escaped to curl wildly about her cheeks. A large dot of flour covered the tip of her nose. The corners of her blue eyes crinkled as she regarded him in a friendly fashion. He could judge little of her age, though he guessed that the voluminous apron she wore hid a figure thickening with the years. A great deal of flour covered her hands and trailed up to her elbows.

She was, quite simply, a mess.

Elias could not abide disorder or disarray. Unkempt women held no appeal for him, though this one might have been presentable enough had she not been pickled and covered in flour. Her bottle-blue eyes held a lively air, and her skin was flushed — from drink he supposed, though perhaps it was due to the energetic fashion in which she was working a thick, shapeless mass on the table with her hands.

"I am seeking someone," he began, surveying the tiny shop and noting with disdain the pastries she'd mentioned. There was nothing from this untidy woman's hands he would risk eating. "Perhaps," he added with little enthusiasm, "you might be of assistance."

Frowning, she blew an errant tendril away from her face. It floated back onto her cheek, and she pushed it away with the back of her hand, transferring a good deal of the flour to her hair and kerchief.

"Possibly," she said. "I know everyone in Worthington. Most are up at the church now. It is just up that path north of the milliner's —"

"I have no desire to visit a church."

"I would be there myself," she said, taking no

notice of his words, "except that I have promised these pastries to Mrs. Gregory today. She has her new in-laws visiting and does so want to impress them. Her petty-patties are quite as good as mine, but she would prefer not to have anything else to worry about, what with Mr. Gregory's temper. Why must some people be so intolerant?"

As if suddenly recalling his presence, she eyed him in dismay. "Oh, dear. I am gossiping to a perfect stranger. Do forgive me."

Elias had no interest in her prattle. He would soon smell like spirits himself if he did not take his leave, and he had no wish to present himself to his new business partner reeking of drink.

He schooled himself to patience. "Perhaps you can tell me where I might find Lady Harriet Worthington at this hour."

She gave him an odd look. "Does she know you, sir?"

"Surely that cannot be your concern." Damned if he would open his budget to a tipsy village maid.

"Very well, then." Her tone was noticeably cooler and her friendly smile vanished. She returned her attention to the shapeless substance on the table, leaving him standing stiffly in the middle of the small shop. She kneaded the mass lightly, then began to roll it out into a long, thin strip.

In this manner passed several silent minutes, as she focused entirely on her dough and he stood there awkwardly.

"Perhaps if I might speak to the proprietor

— your master?" he suggested. A man would understand. A matter of business, Elias would explain, and Lady Harriet's direction would be his instantly, without all this female moodiness.

Removing her hands from the dough, she wiped them on her apron and raised her blue gaze to his. "I have no master," she said evenly. "And that is just the way I like it."

Elias stared at her. "I do not understand."

"'Tis quite simple," she said. "'I am my own mistress."

He frowned. "Do you mean to say that this is *your* establishment?"

"Yes." Her gaze narrowed. "Though I have found that there are those who disapprove of a woman in such a circumstance. I suspect, sir, that you might be counted in that number." With a cool glance of dismissal, she picked up a knife and began to cut the dough into small triangles.

Elias watched, intrigued by the process in spite of himself, as she placed a spoonful of filling from a bowl onto each triangle. Then she folded a thin layer of dough over the top, pinched the edges to seal them, and placed the finished product on a large pan. She repeated the process, seemingly unaware that he was staring at her, until the pan had no more room. Brushing the pastries with a yellowish glaze, she placed the pan into a large oven.

At that point, she turned to a pail of water, plunged her arms in up to their elbows and scrubbed until they were free of flour. Only after she had dried them with a towel did she remove her kerchief, revealing a gleaming mass of auburn hair.

Fascinated at the metamorphosis before him, Elias watched silently as she took off her stained apron, hung it on a hook near the worktable, and turned to face him at last. A smattering of flour still adorned her nose, to rather appealing effect, he decided grudgingly, and without that apron he could see that her figure was not in the least coarse. Rather the opposite. She was slender and decades younger than he had assumed. Close to his own age, in fact.

Crossing her arms, she regarded him with a sharp, clear gaze. He had another realization: She was not at all tipsy.

"Now, sir," she said. "You will be good enough to introduce yourself."

Stung by her authoritative tone, Elias scowled. "And perhaps you will be good enough to remember your manners, miss."

"Indeed, one's manners should always be remembered," she agreed. "They should be the same wherever one is, and with whomever one is speaking. Do you not agree?"

Elias frowned.

"But I have indeed been remiss," she continued. "I have not introduced myself. As I said, I am the proprietress of Loaf of Life, a name that reflects my belief that bread is the very companion of the soul."

Companion of the soul? The woman was obviously an extremist of some sort, Elias decided. He opened his mouth to reply, but she startled him by coming around the table and facing him squarely.

"Bread, sir, is not just flour and leavening," she said. "It symbolizes the very essence of life. People must have a little leavening, or they turn into fossils."

She smiled. "I am Harriet Worthington, though I do not have the *pleasure*" — her emphasis of the word suggested the opposite of its meaning — "of knowing your name."

Elias stared at her. "*Lady* Worthington?"

"I am called Lady Harriet, as I was before my marriage. Since my husband is no longer living, I no longer use his name. I suppose you will think that eccentric."

He could think of no response, nor did she give him time.

"Now you really must introduce yourself, sir, and quickly state your business. I have petty-patties in the oven."

"I am Elias Westwood," he managed. "Freddy's business partner."

She tilted her head and eyed him assessingly. "Ah, Lord Westwood. The man who has sent me so many letters of late."

"Which you did not answer," Elias pointed out.

"I never reply to people who purport to tell me what is best for me." She gave him a considering look. "I believe that one must always keep an open mind, my lord. The man who wrote those letters is as closed as any book."

"I beg your pardon," Elias said, taken aback.

She moved to the little table near the door and

picked up the plate of pastries. "Have a petty-patty," she said. "Perhaps it will improve your symptoms."

"Symptoms?" He frowned.

"A bilious nature can often be soothed by honest food," she said. "Unless, of course, it is a permanent condition."

Though her tone was bland enough, Elias had little trouble detecting her disapproval. To cover his discomposure, he quickly took a pastry and popped it into his mouth, scarcely looking at the thing.

Instantly, a heady mixture of veal seasoned with cinnamon sent an intriguing aroma into his nostrils. A fascinating combination of familiar and exotic hit his palate, and it was no overstatement to say that it propelled his senses into a paroxysm of pleasure. The crust, robust enough to stand up to the meat but delicate and tender as fine French pastry, seemed to melt in his mouth. The meat itself had layer upon layer of bred-to-the-bone flavor that bespoke hours over a smoky fire made with aged wood. The smoke was of mysterious origin — not pine or oak but something distinctly fruity. Mulberry, perhaps. Yes, that was it. The firewood had come from a mulberry tree.

Heaven had not seen meat pies like these. Elias had no words. Indeed, he could only sigh in deep, unadorned delight.

"Is everything satisfactory?" Her tone held a hint of amusement, and he hurriedly swallowed. It took another moment for him to recover from that incomparable morsel. His gaze went greedily to the platter, where several other pies languished. Elias forced his attention back to her and cleared his throat.

"Yes," he managed. "Quite…delicious."

She eyed him steadily. "Perhaps you would care to state the reason for your visit."

It was an effort not to turn toward the platter once more. "Yes," he said.

She waited, but Elias found himself quite unable to think of any words beyond the superlatives that meat pie had summoned.

Her gaze shifted to the oven, then back to him. "You may come for tea this afternoon, my lord," she said briskly. "I have work to do." She turned away.

It took Elias a moment to realize he was being dismissed. He took a deep, steadying breath. Perhaps that was best. After all, the village bakery was scarcely the place to conduct his business. A customer might walk in at any moment.

That sudden realization underscored the strangeness of the situation. A duke's daughter was working in a shop like a common serving girl. Odd business, this. Once more, the heady odor of spirits assailed his nostrils.

"Just exactly what sort of establishment do you run, madam?"

She regarded him with a faint air of puzzlement. "I do not understand."

"The place smells like a brewery," Elias pointed out.

"'Tis the barm." At his blank expression,

she added, "The yeast. I regret that you find it offensive."

"Yeast?"

"I grow my own. In those tubs of ale." She pointed to several dozen large crockery jars, lined neatly along one side of the bakery near the door. "I see that you disapprove. Surely you are not one of Dr. Dauglish's disciples?"

"Who?"

"Dr. Dauglish — a pious soul who has set himself up as an expert on baking. He contends that the unfermented loaf is more wholesome, that fermentation indicates decay and corruption. I gather you have not read his treatises?"

A corrupt loaf of bread. Treatises. This conversation was verging on the ridiculous.

"Madam, I could not care less whether your bread is drunk or sober," Elias declared. "I wish only to settle the business matters between us."

"In that case, come for dinner instead. I keep country hours while in Worthington, so you will wish to be early."

"The invitation was for tea," he pointed out uncharitably.

"Yes, but now I think dinner is best." She opened the oven door, her attention on the steaming meat pies inside. Elias could not help but inhale deeply, savoring the wondrous aroma.

"A man deserves a decent meal now and then," she added. "I sense that your meals have been inadequate. Perhaps that is the source of your biliousness."

Elias knew he must remove himself from this

madhouse before his temper got the best of him. He turned toward the door.

"Good day, my lord," she called after him.

He could not resist a quick look over his shoulder, and saw that her attention was once more on the oven. Furtively, he plucked another pie from the platter near the door and tucked it into his pocket.

It was done quickly, with no one the wiser — he thought.

But the sound of her soft laughter followed him out into the street.

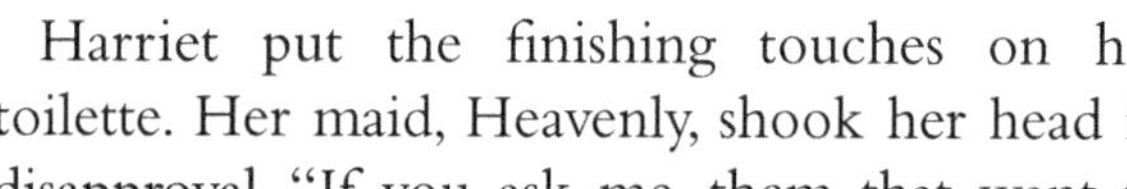

Harriet put the finishing touches on her toilette. Her maid, Heavenly, shook her head in disapproval. "If you ask me, them that want to soften up a man ought to pretty the package a bit."

"I will not cater to that man's twisted notions of proper female behavior — or appearance," Harriet declared. Indeed, she was quite satisfied with her reflection in the mirror. Her hair, normally as unruly as a basket of yarn the cats had got into, was pulled severely off her face and rolled into a tight bun at the nape of her neck. She had deliberately chosen one of her severest dinner gowns, a high-necked black bombazine with long sleeves. She was ready to do battle.

Lord Westwood's sudden visit had been a most unwelcome surprise. For months she had ignored his letters and their increasingly strident tone. She had thought him safely tucked away on one of those Caribbean islands Freddy had spoken about, and the last thing she had expected was to find him in her shop this morning.

"You don't look like yourself, Miss Harriet," Heavenly insisted. "And when a woman don't look like herself, she don't act like herself. And when she don't act like herself, she —"

"Spare me your lectures, Heavenly. I am perfectly myself. Why, who else would I be?" Harriet laughed, though in truth she was a little nervous. Lord Westwood had not been at all as she had expected.

She had imagined a man who wrote such disapproving letters to be a prissy sort, small and bespectacled, balding and pinch-mouthed. But Lord Westwood was large — he'd had to stoop to enter her shop — and much younger than she had envisioned. Indeed, his vigorous appearance put him in the very prime of life. His sun-burnished skin suggested he spent many of his days outdoors, though she could not imagine a man of his hauteur lowering himself to physical labor, even in the service of tending his precious spice plants. Perhaps slaves performed the real work. Alas, she had heard that many of the plantation owners had slaves, despite the reforms forged by Mr. Wilberforce and others.

Lord Westwood looked to be the type of man to use another human being in such a despicable fashion. His eyes, more black than blue, bespoke a censorious, unforgiving nature. Did the man never smile? She doubted that arrogant mouth was capable of mirth. Indeed, Lord Westwood looked to be the very opposite of Freddy, who had certainly enjoyed a good laugh. Had he been laughing, she wondered, when he collapsed and died in the arms of Lady Forth?

"Hand me that shawl, Heavenly, if you please."

"Miss Harriet, you need a shawl like you need another loaf of bread. Any more fabric on those shoulders and you'll suffocate."

Harriet ignored the warning, as she had been ignoring Heavenly's axioms for the majority of her twenty-five years. The shawl gave her something to hold onto, a bit of extra security. For the thought of entertaining Lord Westwood for dinner had, as the day wore on, brought misgivings.

Oh, she would hold her own — she had done so with men for years in her salons and the lively debate they fostered. What bothered her was the prospect of spending an evening in Lord Westwood's forbidding company unrelieved by the distraction of others. Guests were as necessary to a meal as yeast to bread. Harriet rarely dined alone, and never alone with a man.

"I wish I had invited Squire Gibbs. Or the Tanksleys," she said.

"Squire would spend the evening trying to get that mill away from you, and Mrs. Tanksley would go on and on again about why you should marry her son," Heavenly muttered.

"Well, I do not intend to sell the mill, and I certainly do not intend to marry again, so that is that," Harriet declared, rising.

She swept down the grand staircase that had

been one of Freddy's proudest accomplishments. He had ordered the pink marble from Italy and the gold from Africa. Craftsmen from Ireland had applied the gilt to the mahogany railing carved by Thomas Sutterly, one of the country's foremost wood-carvers. Harriet had never seen anything half as grand, even in her father's house. Personally, she thought the carvings of naked cherubs twining up the banister a bit much. But she had always believed in tolerance. If tolerating her husband's eccentricities had sometimes been challenging, she had nevertheless managed to do so. She suspected her dedication to that principle would face yet another test in Lord Westwood.

Downstairs, Harriet checked the table arrangements, though it was unnecessary — Horace always followed her instructions to the letter. Her quick trip into the kitchen was likewise unnecessary, as Celestial had everything well in hand. Heavenly and Celestial had been employed in her father's household for as long as she could remember and had joined her staff upon her marriage to Freddy — though perhaps "joined" was the wrong word for two such strong-willed women. In truth, they had invaded it, giving Horace, Freddy's butler, fits. Freddy had been appalled by the easy familiarity Harriet enjoyed with the twins, but then Freddy had been a bit of a snob, albeit a good-natured one.

Lord Westwood had more than a touch of the snob in him. The man's nose looked positively regal, and it was clear he viewed himself as superior to the rest of the world. He carried himself like the wealthy nabob he was — stiff and forbidding, encased in rather prickly armor. No doubt he lived like a king, with all the trappings his riches could provide.

Wealth, Harriet had found, meant very little in the overall scheme of things. Her father was as rich as Croesus, but her enormous dowry had been woefully unable to purchase wedded bliss. Freddy had piddled away most of her funds on his gilt banisters and gilded women. She had been surprised as anyone to find herself part owner of a West Indies spice business, but what did any of it matter? Money was not the measure of a man — or woman.

Unfortunately, she was doomed to spend an evening with Lord Westwood discussing that very subject, for the man's letters had been rife with talk of profits, loss, capital, investments. Apparently he intended for her to consult him on every business move. The more Harriet thought about it, the more she resented the intrusion upon her time that this evening would mean.

But when Horace ushered Lord Westwood into the drawing room, her resentment faded as she took in his appearance. His height, so noticeable in her tiny shop, ensured that he would dominate any room, large or small. The black superfine tailcoat fit his broad shoulders with nary a hint of padding. His white breeches hugged his well-formed calves like a second skin. A cravat, tied in an unfamiliar but restrained style, framed his chin and set off his dark features to gleaming perfection. His tousled black hair graced his high forehead with natural ease and with none of the dandy's conceit or artificiality. Perhaps the flour had clouded her vision earlier, for she had certainly failed to take note of his considerable physical attributes. Then again, a man's measure was not decided by the package in which it was wrapped, however appealing that might be, Harriet reminded herself sternly.

He smiled politely, revealing a slight indentation in one cheek — could that be a dimple? Harriet was forced to concede that without a disapproving look upon his features, Lord Westwood was devastatingly handsome.

She steeled herself against that unexpected smile. No doubt he intended to charm her into signing over Freddy's part of the business. Well, he would soon learn that she was no easy mark.

"Good evening, Lady Harriet."

"Lord Westwood," she acknowledged, suddenly feeling stiff and unfashionable in her black bombazine. He bowed formally and, at her gesture, seated himself in the chair next to hers. Horace poured out sherry and discreetly left the room.

Harriet decided not to mince words. "You should know at the outset, my lord, that I have no intention of selling my part of the business to you. Nor do I intend to consult you on decisions I make regarding my investments."

The polite smile faded from his face. They regarded each other for a long moment.

"How is it, madam," he said finally, "that you

possess such an extraordinary amount of freedom in the matter?"

The assumptions behind his question irritated her. "This is the second time today, sir, that I appear to have shocked you by being my own mistress," she said, unable to keep the annoyance from her voice.

Even to her own ears, the words sounded shrill. "I beg your pardon," she added quickly. "I have rather strong opinions on certain matters, but it is not my wish to inflict them on you, especially since our acquaintance is of such short duration." Feeling excessively awkward, Harriet fell silent.

Lord Westwood's brow furrowed. He did not immediately respond.

She was making a muddle of things, Harriet realized. She took a deep breath. "As to your question, Freddy's estate came to me without preconditions, although my father remains a trustee. For whatever reason, after controlling me for half a lifetime, he has allowed me to do as I wish." The reason, she suspected, was so he would not have to be bothered with her.

"Lord Worthington had no heir?" the earl asked.

"No. It is a worthless title, at all events." She hesitated. Lord Westwood was her business partner, so perhaps it was best to be forthright. "My father took care of Freddy's debts before our marriage."

"Your father is a generous man," he observed in a noncommittal tone.

"There was a price for his generosity." With her father, there was always a price. "Though Freddy had no immediate heirs, my father preferred not to take the chance that his investment would be squandered. He dissolved the entail."

He regarded her in surprise. "An Act of Parliament?"

"My father is a powerful man. It was not difficult."

"I see."

Harriet wondered what he thought of such a tale of money and manipulation. She was fortunate to have free rein over her own affairs, though it galled that she owed that very freedom to her father. Men were always trying to arrange things, never troubling themselves to ask whether their machinations were welcome.

Lord Westwood was studying her. "The business has lost a great deal of money since Freddy's death," he said.

Now they were at the reason for his visit. "That is regrettable," Harriet replied. When he did not answer, she eyed him curiously. "Surely you do not hold me to blame."

There was a pause. "I do."

"What? Why, that is silly. I have done nothing."

"That," the earl said, "is precisely the problem."

Harriet frowned. "The loss of a few pounds could not have seriously altered your finances."

"Thirty thousand."

"I beg your pardon?"

"Thirty thousand," he repeated. "The decisions I have been unable to implement because of your refusal to respond to my instructions have resulted in the loss of thirty thousand pounds since November last. A king's ransom, madam. It also appears you have sold some of the stock and availed yourself of a significant sum of cash. Ten thousand pounds, to be precise."

Harriet was surprised. It was rather a formidable sum. She had not kept track, for such things did not concern her.

"It was my part of the business to do with as I wished, my lord," she said. "At all events, I have put the proceeds to good use."

"And what might that be?" His gaze was hard.

Was he trying to intimidate her? "Necessary improvements," she replied crisply.

"Please explain." A clear command.

"It is quite simple," she said, trying to keep the edge from her voice. "I sold some stock to pay for the Whitmires' wheat crop, which was devastated by the rains last year. Now they can plant winter wheat, which many think is a superior grain and —" She broke off. Lord Westwood's expression had darkened considerably.

"You sold stock in Westwood Imports to pay for a neighbor's wheat crop?"

"There was also Mrs. Gibson's cow, which died suddenly last month," Harriet said. "A family cannot subsist without a cow," she added defiantly.

"A cow," he echoed.

"It cannot have escaped your notice, my lord, that the village is in need of repair. Its fortunes have fallen over the last few years, and there is much to be done. And it does bear the Worthington name, a remnant of a time when Freddy's family owned much of the land. I have a responsibility here."

"I see," he said.

"The mill needed to be rebuilt," Harriet continued. "Squire did not keep it up, and Freddy had done no repairs after winning it from him in a card game. People depend upon the mill. But before the mill could be useful, we had to tear down the old dam, which was diverting the water power and flooding an old pasture. The Reeds needed water to irrigate their fields, so we built a new dam, and everyone is quite happy now. Especially the Smythes, who owned the old swampy pasture. Now they can use it for grazing land. Of course they did not have any grazing animals until —"

"You bought them a herd of sheep."

Harriet beamed. "How did you know?"

Lord Westwood exhaled slowly. For a moment he did not speak. "Lady Harriet," he said finally, in a constricted tone, "I am certain that your neighbors are grateful for your assistance. But you have succeeded in severely depleting the assets of a business which I founded, which bears my name and which until last year was extremely profitable, without consulting me. I cannot imagine that you think that is fair."

She frowned. "When you put it that way, my lord, perhaps not. But perhaps you had too much money to begin with."

He eyed her incredulously.

"The business never did Freddy any good, if you must know," Harriet explained. "He had a most unfortunate gambling habit and frittered away his money on unhealthy pursuits. In fact, I believe the business hastened his death."

"Whatever pursuits in which your husband was engaged," Lord Westwood responded, "it is hardly fair to take your anger at him out on my business —"

"Oh, I am not angry," Harriet assured him. "Not at all. Freddy was entitled to do as he wished. But he could not handle wealth, and I believe it shortened his life."

"I see. So you decided to give the wealth away."

"It may please you to paint me as a spendthrift, my lord, but the truth is I have used the money for greater good. Reapportioned it, one might say, for a better purpose. As is my right, I believe."

Lord Westwood rose. He wore an odd expression. A rigid one, she thought.

"I thank you for the sherry, but I cannot stay for dinner," he said. "To be quite frank, madam, I am having great difficulty controlling my temper. It is a character flaw, to be sure, but there it is, nevertheless. We will continue this discussion on another occasion."

Harriet regarded him regretfully. "Oh, dear," she said. "And I had Celestial prepare broiled salmon with caper sauce."

"Caper sauce?"

"I find it marries quite beautifully with the raspberry vinegar-marinated asparagus, though one might be forgiven for assuming that the pungent flavors would do battle. They do not, I assure you."

The earl set his glass of sherry on the table. "I suppose you cook the life out of it."

"The asparagus? Oh, no, my lord. We steam it slightly just until the color sharpens. Then we plunge the stalks into cold water to stop the cooking. They are quite crisp and more than hold their own with my crusty French rolls. Did I mention the buttered prawns? We dress them with plenty of garlic so they do not fade away amid the other dishes. I like food that makes one sit up and take notice."

Lord Westwood squared his shoulders and took a deep breath. "I am sure it is delicious, and I regret ruining your dinner, but I have learned over the years that my temper is not to be trifled with. I am afraid I must —"

"Trifle? Oh, dear." Harriet rose quickly. "We were to have a trifle for dessert — 'tis my own creation, something of an international dish. Prime English custard layered over a cake soaked in Madeira wine, overspread with candied fruits from Italy. I finish it with ice cream flavored by Turkish apricots. But since you are not staying for dinner, I must tell Celestial not to unmold the ice cream, else it will be ruined. Please excuse me."

She moved toward the door.

Lord Westwood cleared his throat. "Lady Harriet." His voice sounded strained.

"Do not worry," she assured him, waving a dismissive hand. "I am not in the least offended by your premature departure. I have a most open mind about masculine behavior. But that is neither here nor there. Good evening, my lord."

"It is just —" He broke off.

She turned. "Yes?"

"I would be loath to..." He hesitated.

Harriet smiled encouragingly.

"To ruin your trifle," he finished.

Harriet frowned. "Does that mean you wish to stay for dinner after all?"

But before he could answer, the door opened and Horace stood at the threshold. "Dinner is served," he intoned.

An aroma of freshly broiled salmon, pungent caper sauce, raspberry vinegar, prawns heavy with garlic, and musky exotic fruits filled the room. Lord Westwood took a deep breath, pulled out a handkerchief, and wiped his brow. He closed his eyes.

"Yes," he declared in a ragged tone. "I believe I do."

CHAPTER TWO

HIS NOSE HAD betrayed him. Elias had been ready to walk out of Lady Harriet's parlor, taking his anger safely into the night before it brought disaster. But his nose had sabotaged him, and now he sat at her table, consoling himself with raspberry vinaigrette and capered salmon.

It was no small consolation. A rich fish like salmon deserved a zesty accompaniment. Most cooks never understood that. Harriet Worthington did. She also knew the lush, pink flesh should be cooked just until the edges lightened, leaving a deep band of pink inside.

"Otherwise it dries out," she told him. But there was no need to explain to Elias. He had been eating salmon for years. He hated it dry and meaty like worn-out beef. Lady Harriet might be an abysmal businesswoman, but she was the first hostess he had met who truly understood salmon.

"I quite agree," he found himself saying, before he remembered that she was his opponent, the woman single-handedly depleting his fortune and turning his business into an agrarian charity.

But as he stared at the trifle and the thick

topping of sumptuous ice cream, Elias knew he would not regain his common sense until this heady experience of taste and smell was behind him, until Lady Harriet rose and declared the dinner over and he could prevail upon her to continue the discussion in more neutral territory.

Someone with the improbable name of Celestial had prepared the food, but Lady Harriet had obviously supervised every dish. Elias could not help but admire a woman with such skill. Though she had swathed herself in black bombazine — a concession to mourning, perhaps, though Freddy had been dead a full year — he found himself wondering how she would look in a different gown. One that, like the Turkish apricots adorning that ice cream, complemented a more sensual essence.

In the bakery, her reddish-brown hair had formed an appealing tangle of curls. Tonight it was tamed into an unflattering bun that, with that dreary black frock, made her look hopelessly austere. Austere did not suit her. No, the woman in the bakery had an earthier appeal, as if she knew what it was to run barefoot through a meadow, hair fanning out from her flushed face, blue eyes reflecting the glory of a clear sky.

Yet there was nothing coarse about her. Elias realized that now. Even in that flour-dusted apron, she had carried herself with quiet assurance, her eyes reflecting a calm self-possession. But something about her hinted of hidden currents beneath those still waters.

What had she said? That she was her own

mistress, that Freddy had been entitled to do as he wished, that she had a "most open mind" about masculine behavior. Slowly, Elias began to wonder about Lady Harriet's marriage.

Whatever "unhealthy pursuits" in which Freddy had been engaged — and Elias could guess at some of them — had Lady Harriet sanctioned them so that she could enjoy a similar freedom? His eyes narrowed assessingly. Beneath that dreadful gown and constricted bun was a woman who understood appetites. Perhaps all sorts of appetites.

Might there be another way around his difficulty with her? He inhaled deeply, savoring the bouquet of the fine Madeira. When it came to dealing with females, he had never possessed much drawing room charm. He was not one for empty flattery and pretty compliments. Still, how difficult could it be to persuade one woman — a lonely widow at that — to entrust her share of the business into wiser, more skilled hands? Of the two partners in Westwood Imports, Elias had always been the one to make the hard decisions and to execute them ruthlessly. Yet ruthlessness need not always mean outright confrontation. Sometimes an oblique approach was more effective.

There was no doubt Lady Harriet needed a firm hand. Sooner or later she would see the wisdom of ceding the business decisions to him. But perhaps he could afford to be patient.

To be sure, there were worthy distractions to help pass the time. Indeed, he had just consumed one of them. Elias placed his napkin on the table. "I do not know when I have had a more delicious meal."

"Thank you." She looked briefly amused, then wary. Perhaps she distrusted compliments. He must remember that. It would not do to overplay his hand.

"Would you favor me with a turn in the garden?" he asked. "A rich meal ought to be followed by a bit of exercise."

She hesitated.

"You might call your maid to accompany us if you prefer," he added quickly.

She gave him an easy smile. "Heavenly would jump at the chance, but I do not need a chaperon. 'Tis merely that I must rise very early tomorrow to see to things at the bakery, and I confess I am rather tired. But by all means, let us take the night air. The garden is lovely in the evening."

Elias did not know who Heavenly was, but the image of Lady Harriet toiling in the village bakery jarred anew. "Most women of your station do not occupy themselves in such pursuits," he observed, striving for a neutral tone, as she led them out of the house and past a stoned-lined flowerbed and terrace.

She slanted a gaze at him. "Yes, my friend Mrs. Tanksley is forever telling me so."

At least there was one voice of reason, Elias thought.

"But I pay her no mind," Lady Harriet went on. "She does not understand the pleasure — indeed the complete gratification — I find in my shop."

Beyond the terrace, lanterns illuminated a path that opened into a large, sprawling garden. Elias found it useful to focus on that, rather than Lady Harriet's odd declaration. He noticed a profusion of erect green plants and inhaled deeply, glad for the distraction.

"Mint," he observed. But there was more, he realized. "Savory as well. Thyme over in that direction, rosemary under that ornamental cherry."

Lady Harriet stared at him. "Are you a gardener, my lord?"

He waved a dismissive hand. "Merely cursed — or gifted, I suppose — with a heightened sense of smell. It has been useful in my business."

She regarded him with interest. "You identified my herbs perfectly — those I use in the kitchen, anyway. Celestial planted them, along with a few others I cannot name which she uses to treat various ailments."

"I find it most untoward that you run a bake shop," he said bluntly — only belatedly recalling that he intended to avoid outright confrontation.

Instantly, her expression tightened. She walked ahead of him to maneuver around a bush that intruded into the walk. Then she turned to him. "Bread is the very essence of nourishment, my lord," she said. "It is a gift of the land, as much as those spices you cultivate."

"Nonsense," he said. "I can pluck a pepper from a bush, dry it out, grind it into powder, pack it in a container and ship it far and wide. You cannot compare that to a loaf of bread."

She regarded him pityingly. "Just as your process creates a spice, mine grinds grain into flour, adds water and a yeast broth, transforming it into dough. With time and heat its diverse elements are joined in glorious harmony. There is no difference between my process and yours. Except that mine is uplifting, perhaps even spiritual."

"Running a bakery is commerce, and commerce is not for gently bred females," he insisted.

"Or gentlemen?" she rejoined. "Come, my lord. Peers of the realm do not engage in commerce either. Has no one pointed that out to you?"

Perhaps he had deserved that, Elias thought. "A peerage, Lady Harriet, is deuced expensive to maintain."

She regarded him with a thin smile. "I see. Your thriving spice business keeps the wolf from the door and thus is a necessary evil in the service of your title. I do not criticize you for conducting such commerce, so I cannot imagine why you feel free to criticize me for working in my own bakery."

Elias regarded her. "Surely, Freddy did not allow you to engage in such activities when he was alive."

"I never presumed to tell my husband what to do, and he never presumed to tell me," she said coolly. "We had an egalitarian marriage. I see no more reason to restrict my behavior as a widow than I did as a wife."

The Duke of Sidenham must have demanded monstrous promises from Freddy in exchange for Lady Harriet's hand, Elias decided. He could not imagine any other reason a husband would allow his wife such outlandish freedom.

"I did not intend to bring up painful memories," he said. "You are still in mourning."

"I was never in mourning," she corrected. "I do not believe in mourning the dead when one can be celebrating the living."

That took him aback.

"You wear black," he pointed out carefully. Each topic of conversation seemed to send him further into a maze in which every turn opened into a thicket of thorns.

Lady Harriet looked down at her gown. "Oh, this. This was for you."

Elias blinked.

"Silly of me, was it not?" she said. Was that a flush on her features? "I suppose I did not want to appear too..." She hesitated.

He waited.

"Too feminine — I suppose that is the proper word," she said. "I have no interest in being perceived as flirtatious or womanly." She eyed him speculatively. "There are men who would exploit that."

Lady Harriet's quiver contained quite a few arrows, Elias reflected. So that stern fabric she wore was a weapon. He wondered anew how she might look in a gown that was less austere. But the image his mind's eye gave him was not of some lush, revealing ball gown. Instead, it was of her in the bake shop, with smudges of flour on her face, elbow deep in kneading her dough. Strangely, it was a far more arresting image.

When he did not respond, she laughed softly. "Come now, my lord. I know that your only purpose in coming here was to call me to account, to persuade me to turn my part of the business over to you. If it suits me to don bombazine armor, who are you to challenge that?" Her mouth twitched in amusement.

Elias opened his mouth to respond, but she waved a dismissive hand. "Nay, do not deny it. You must own that your intention is to persuade me to let go of my shares, and, failing that, to try to control what I do with them. Indeed, you have said as much."

"'Tis obvious, madam, that you have no ability for managing finances," he returned. "But I would happily leave you to your spendthrift ways were it not my money you were so eagerly spending."

"*Our* money," she corrected.

It was perhaps time for a change in strategy.

"I am a man of business," Elias said carefully. "And I confess to some impatience to settle the business matters between us satisfactorily."

"By which you refer to *your* satisfaction," she said.

"I am not incapable of objectivity, Lady Harriet."

She studied him. "As to that, I expect we shall see." Unexpectedly, she smiled. "I am not your enemy, Lord Westwood."

"Perhaps not," he conceded. "But you are exasperating, madam. And that bombazine is a crime against nature."

Her brow furrowed.

Good God. Had he actually spoken those words aloud? Elias cleared his throat. "That was excessively familiar. I regret —"

Her sudden smile caught him by surprise. "I am certain I should tap you roundly with my fan or blush prettily, but I do not possess such skills."

The smile transformed her features. Her upturned lips and twinkling blue eyes banished all thought of that unforgiving black material, and Elias found he could not quite take his gaze from her face.

"In truth," she added with a sigh, "although I am at ease in large groups, I do not have the slightest idea how to entertain a solitary gentleman. I do not even own a fan."

Into what foreign territory were they venturing? Elias wondered. Neither his military training nor his commercial endeavors had taught him how to deal with an opponent who possessed Lady Harriet's unnerving candor.

"As to that," he heard himself saying, "you have entertained me quite adequately, and we have only just met so I imagine that your ability is quite, er, passable." He managed a game smile.

It was too dim in the garden to tell whether his ham-handed compliment had made her blush. Indeed, the path toward persuading Lady Harriet to comply with his wishes was suddenly less clear. It was as if his target had shifted or changed shape. Certainly, it had become more interesting. Yes, perhaps he could afford to bide his time. The caper sauce alone was worth it.

They had now come round to the beginning of

their walk. It was time for him to take his leave. Elias made her a deep bow. "I am in your debt, for the exquisite meal. We will continue our business discussions on another occasion."

"Yes, I expect we shall," she said.

Elias quickly took his leave. Dinner might be over but the evening would linger in his memory. He needed to ponder that very unsettling fact.

"Now, Squire, we have covered this ground. I have no intention of selling you the mill." Exasperated, Harriet pushed a rebellious strand of hair away from her face with the back of her hand, the only part not covered in flour. It was just like Cedric Gibbs to show up when she was distracted by the vagaries of her new sourdough culture.

"But, Harriet," he protested, "Freddy never meant to keep the thing. He was to offer me a chance to buy it back at the first opportunity. Had he not died so suddenly —"

"Nevertheless he did," she interrupted, "and he never said a word to me about returning the mill to you."

His face reddened. "Nonsense. That was his wish."

"You had let it sink into the most deplorable state," she continued, "whereas I am happy to make the necessary repairs. It is much better off in my hands. The village needs a working mill."

Cedric's florid face made him look rather unwell, Harriet observed. The man was not much above middle age, but, like his mill, had deteriorated. He was overly fond of drink and it showed in his mottled complexion and a rather rotund form that was clearly unaccustomed to any physical exertion besides lifting a pint. Still, his lot was not an easy one. He'd lost his wife several years ago, and had a number of young children. But Cedric made things worse with his grating disposition and temper. The man had offended just about everyone in Worthington at one time or another.

Monica Tanksley insisted that losing the mill to Freddy had improved Cedric's character. He *had* been rather amiable lately, but Harriet suspected it was all for show. The squire's family had controlled the mill for decades and made a comfortable living by charging people enormous sums to grind their grain. Though Harriet allowed him to use the mill for free — as she did all of her neighbors — she knew he would not be satisfied until the mill returned to his ownership.

His latest tactic was to try to woo her for it. He had not yet worked himself up to an offer, but it was only a matter of time. His sudden appearance in the bakery this morning, when she was alone, did not bode well.

"Please excuse me," Harriet said briskly, turning her attention to her worktable, where a large tub of her culture bubbled happily. She loved her table. It was white oak, the same material from which the mill was constructed, and it was long enough to hold as many tubs and loaves as she liked. "I have work to do."

"*My* work has become considerably lighter without my mill," he responded acidly.

"Yes, and a great deal less profitable, since you are not able to charge twice the going rate."

Cedric regarded her through narrowed, bloodshot eyes. "With all due respect, Harriet, you have not lived in this community for a lifetime, as I have. I am a fair man. Anyone who could not pay their shot had no trouble finding credit with me."

"For triple interest," she pointed out.

His color deepened. "I would certainly consider your suggestions for revising my fees," he said magnanimously, though the bulging vein at his temple betrayed how much that statement cost him.

Harriet eyed him sharply. "That is pure blather, Cedric. We both know that you have not the least interest in doing so. You are only saying what you think I wish to hear."

"Are you calling me a liar, Harriet?" he demanded.

She sighed heavily and returned her attention to the culture. It was unusually pungent, a good sign.

"Bloody blazes!" he snarled.

Harriet scarcely heard him, focused as she was on the bubbling mass. Lady Hester Stanhope, with whom she had developed a friendship several years ago in London, had recently sent her several dried cultures from her travels. This one was Egyptian. She wondered how long the Egyptians had allowed the mixture to ferment before deeming it ready to use. Too short a time and the mix would not develop the sour flavor she was after; too long and the culture would lose its power to make the bread rise sufficiently.

"It may suit you to pretend that you have no use for men, but you are not fooling me," he insisted. "Women need to be shown the correct path in life."

Harriet was only vaguely aware that he had spoken. Her first attempt to produce the Egyptian sourdough had resulted in a brick-like loaf unsuitable for anything but the crows. But she was determined to succeed. It would be nice to serve something special for dinner, when the Tanksleys would join them. Perhaps she would even invite Lord Westwood, though the man's snobbery was certainly off-putting.

Her instincts told her the culture was almost ready. It was time to mix the dough.

"You have been a year without a man — far too long," Cedric was saying. "I can give you a ready-made family: eight children, all in need of a woman's touch, what with my Hilda gone these four years. With your money and the only working mill for fifteen miles, we will be quite secure."

Whatever was he talking about? Harriet wondered, her thoughts occupied with plans for the dinner. Lord Westwood seemed to appreciate adventurous cooking. To be sure, he was an annoying man, but she had found herself softening — slightly — toward him last night.

"The Gibbs name is a good one. You may be

well-born, but you are not above manual labor," he said approvingly, surveying the shop. "You would do well to take a page from Hilda, God rest her. She was as eager to please as a good sheepdog. Never ran on at the mouth like a man, never criticized."

So intent was Harriet's concentration that she did not realize Cedric had moved around to her side of the table. "Yes, Harriet, I do believe it is time that I took you in hand."

His large hand clamped down on her shoulder, startling her into a little shriek.

"Now, Harriet," he said in a soothing tone, "there is no need to be coy. I know how lonely a bed can be."

"You will remove your hand from my person," Harriet said firmly, tamping down a vague feeling of alarm. She had risen early so as to have the bakery to herself this morning. She had always considered Cedric quite harmless, but there did seem to be an intensity about him this morning.

Instead, Cedric pulled her closer. Harriet cringed as his face neared hers. The man's breath would fell an oak. "Stop it, sir, this instant!"

"No need to play the reluctant virgin," he said thickly. "You have been a married lady. You can trust me with your deepest desires."

"My deepest desire, Cedric, is that you remove yourself from my shop." Harriet tried to extricate herself, but he had trapped her against the long side of the table.

"Nonsense. You have been a year without a

man. A man is necessary for protection — and pleasure."

Harriet fixed him with a stony glare. "You could not be more wrong. I must insist that you leave this instant."

"A woman needs a man, none more than you. Why, look at you mucking about in this shop by yourself. 'Tis not safe." With that, he closed what little space remained between them and tried to kiss her.

Harriet turned her face away.

"Do not pretend you are holding out for that pup Eustace," he warned. "I know Monica Tanksley has been trying to match you up with her young fop, but you need a real man."

He grinned, and put his wet lips on hers. Harriet fumbled blindly behind her, searching for anything that might serve as a weapon. Just as her fingers found the bowl containing the culture, she heard the door scrape open.

"What the devil is going on here?"

Harriet instantly recognized the deep voice. "Lord Westwood!" She did not bother to disguise her relief.

Cedric took one look at the tall figure filling the doorframe of the shop entrance and released her. Unfortunately, Harriet had bent so far backward over the table that when his arms fell away, she lost her balance and slid to the floor.

In the next instant Lord Westwood was pulling her to her feet. He regarded her assessingly for a moment, then turned to Cedric and slammed the squire against the wall. As the earl was a good deal larger and a head taller, the squire was clearly on the wrong end of the matchup.

"You struck her," Lord Westwood growled.

"No, no!" Harriet protested as the earl's hands went around Cedric's throat. "I simply lost my balance."

At her words, Lord Westwood turned toward her, a momentary lapse that allowed Cedric the opportunity to vent his own displeasure. He landed a blow on Lord Westwood's jaw.

Instantly, the earl grabbed Cedric by the collar and yanked him upward. Cedric responded with a furious kick aimed at Lord Westwood's midsection.

The two men crashed against the table, sending pans clattering to the floor. "Stop it!" Harriet cried. "Stop this very instant!"

Neither man paid her heed. Harriet feared for the fate of her shop. A pan of newly risen rolls awaiting a trip to the oven was among the casualties now strewn on the floor, a morning's work lost. This simply would not do.

The bowl containing the sourdough culture was on the edge of the table, within her reach. Harriet picked it up and, in one motion, heaved the contents over the combatants.

With a collective roar, the men separated, which almost — but not quite — compensated for the loss of her precious culture.

"The devil!" Cedric struggled to his feet. His hands and arms were covered in the thick mass. He looked as if he wished to strangle her. But he only glared at her with pure fury, and marched out into the street. The door slammed behind him with such force the windows rattled in their frames.

Cedric had not gotten the worst of it, however. That unfortunate privilege belonged to the earl, whose head and shoulders were covered in her prized culture. It oozed over his black superfine coat and down what must have been a fashionable brocade waistcoat. It sank into the folds of the swath of linen tied at his neck.

Lord Westwood stood perfectly still, as if he could not believe what had occurred. His hair was covered in the culture, which also dribbled down the side of his face. Wordlessly, Harriet handed him the towel that had covered her rising rolls. But it had been dusted with flour to prevent the rolls from sticking, and when he brought it to his face, the flour only added to the pasty mess.

The culture's pungent odor, which was to have imparted such a wonderful taste to her bread, brought a revolted expression to his features.

"What is this putrid muck?" he growled.

"An Egyptian sourdough culture," she explained. "I am developing a special bread recipe..." Her voice trailed off as his expression darkened further.

He began to apply the towel to his head, but the fetid residue clung to his hair like thick glue. It was a hopeless task. Nothing less than a complete dunking in a hot bath would repair the damage. Harriet guessed he was staying at the Boar's Head Inn, which was not known for hot baths — or any baths, the proprietor being notoriously stingy.

At all events, she could not imagine Lord Westwood presenting himself at the inn in such a state. He would be a laughingstock.

"It is still early in the day, my lord," she ventured. "There is scarcely anyone about yet. Perhaps you would care to come back to my house. I will ask Horace to prepare a bath so you can repair your appearance."

The rigid set of his jaw told her that slinking into her house for a bath was the last thing he wished to do. But he must also have seen that it was the only way.

For a long moment he did not speak. Harriet shifted uncomfortably. She had repaid his gallantry — misguided though it had been — by dousing his clothes and his person, and yet, at the time she had seen no other way to stop the fight. "My lord, I regret —"

"Enough," he said in a clipped voice.

Harriet waited for a snarled reproach, a scathing denunciation. But he merely stood rigidly, keeping himself in check. She moved quickly toward the door.

"The gig is just out front." Harriet tried to sound cheerful.

"Thank you," he said, in a voice of unnatural calm.

CHAPTER THREE

ELIAS DID NOT trust himself to speak. He remained silent during the minutes — which felt considerably longer — that it took the gig to travel to Lady Harriet's home. And during the half hour he stood in her foyer as servants hurried to heat water for his bath.

As he stood there in his fetid clothes, his hair coated with the stinking substance that evidently was part of Lady Harriet's culinary magic, his dignity suffered mightily. Most well-trained servants would have gone about their business without remarking upon his appearance, but Lady Harriet's apparently had no thought of restraint. The servant whom Lady Harriet called Heavenly quickly fetched another woman from the kitchen. Putting their hands up to their faces, the two women stared at him, then dashed away, no doubt to collapse in utter merriment. Only the butler maintained some decorum, but it did not take a genius to read the gleam in the man's eye.

Elias tried to suppress his chagrin. Thanks to Lady Harriet, he had become a putrid specimen of humanity, lost to odoriferous indignity. The very instrument of his humiliation now appeared in the foyer to summon him.

"This way, my lord," Lady Harriet said in a cheerfully cajoling tone one might use with a recalcitrant child.

Silently, Elias followed her up an excessively ornate staircase and into a room that held a large copper hip bath. Steam warmed his nostrils. Staring at the enormous tub, he knew a faint glimmer of hope.

"Horace will fetch your clean clothes from the inn," she said. "Are you traveling with a valet?"

What he would not give to place himself in Henry's capable hands. But Elias had seen no need for the batman to accompany him on an errand that was to have occupied only a day at best. As a result, Henry was in London, enjoying a respite from his duties and doubtless draining his employer's stock of French brandy.

"No."

"Horace will serve in his stead. He has laid out a dressing gown for your immediate use, but you may be assured that he will return with your clothes as quickly as he can." She paused. "Unless you wish him to stay and assist you in the bath."

"No."

"Yes, of course. Well, I will leave you now." She turned and left the room.

With that, Elias ripped off his clothes and plunged into the steaming tub. He ducked his head under the water and let it wash away the morning's indignities.

He had risen early, knowing that it was her

intention to work at the bakery. He had hoped to find her more receptive to his business proposal with the light of a new day — and, it must be acknowledged, to sample more of her meat pies, or anything else from her oven. Instead, he had encountered a florid-faced ruffian pressing his attentions on her — nay, mauling her — in a manner that left little doubt as to his ultimate intention. That Lady Harriet did not welcome the lout's attentions was obvious, underscoring once again the foolishness of her habit of working in the shop alone. Had he not come by, God knows what might have happened.

Still, the episode had taken him into dangerous territory. He liked to think that most disputes could be settled without fisticuffs — though there was a time in his younger days when his temper controlled him rather than the other way around. Still, the ruffian had abused Lady Harriet and landed the first blow against him, so Elias did not overly regret his behavior. It was perhaps another reason, as if he needed one, to finish his business here and quit Lady Harriet's troublesome company.

Sliding the soap over his skin, Elias detected the scent of lime — with a hint of cinnamon, of all things — and found himself wondering wildly whether Lady Harriet's soap was edible. Even the soap in this household did wondrous things to his senses. As he sank into the comfortable oblivion of his bath, Elias could not help but wonder whether Lady Harriet was the regular recipient of such boorish advances. By paying no heed to the cautions necessary for one of her gender, she had made herself an easy target.

Nevertheless, he was not here to change Lady Harriet's habits, however ill-advised they might be. It was enough to ponder how he would persuade her to relinquish her disastrous hold on his business. Though the answer had not yet presented itself, Elias had every confidence that he would ultimately prevail. His business would be his again.

To be sure, he had lost ground today. She doubtless would not soon forget the stinking spectacle he made as he stood dripping and oozing muck in her foyer — the very opposite image of a man of serious purpose. The bath was a godsend, however. He would eventually be presentable again. And then perhaps he would regain his dignity.

Harriet had caught the merest glimpse of Lord Westwood's bare back as he plunged into the bath. She'd but lingered a moment out in the hall in the event he needed something that she had not foreseen, and had glanced quickly back into the room. Truly, she was only being a good hostess, she told herself. But the door was not fully closed when he ripped off his shirt. And though she ought to have been shocked and mortified, gratified more accurately described her reaction as she quickly averted her eyes and tiptoed away down the hall.

She had seen enough to realize that his superbly tailored clothing concealed a well-toned physique. Blushing deeply, she felt mortified at having spied on him, however inadvertently.

Freddy had not possessed rippling muscles. His physical assets suffered from inactivity and debauchery, and no one knew better than she how he had squandered his resources, masculine and otherwise. Harriet had not held that against him — she liked to think of herself as without prejudice. Still, to compare Lord Westwood with Freddy was, perhaps, inevitable.

Harriet willed that thought away. The man might be wrapped in an appealing package, but he was mired in rigidity, especially when it came to his notions about women. She could have handled Cedric, for instance. The man was harmless. Oh, perhaps she had taken a small — *very* small — pleasure in Lord Westwood's rushing to her rescue, but she needed no Galahad. She was quite capable of managing her own affairs.

"I do hope your bath was restorative," she murmured an hour later as she poured out coffee for Lord Westwood's breakfast, then realized that was an exceedingly improper thing to say. One simply did not refer to a gentleman's hygiene — certainly not when the gentleman was someone she barely knew.

But he accepted the coffee without a word, choosing neither to notice nor respond to her comment, to her relief. At least he could have no complaint about the food. The sideboard was laden with ham, kidneys, eggs with nutmeg sauce, and fresh bread. He would not have eaten so well at the Boar's Head Inn.

When she asked whether she could fill his plate, he nodded his assent. Though his prolonged silence was disconcerting, Harriet told herself he simply preferred to concentrate on his food.

His hair still bore a faint sheen of moisture from his bath. In his fresh burgundy jacket with fawn trousers, he looked like a typical country gentleman finishing off a deeply satisfying breakfast. Indeed, he ate everything she set before him. But when he placed his napkin on the table and met her gaze, he looked anything but satisfied.

"Has that man struck you before?" he asked.

"Squire Gibbs?" Harriet eyed him in surprise. "He did not strike me. You mistook the situation. I merely fell because he released me so abruptly."

"You were struggling with him."

"Yes, but he would not have done me harm —" Harriet broke off. Perhaps she *had* been the tiniest bit afraid. For though she had known Cedric Gibbs for years, she also knew that in recent months he had become rather desperate in the matter of the mill.

Lord Westwood arched a skeptical brow. "Surely, you do not wish to convey that you welcomed his advances? That his appearance in the shop this morning was expected?"

"Certainly not!" Harriet replied indignantly. "I do not arrange rendezvous with men in my bakery. Or anywhere, for that matter."

"And yet, you make a habit of working alone, where anyone might happen in."

Harriet made a dismissive gesture. "I know everyone in the village and there is not one person who wishes me harm, Cedric included," she insisted. "He only wants to buy back the mill Freddy won from him during a card game. He has exhausted all verbal means of persuasion, and I believe he has the misguided notion that if he seduces me, I will give him what he seeks. Despicable scheme, is it not?"

Lord Westwood did not respond.

"Some men cannot get it into their heads that women are better off without them," she continued.

"Are they?" He regarded her over his coffee cup.

"Oh, yes. But you will be thinking me disrespectful of Freddy. I am not glad he is gone, my lord, but I have managed quite well by myself."

"This morning was proof of that, of course."

Was that sarcasm in his voice? "I was grateful for your assistance, Lord Westwood," Harriet said quickly. "I have not thanked you properly."

"You have done more than enough, madam."

This time, Harriet had no trouble recognizing the ironic tone. She flushed. "I am sorry about the sourdough culture. I was simply trying to stop the scuffle while my shop was still in one piece."

"Indeed."

His expression was unreadable. Was he angry? It was not the first time she had failed to foresee the disastrous ramifications of her actions. She ought to have learned something from that very first disaster — her marriage to Freddy — but she had only grown more impulsive since then, not less. "I cannot say again how sorry I am. Is there anything I can do to make it up to you?"

"Sell me the remaining shares of my business," he said.

"You are very blunt, my lord."

"I like to put my cards on the table."

"Very well," Harriet said. "I will be frank, too. The shares are mine, and I intend to keep them to help the people of this community as their needs arise."

He made an impatient sound. "I will pay you well. Then you may use the money to buy cows, or pigs, or anything you like."

"It is not the same."

"Damnation, woman," he growled. "You are selling off my business for a pittance. And whoever is brokering the transactions is probably stealing you blind, having long ago figured out that you do not have the slightest idea what your shares are really worth."

"Mr. Stevens was Freddy's solicitor," Harriet protested. "I am sure he is honorable."

"Freddy's solicitor?" Lord Westwood gave a scornful laugh. "Now there's a recommendation." He leaned forward. "I will pay you twice what those shares are worth just to have them in my control once more. My offer is more than fair."

Harriet rose. "I do not wish to have my shares in your control. I do not wish to have anything of mine in a man's control. I am my own mistress."

She turned away, but he had risen as well and his hand touched her arm.

"So it is your much-vaunted independence that is the real issue," he said. "Beware, madam. I will have them from you. I have never met a woman who possessed the business sense of a man. You are no exception."

"And you are extraordinarily condescending," Harriet retorted. "How like a man to think that he knows best. You are no better than Squire Gibbs."

"There is no similarity between me and that ruffian."

"No?" she challenged. "Both of you want something from me. The only difference between you is that he has the effrontery to think he can win the mill by seduction. At least you do not have that shameful notion."

Harriet's face flamed as she heard her own bold words. But she stilled at his reply: "Do not be so certain."

She stared at him. The stormy seas in his dark eyes had given way to something more unsettling. "That, I am afraid, would be quite useless," Harriet assured him. "I am quite immune to men."

He arched a brow.

"I do not celebrate Freddy's death, but I am my own person now," Harriet said quietly. "I have no need of a man."

Lord Westwood was silent for a moment. "That is quite a manifesto," he said at last.

"Nay, 'tis simply the truth," Harriet replied.

"Immune, you say?"

"Quite," she assured him.

"Utterly without passion, I suppose?"

Harriet flushed. "I have passions, but they are not the sort you mean."

"What sort are they?" His gaze was bland.

She hesitated. "Perhaps it sounds silly, but I am passionate about bread. Indeed, about anything I can create in my kitchen. And, I am quite passionate about ideas."

Lord Westwood looked puzzled.

In spite of herself, Harriet smiled. "Is the word foreign to you, my lord? I assure you, it is not to me. Or to those I entertain in my salon in town."

"Ah. A salon. You are one of *those* women."

"I beg your pardon?"

Lord Westwood's gaze slid to the mantel clock. "Never mind. It is far too early in the day to discuss politics."

"It is never too early to discuss politics," she said. "I did not know that you enjoyed political discourse, my lord. How delightful! We could —"

"No, we could not." His voice held a note of finality. "If you will excuse me, madam, I will take my leave."

His gaze drifted to the table and the remnants of the meal. "I hope you will reconsider my offer," he said. "You'll not find a better one."

"It matters not," Harriet rejoined. "I shall not sell."

He sighed. "Thank you for breakfast," he said. "It is no overstatement to say I have not seen its equal."

And with that, he was gone.

Elias could not fault Lady Harriet's passions. He himself had long since given up any hope of taming his own passion — his highly developed olfactory sense. Indeed, it had been the inspiration for his business, which had begun as a diversion and quickly blossomed into his lodestar.

As his father's only heir, he'd been discouraged from dabbling in unsuitable matters — the kitchen was the province of his father's London-trained chef and female minions; the herbal garden and vegetable fields were tended by workers his father considered beneath his notice. Elias had been schooled instead in the manly arts of boxing and swordplay, the scholarly texts of Latin and Greek, and the gambling and raffish behavior that was *de rigueur* among his class but, to Elias, utterly boring.

Finally, his father — despairing of any other way to engage his son in preparing to shoulder the weight of an earldom — sent him to the family properties in the West Indies in the hope of impressing upon him how far-flung were his responsibilities. Only then did Elias find what it seemed he had been searching for the whole of his entirely useless boyhood.

Ginger, nutmeg, cinnamon, thyme, dasheen, chilies of every color and heat, chutneys, curries — there was no end to the surprising aromas and culinary creations permeating the air in the islands that sat like tiny jewels in the crown of the Caribbean. On Jamaica Elias discovered the pimento tree, whose berries and wood were central ingredients in a pungent paste used to slow-cure dried meat to an unforgettable balance of fire and sweet. Beet sugar, cloves, coriander, mango, coconut, hot sauce made from peppers in a rainbow of colors — the islands were a veritable heaven of flavors and seemingly endless possibilities.

Still a youth with scarcely twenty years on his plate, Elias was already spinning a future in which he ran the family plantation when word came that his father had died. It was perhaps to his everlasting shame that Elias's grief was less for the man he scarcely knew than for the fact he was forced to leave the island behind, knowing that his duties now would be very different from those in which he had so happily immersed himself.

Impatient to return to the only place that had set him afire, Elias paid little attention during the reading of his father's will, and even less to the bothersome title that became appended to his name. Only later, meeting with his father's solicitors, did he discover how badly in debt his father had been and how, even as Elias had been exploring those island properties, his father had been forced to deed them over to his creditors.

And so it was gone, all of it, before Elias could make his dream a reality. A great portion of his father's estate was encumbered or to let, and when all was said and done, Elias could not have purchased one pimento tree in Jamaica had his life depended upon it. The military had seemed the only option, and he took it. Indeed, it was the closest thing to a family he had ever known, his mother having died early in his childhood.

Afterward, he'd met Freddy. A scapegrace, to be sure, but a thoroughly charming one. They'd shared a bottle at White's, which cared less for a man's financial circumstance than his pedigree. Freddy was flush with his winnings at a local hellhole and eager to invest in an exotic business venture. One thing led to another, and before the evening was done, Elias and Freddy had become business partners. Money from Freddy's gambling wins was sufficient to purchase the property in the Caribbean that would become the foundation of their business.

Elias's nose unerringly directed him to the spices that most appealed to the English palate, like ginger and nutmeg, heretofore available only in the East. To those he added pimento, the magical berry that combined the taste and aroma of those spices as well as pepper, cloves, and cinnamon.

Before long, their modest import business showed promise of providing them a comfortable existence. Moreover, it kept Elias — happily, in his view — far from home. They might have continued profitably for years, but Freddy was not one to hold on his funds. His taste for gaming hells ensured that money slipped through his fingers like sand. Even though the business had begun to turn a profit, there was little available for the investment needed to expand and thrive. But Freddy had become enamored with a duke's daughter, and his attention to business details, never meticulous, evaporated altogether as he rushed headlong into the wedded state. Marriage gave Freddy less time to gamble, and soon Westwood Imports had the cash it needed and was flourishing beyond Elias's expectations. Then Freddy had met an untimely end, and Elias found himself saddled with an unreliable partner once more.

Alas, the longer he spent in Lady Harriet's presence, the more he realized that persuading her to sell her shares was perhaps his greatest challenge to date. Thus he was surprised at the Boar's Head Inn some hours later to receive a missive in a neatly scripted hand suggesting they could perhaps resolve their business matter over tea later that very day and, assuming all went well, at dinner that night.

It was an overture he readily accepted, knowing that he would be better prepared this time. She had her passion, and he had his. All he had to do was figure out how the two might align.

Tea proved something of an ordeal. Oh, there were the light-as-air tea biscuits, confections that by now Elias had come to expect from the supremely talented Lady Harriet. Were it not for the fact that Elias was focused single-mindedly on his mission of buying her out, he might have enjoyed them more. He willed his thoughts away from the biscuits' mesmerizing combination of sweet and savory — vanilla and thyme, if he did not miss his guess — and to the matter at hand.

Lady Harriet, he was somewhat gratified to see, had abandoned her dreadful black of yesterday and wore a sprigged muslin frock that, while perhaps too pale and insipid for her coloring, at least did not assault one with the grim purpose of that unrelenting bombazine. The lady herself was rather quiet. He took that as an invitation to resume their business discussion.

"I recognize," he began, careful to keep his tone conciliatory, "that my appearing here in the country may have come as something of a shock, notwithstanding my many previous written communications to you."

"Shock?" She studied him. "Do you think me fragile, my lord?"

Elias all but stifled a groan. Though he had become accustomed to this woman challenging him at every turn, it still annoyed him. He schooled himself to patience.

"Unprepared as you must have been to face a tangible reminder of your late husband in the form of his business partner," he continued, ignoring the mutinous spark in her eye, "you must have recoiled, as anyone would, from a course that would permanently separate you from the last connection you have with him."

She frowned.

"Yet I imagine that the details of the business must be a nuisance — a trial — for one such as yourself," he went on. "It can only be a relief to know that I am willing to take on the entire burden of the business myself."

She set her teacup on the tray, forcefully enough that it rattled the saucer.

"In short, I deeply regret if my previous

business proposition was insensitive," he added, striking what he hoped was a mixture of concern and remorse. "I have always been one for plain-speaking, and —"

"Nonsense."

He blinked. "I beg your pardon?"

Her amused gaze met his. "You suggest that I am too overwrought to consider a business proposal. That is subterfuge, as you can see with your own eyes that I am not in the least overset. Therefore, your statement qualifies not as plain-speaking, but rather as a negotiating ploy."

He stared at her.

"I have made my peace with Freddy's death," she continued. "That does not mean, however, that I wish to relinquish my shares."

She leaned forward in her chair. "I do not know why you persist in the belief that I am a fragile female lacking the wherewithal to continue living my life in the solitary state."

What in blazes had Freddy seen in this singularly confounding woman? Elias wondered darkly.

"Come now, Lord Westwood." Her mouth twitched. "Have you never encountered an independent woman?"

For that, it seemed, there was no answer. Nor did she seem to expect one. One thing was certain: Harriet Worthington was the most irritating woman he had ever encountered. She kept him off-balance — undoubtedly her intent. But Elias did not intend to dance to her tune.

"Certainly not one so strident," he replied. "Nor one so obsessed, apparently, with pointing out her independence at every turn. I assure you, madam, once would suffice. I have lost count, but it is surely a half-dozen times, perhaps more."

She looked taken aback.

Elias rose. "You led me to believe we might resolve this matter over tea. Instead, I am treated to a polemic."

"But we have resolved it, have we not?" she responded. "I considered your offer. I have rejected it. It is decided."

So they were quit. That signified only insofar as it was now necessary for him to pursue other options. He should have known better than to put faith in his powers to persuade a member of the opposite sex to see things his way. That question had been painfully answered in the negative years before. Yes, he definitely should have known better. He moved to the door.

"Never say you will be going," she protested. "Why, there are biscuits left on the tray." There was the hint of a self-satisfied smile on her face, which was all it took to blacken his mood further. It was a moment or two before he could trust himself to speak.

"It may please you to play Lady Bountiful," he said finally, "to gift your neighbors with cows and mills and the like. Undoubtedly, they revere the grand lady who makes a show of her workaday labor, of rising early to bake bread without a care as to the quantities of flour on her clothes or person, and who returns to this well-appointed house atop the hill, where her every wish is attended to."

Elias heard her sharp intake of breath, but he was not yet done. He fixed her with a dead gaze. "You are aware, are you not, that you are merely pretending to be one of them? Perhaps no one taught you that one person's amusement is another's livelihood."

He turned away from her, knowing he had let his temper get the best of him. But pretending to be something one was not in the spirit of false egalitarianism had always struck him as a rather corrupt form of *noblesse oblige*. What drove Lady Harriet's behavior he neither knew nor cared. His father had practiced the same sort of condescension, and thought it a great joke when Elias said he had worked on the island property alongside the laborers.

He had wasted quite enough time on this futile errand. The woman had her head in the clouds, doubtless filled with images of herself handing out bread to her grateful tenants, while word of her generosity spread far and wide.

Now, at least, his course was set. He would direct his solicitor to take legal steps to dissolve their partnership on grounds that she was an inferior business partner — indeed, a destructive one, whose improvident spending was destroying a heretofore thriving business. That would delay things considerably; the matter was likely to end up in court and in the meantime Lady Harriet would have spent down his shares further. Still, it appeared to be the only way he could regain control of his business.

Behind him, Elias heard her quickening steps.

He felt a hand on his arm. He turned, just as she collided rather forcefully into him.

"I beg your pardon," she said, and hastily took a step backward — which would have been possible had not Elias instinctively reached out to prevent her from falling and in so doing trapped her within his arms. And so they stood there awkwardly, inhabiting a physical space rather too small for people who were not more intimately acquainted — and who were at *point non plus,* besides.

Instantly, Elias released her.

She wasn't prepared for that and teetered briefly — until she placed her hands flat against his chest for balance. Elias's gaze slid to her hands, and he briefly registered the fact that the long, graceful fingers pressed against him bore calluses, underscoring, perhaps, the unjustness of his accusations.

Flushing deeply, she took another step away from him. She looked chastened, uncertain.

"Let us not prolong this ordeal between us," Elias said, not unkindly. "My words were ill-considered and mean-spirited, but perhaps they serve to demonstrate how wrongheaded my trip here was."

"I only mean to tell you that you have misread my character," she said quietly.

Had he? He doubted that. It did not matter in any case. They were quits, and tomorrow he would see his solicitor.

"Whatever you think of me," she continued, "and I understand that it is not flattering in the least, I ask you to believe that I do not seek my neighbors' approval out of any vainglorious attempt to persuade them to think well of me. For that matter, I do not seek your approval either, which is fortunate since clearly I do not have it."

Elias regarded her. "And yet you are at pains to correct my misimpression."

"Only of my motives. I am no Lady Bountiful, sir."

Hearing his characterization of her repeated, Elias winced. "I meant no offense." He paused. "No, that is untrue. I let anger rule, and I can say with some conviction that my intentions were as base and offensive as you took them to be. I think we will both agree that our talks have been futile and we will both be better for abandoning them."

"I wish to explain."

He eyed the door wistfully. "That is not necessary. Now, if you will pardon me, I will take my leave."

She stepped between him and the door.

Elias stopped himself — just barely — from reaching out and setting her from him. Indeed, their proximity was muddling things again. Suppressing a sigh, he waited. Obviously, she intended for him to hear her out.

So it surprised him when he saw the shimmering in her eyes, the slight trembling about her lips. To be sure, he'd been unnecessarily judgmental. But why the devil were women so sensitive? "Lady Harriet —" he began.

"I do not expect you to approve of me," she said. "But the truth is that I am endeavoring to do right by this inheritance. I mean to use it for good." She hesitated. "You see, I am responsible for Freddy's death."

Elias stilled.

"That is why I intend to set things right, to put that money toward good. I am not trying to impress anyone with my charity. It is what I *must* do." Her voice wobbled on the last. A tear threatened to spill over onto her cheek.

"According to the account provided to my solicitor," Elias said carefully, "Freddy's heart simply gave out. There is nothing you could have done."

"I will never know. He was not at home that night. He was with another woman."

Egad. That was a detail he had no wish to hear. To be sure, Freddy had always been one for the ladies. Still, to learn such a thing from his widow, to be confronted with her pain — Elias could think of no response. So he did the only thing he could, which was to search his pockets for a handkerchief and, that failing to produce anything suitable, untie his neckcloth and offer it to her to dry her eyes.

She looked surprised, but accepted it silently.

Elias hesitated, uncertain whether it was fitting to wade into such murky waters. But she had broached the subject, so perhaps she wished to discuss it. "If Freddy was with someone else," he said at last, "I fail to see how his death could have been your fault."

Lady Harriet shook her head. "Please understand: I did not object to his liaisons. Indeed,

I tolerated them, a fact I still do not regret. Freddy deserved to be happy, and I was unable to give him that. I drove him to the very excesses that led to his death."

"Nonsense," Elias said sharply. "Freddy Worthington was incapable of fidelity."

She eyed him in surprise. "So you knew of Freddy's...proclivities. I suppose the whole world knew. No matter. He would have been true to the right woman."

"Again, madam: utter nonsense."

"He would not have spent his days wrecking his health with drink and other...pursuits had I been able to please him," she persisted.

Elias heartily wished to be anywhere else but here, listening to this too-intimate confession. He also wanted to shake some sense into her. "You are not responsible."

"I am," she said softly. "He went elsewhere because I could not please him. Not in the way a woman is able to please a man."

That sentence hung there, in the space between them, as if she had shouted it to the skies, when in reality she'd spoken in a quiet, pensive voice.

"Freddy had a defective heart," Elias said. "It is useless to blame yourself."

But she would not be swayed. "You cannot know how it embarrasses me to confess such an inadequacy. But it is the truth."

If only it were possible to look away from those shimmering blue eyes. Now a tear did spill over, and without thinking he reached out and brushed it away with his thumb, a shocking intimacy, he belatedly realized. But she scarcely seemed to notice.

"You may think me a tiresome bluestocking," she continued. "But I did wish to please Freddy. I *did*." Her voice broke on the last.

Elias found he could not take his eyes from her face. The rosy warmth of her cheeks contrasted with the cool blue of her eyes, and seemed to grow warmer as their gazes held.

"Lady Harriet," he said gruffly, "if Freddy was not satisfied in your arms, it was his own damned fault."

As her watery gaze held his, Elias told himself he meant only to comfort her, as one might comfort a child. Gingerly, awkwardly, he patted her shoulder. But she bit her lip, and he could see the effort it cost her to keep her emotions in check. And so he extended his arms — stiffly, like two sticks of wood. After a moment's hesitation, she leaned toward him and put her head against his chest. He heard a soft sob.

He did not know what to do with his arms, exactly. They seemed to want to close around her, and so they did — tentatively, uneasily, as if they could not quite negotiate the distance between confronting his adversary and extending her charity.

And so they passed a long — very long — moment, during which Elias grew keenly aware of the softness of her form against his and the warmth of her skin through the muslin of her frock, the muslin he'd earlier thought insipid but which now taunted him with rough-textured fibers that awakened his senses.

Finally, she looked up at him. Why had he never noticed her eyes were the color of Caribbean seas? He realized he was staring, so he dropped his gaze lower and found instant consolation in studying the smooth rosy flesh of her mouth.

Not good, he thought, and wrenched his gaze away. It fixed lower still, on the graceful curve of her neck, then the slope of her shoulders — some pale freckles there, he noticed — and then, alas, on the slight rise of her breasts, very little of which was actually exposed, that muslin frock being the soul of modesty.

Freddy, God rest him, was an idiot. Strident though she may be, this woman huddled against him possessed a spellbinding sensuality. It shocked him to realize that.

Elias felt in danger of losing his moorings. All he intended was to offer his assurances that she had been blameless in Freddy's death, but his mind had taken him on another journey. At last she gave an audible sigh and stepped away from him.

"I appreciate your kindness, my lord," she said in a shaky voice. "But I am well aware of my faults."

"I am not kind," he said.

That startled her. Elias thought it was well that she had severed their physical connection, because otherwise he would be tempted to reach out and touch her chin, perhaps tilting it slightly upward for closer inspection of those rosy lips.

He would slip his other hand around her waist and pull her close, savoring the soft fullness of her breasts against his chest, though perhaps this time with more leisurely appreciation.

"Harriet!" said a shrill voice. "Whoever is this man? And what is he doing to your, er, person?"

'Twas no fantasy, Elias realized, suddenly and acutely aware that his own mouth was but a hair's breadth from Lady Harriet Worthington's lovely lips. And that he had, in fact, pulled her once more into his arms.

CHAPTER FOUR

"POOR EUSTACE!" DRAPING herself in a chair, Monica Tanksley took refuge in her smelling salts. "I cannot believe you have betrayed me like this, Harriet. Poor, poor Eustace!"

Harriet, mortified that she had succumbed to guilt and self-pity in the presence of Lord Westwood, had quickly recovered her poise and summoned more tea. Monica was inclined to grow overset over every perceived slight to her only son, regardless of whether it was intended. On second thought, Harriet decided, sherry was called for.

She signaled to Horace to bring that and the little iced cakes her neighbor loved.

"Now, Monica, it is not what you think," Harriet began, then trailed off. In truth, she could not have explained what had transpired. One moment Lord Westwood was comforting her, and the next — well, she did not know exactly how to describe what had happened next. "Anyway, Eustace has no more regard for me than he does for that chair. It is useless for you to persist in the notion that we should suit. At all events, I am far too old for him."

"By but a handful of years," Monica replied plaintively. "And you are young enough that I may yet hope for grandchildren. Moreover, I am quite certain you would keep him out of trouble."

Harriet sighed inwardly. The older woman's belief that her best friend and son would make a good match was more than wrongheaded; it was bizarre. But she knew the notion was born of Monica's dismay that Eustace had surrounded himself with some unsavory companions of late — and the futile hope that Harriet could negate their influence. The wife Monica envisioned for her son was more of a guardian than a helpmeet.

Her friend was more than a decade older than Harriet, slender and with thin, light brown hair that would likely gray within a few years. Her sharp-set nose and angular features gave her a saturnine appearance in the happiest of times, but now more than adequately conveyed her disappointment. "You do not know my son as I do," she added mournfully. "He is a dear, sensitive soul. To learn that you have given yourself to this...this rakehell, will be more than he could manage. He will be inconsolable."

A dry cough from Lord Westwood, who had remained ominously silent throughout Monica's hysterics, drew Harriet's attention. Conspicuously absent his neckcloth, which Harriet had laid carefully on a chair, the earl stood stiffly in the middle of the room, undoubtedly eager to take his leave but perhaps too much the gentleman to depart in the midst of Monica's hysterics.

"Monica, allow me to introduce Lord Westwood. He is — was — Freddy's partner in the spice company. He is here to consult with me on business matters." Harriet was well aware that benign explanation would not satisfy Monica's curiosity over her relationship with the earl, which had doubtless appeared rather the opposite of businesslike when Monica came upon them.

Monica cast the earl a jaundiced eye.

"My pleasure, madam," Lord Westwood said politely, with a quick bow.

"I imagine it was," Monica retorted meaningfully.

The earl opened his mouth to respond, then evidently thought better of it and lapsed into silence once more.

Eager to head off any fireworks, Harriet hastily grabbed the plate of iced cakes and passed them to Monica and the earl. Lord Westwood shook his head, clearly impatient to leave. But she held the plate in front of him for another moment and, with a barely perceptible sigh, he gave in. Absently, he took a bite, then looked up quickly in surprise. In the next instant, the entire piece had vanished.

"Exceptional," he murmured, reaching for a second piece.

Monica glared at him. "It is the rose water that makes it special."

He tilted his head consideringly. "It is the mace," he corrected. "It marries well with the sugar but does not eclipse the underlying tartness that keeps the cake from being cloying."

"Lemon juice," Harriet put in quickly as Monica's expression darkened. "Just a dash, mind you. It is one of my favor —"

"I still say it is the rose water," Monica groused, but she regarded Lord Westwood with new interest.

"The hint of roses is all to the good," he conceded, "but you must own that the sweetness of the spice and sugar harmonizes perfectly with the citrus."

Monica eyed him with grudging respect. "I have never met a man with such comprehension of taste."

"Lord Westwood is in the spice trade," Harriet said. "He searches the West Indies for products that might appeal to English tastes and ships them here to enliven our ordinary cuisine with a bit of the exotic."

The earl looked at her in surprise. "Never say that you actually have an inkling of what my business is about?"

"*Our* business," Harriet corrected. "I hope you did not think me entirely ignorant, my lord."

"No, merely someone who sells off shares of a hugely profitable business for a fraction of their worth."

Harriet snatched the plate of cakes away just as he was about to snare another one.

The tart exchange was not lost on Monica. "Perhaps I misconstrued things," she said, studying them. "I expect it is only a fleeting attraction between you. I have heard that these things can happen." She paused, then added wistfully, "Not, unfortunately, to me."

Harriet flushed. "Lord Westwood and I are merely business partners."

Monica only returned her a knowing look and reached for another cake.

But Lord Westwood had had enough. "Let me assure you, madam, that the only commonality Lady Harriet and I share is one for exceptional gastronomy." Bowing deeply, he left, not bothering to retrieve the damp swath of linen that had served as his cravat.

Harriet stared after him for a moment, then felt Monica's gaze on her and managed a weak smile. "Truly, Monica, there is naught between us."

Monica simply shook her head. "Oh, dear, Harriet. Oh, dear, dear, dear."

<hr>

"I know what I saw, and it weren't any business discussion." Heavenly eyed her sister meaningfully across the kitchen table. "They were closer than the icing to those cakes of yours."

Celestial sighed. "Wouldn't be a bad turn of events. The man does have a robust appetite," she said approvingly. "That husband of hers never showed the least bit of interest in her before his port. More often than not he was too castaway to eat. Lord Westwood's plate comes back clean as a whistle."

"Lord Westwood has an appetite, all right."

Heavenly frowned. "And herself having no idea about men. She might as well be a green girl."

Horace tried to look stern, but in truth he was just as interested in what had transpired between his mistress and the earl. He had followed Mrs. Tanksley into the drawing room in a vain attempt to announce her presence and had thus witnessed the same…closeness that Mrs. Tanksley had. Heavenly, he soon learned, had been watching from the adjacent parlor.

"Lady Harriet would be distressed to know you had been spying," he said disapprovingly.

"Who's to tell her?" Heavenly retorted. "Not me."

"Nor I," Celestial promised.

"If only you had seen her, Celestial." Heavenly shook her head in wonder. "Wasn't an ounce of daylight between them."

"He must have started it."

"Aye. Lady Harriet wouldn't have," Heavenly said.

"Not a bit," Celestial agreed.

But Heavenly looked thoughtful. "Could be our lady is coming into her own," she offered.

Celestial considered that. "Wouldn't be a moment too soon. After what that husband of hers put her through, she deserves to be happy."

"Was a scoundrel, that one," Heavenly agreed.

"You are speaking of our dear departed employer," Horace said reprovingly. As he'd been part of the viscount's household before his marriage to Lady Harriet, he usually rushed to his late employer's defense. Still, there was no denying facts.

"Wasn't nothing dear about him," Heavenly retorted.

Horace remained tactfully silent. Lord Worthington had been, by any reckoning, something of a cad. But he would not indulge in kitchen gossip, either. Or at least he would not appear to.

"It has been a year since the viscount's death," he said in a neutral tone. "It is perfectly understandable that Lady Harriet wishes to enjoy a gentleman's company once more."

"No, it ain't," Heavenly corrected. "She is scared to death of men."

Horace frowned. "She runs that bakery, lives here on her own, throws all those parties in town by herself. Why, Lady Harriet fears nothing."

Heavenly exchanged a meaningful look with her sister. "Men are so ignorant," she said."

Celestial regarded Horace pityingly.

The trouble with living near a small village in the country is that the only people available to invite to dinner were those one saw every day, Harriet thought glumly as she put the finishing touches on the meal. She had invited the Tanksleys and Squire Gibbs to dinner before the morning's unfortunate events. She assumed Lord Westwood would return for dinner, despite their very odd encounter over tea. But her earlier note to him had neglected to mention that his dinner companion would include the man with whom he had so recently been at fisticuffs. There being no fitting way to send a message round to either man at this hour informing him of that fact, Harriet suspected her dinner would be a complete disaster.

Fortunately, she would soon remove to London, where her salons would be as lively and fascinating as ever, and where people knew how to comport themselves even when the discourse grew outlandish.

She spent every Season in town — not for the parties and social whirl but for the stimulating talk that accompanied the arrival of Parliament. Over the years, her town house had become a gathering place for all manner of political figures from radicals to Tories. What flourished was a yeasty mix of ideas as scintillating as the food she served to accompany them. Her invitations were prized, although Freddy had often preferred to spend his evenings elsewhere.

Last Season she did not go to town. It was not because she was in mourning. She had simply not wished to encounter Freddy's friends — especially Lady Forth, who knew all too well Harriet's failures as a wife.

Throughout her disastrous marriage, Harriet had kept an open mind, reasoning that Freddy had every right to seek his own happiness when he could not find it at home. She did not regret her decision. But she did regret that all of London knew that Caroline Forth was Freddy's mistress. And Cecily Browning before that. And Lady Iris before that. And any number of dazzling stars in the *ton's* firmament.

Before her marriage, which had followed close on her first and only London Season, Harriet found Freddy a captivating diversion from the suffocating existence she had led in her father's gloomy castle. She had grown up lonely, her father having retreated so far into his grief over her mother's death as to appear as cold as those Cornwall winters.

Harriet had never seen a man so full of life as Freddy. He had swept her away with his flattery and romantic ways. Harriet had wanted to believe that he cared for her; she yearned to find in another human being the warmth she had never known — and yes, she had been eager to share his bed. Early in her marriage, however, she discovered that she had mistaken his practiced charm for sentiment and that Freddy had fallen in love with her dowry, not the woman attached to it. And although he granted her all the freedom a wife could want, he had no intention of conceding his own.

Marital intimacy had left her feeling empty and disregarded. Indeed, intimacy had only deepened the wedge between them, for it threw into sharp relief the hollowness of their union. How, Harriet had often wondered, was it possible to share such intimate touching yet remain such perfect strangers? Freddy's eyes had looked past her, and that chilled her more than anything else. Later, after she discovered the true state of his allegiance, which was to say none, Harriet thought that perhaps things had worked out for the best after all. She did not try to cajole or wheedle or reproach her husband, accepting that her initial attraction to him had been misguided and that his for her had been nonexistent, merely a reflection of her own fantasies.

Over the five years of their marriage, she immersed herself in her salons and in her baking. In time, she almost forgot about Freddy's dalliances.

Every time she encountered Lady Forth at a party or the opera, she remembered, of course. It was there in the woman's pitying eyes, in the cool contempt with which she regarded Freddy's eccentric wife. At such times Harriet's resolve and confidence faltered, and it became more difficult to tell herself she was not to blame for Freddy's straying. She considered whether her ignorance of men might have contributed to his rejection. That thought made her feel small and inadequate, but she did not know how to overcome her deficiencies.

Nor did she know how to reconcile her failure to please Freddy with her insistence since his death that she needed no man, that her world was complete as it was. It was as if she endeavored to compensate for her failures by removing any possibility of being judged for them. She was not unaware of the irony but, as with Freddy's dalliances, chose not to dwell on it.

A finality had settled over her since Freddy's death, a peace of sorts. After all, it was but one more way in which he'd left her. Still, she could not help but conclude that marriage was overrated and desire but an illusion. This thing between women and men that had inspired poets and flowery words over the centuries was vastly inferior to the lofty literature it had spawned.

Or so she had thought.

That very strange moment with Lord Westwood, that embrace — if that's what it was — had unsettled her. Reflecting on that moment now, she was mortified that she had confessed to him her torment over her marriage, that she had given in to emotion and weakness.

It had been oddly comforting to linger within the circle of his arms. And there was something else: a heightened awareness of how nicely she fit within them. But that was a silly notion, another misguided fantasy. Men and women did not "fit" together. That was an illusion akin to that which led her into marriage with a man oblivious to any needs but his own. She might be a good judge of recipes, but she was a dreadful judge of men.

And yet, it struck her that Lord Westwood would be an excellent teacher. He was not like Freddy. He was sober and serious, and not in the least frivolous. Certainly, he was not charming or diverting. But neither did he look past her. Indeed, when he fixed her with those dark eyes and bluntly stated his wishes, she did not doubt the truth of his words. He might be capable of negotiating ploys in the service of his business interests, but he was not a man to shun honesty.

In recent weeks, Harriet had thought she was ready to return to London for the first time since Freddy's death, ready to face her husband's friends, perhaps even his mistresses. Not that she *wished* to face them. There would be whispers — perhaps even open comments — about Freddy's scandalous exit from the world. She would not mind the whispers as much as the pity.

Still, it was past time to leave the countryside. Squire Gibbs's behavior was becoming boorish. Monica's scheme to match her with Eustace was silly in the extreme. Harriet had grown so preoccupied with the drama around her she could not even think clearly.

But she had grave doubts: Was she truly prepared to face Lady Forth and those who would salivate at seeing the two of them at the same social events? Was she strong enough to pick up the threads of her life again? In the immediate aftermath of Freddy's death, she had thought so — only to lost heart and flee to the country instead. Here in Worthington she had stayed busy, immersing herself in her shop and her baking, avoiding confrontation with the menacing forces her marriage had spawned.

Could she face those alone? Harriet had no answer.

With a sigh, she went to the kitchen to survey the last-minute preparations for dinner. "Do not forget to add the juice of an orange, and perhaps a bit of the peel," she told Celestial. "Curry welcomes a bit of tang."

"Yes, Miss Harriet. Is that nice lord coming to dinner?"

Harriet eyed her sharply. "Lord Westwood dines with us. Why do you ask?"

Celestial shrugged. "No reason."

Harriet studied her. "Is there something you wish to say, Celestial?"

"If I had my way, I'd have a sweet-goer, too," Celestial said, "but Heavenly won't hear of it."

Harried frowned. "Sweet-goer?"

"A gent," Celestial said. "Maybe not a prime one like that earl of yours, but a swell who knows a thing or two about —"

"Lord Westwood is a business associate," Harriet insisted. "He is not my, er, gent. I cannot imagine why you would conclude such a thing."

Celestial did not reply.

Harriet studied her. Celestial had always been the more restless of the twins, Heavenly the more dominating. Both held strong views and did not hesitate to voice them, viewing it as their prerogative for their long years of service. Indeed, they were more family than her own father. Celestial had treated Harriet's rare illnesses with potions made from her plants, and she was a kindred spirit in the kitchen.

The sisters were tall, with dark brown hair that set off their ruddy features, their chief physical difference being that Heavenly alone possessed one green eye and one blue one. When Heavenly turned the full force of her gaze and sharp tongue on someone with the bad judgment to cross her, the effect was as if a spirit from the underworld was let loose upon the hapless offender.

Harriet had often wondered why neither had

married. Then again, they presented a formidable front, as if they were united against the world. Perhaps no man was brave enough to try to part them.

"What say has Heavenly over any gentleman of yours?" Harriet asked.

Celestial set down her spoon. "It's because we are twins. She doesn't want us to part. I told her it wouldn't be like that, that we'd always be close, but she don't believe it. Every time a man pays me any mind, she takes it as a betrayal."

"But you are a grown woman," Harriet protested.

"Aye. Thirty-three years on my plate," Celestial said mournfully. "Most women my age have birthed their children. Some even have grandchildren. I won't ever have a family if Heavenly has her way."

"You are old enough to make your own decisions," Harriet said.

Celestial just shook her head. "Heavenly does things her own way. Not a man alive strong enough to change that."

Harriet regarded the other woman intently. "Is there someone who has caught your fancy, Celestial?"

Celestial shook her head, but Harriet did not miss the shadow that crossed her face.

"The monarchy is out of touch."

"Eustace!" his mother said reprovingly. "That is unacceptable talk."

"Come now, Monica," Lady Harriet said. "The country is rife with criticism of the Prince. Eustace says no more than what has already been said."

All eyes went to the young man posed stiffly at the mantelpiece, his pale blue eyes radiating an air of defiance.

"There are many who think the current movement to reform Parliament must extend even further — to the royals themselves," he declared. "Why do we need them? That fat Prince does nothing but squander our money —"

"Treason," pronounced Squire Gibbs, one of the few words he had uttered all evening. "Pure treason."

Mrs. Tanksley's gaze lingered on the squire. "I cannot think what has put such radical notions in Eustace's head," she said sorrowfully.

"Why, the state of the country, of course," Lady Harriet replied. "The soldiers who fought so bravely abroad have no jobs at home. Riots erupt over the price of bread. Taxes are high, yet the Prince demands more and more money from Parliament to pay his debts."

May the fates spare him the company of a woman who dabbled in politics, Elias thought grimly. Though he had no great love of the Regent, Elias had fought for the very government Lady Harriet scorned and would never join the ranks of its public critics. He was determined, however, to keep these thoughts to himself, as he had no desire to prolong the current discussion.

And, if truth be told, his mind was occupied

with more troubling concerns. The very brief interlude with Lady Harriet this afternoon had been inappropriate. Indeed, it was dawning on him that the scene onto which Mrs. Tanksley had stumbled could be viewed — were Lady Harriet an innocent, which as a widow she was not — as compromising.

To be sure, he had only meant to comfort her. His conscience was clear on that score. But even widows, unless they wished to ruin their reputations, did not engage in such close contact with men in easy view of any servant or friend who might drop by.

And though Elias had little regard for society's musty strictures, his own code did not include publicly embarrassing any woman. Perhaps more importantly, he hoped he had not left her with an impression that he was drawn to her in that way. If there were ever two people in this world who did not suit, it was he and Lady Harriet.

She was an excellent cook, of course, as tonight's dinner again underscored. It began with a broth of beef bones with wild mushrooms that provided deep, earthy notes. It was followed by roasted squab, green beans so delicate and thin that they stood in perfect counterpoint to the toasted slivers of nuts and caramelized onions that adorned them, a rack of lamb, and, for the finish, raspberries in orange liqueur. There was not a wrong note anywhere. Then again, Elias had come to expect no less.

Conversation that accompanied dinner, however, had been strained. That oafish Gibbs fellow had said very little, but Mrs. Tanksley more than made up for that with her endless commentary on the vagaries of the weather.

Afterward came more stilted conversation in the drawing room. The convention of the gentlemen's port had been dispensed with, it being tacitly conceded that he and Squire Gibbs could have little wish to engage in polite discourse after the events in Lady Harriet's bake shop.

It would soon be time for the guests to take their leave. Elias's conscience told him that conversation by way of apology was perhaps needed between Lady Harriet and himself. He could ignore the incident — he certainly had no wish to embarrass her by reminding her of her distress, which was doubtless the only reason she had sought refuge in his arms, however briefly. Ignoring things was not his way, however. Therefore, he would speak with her. He did not know what he would say or how he would do so without attracting the notice of the others.

Help came from two unexpected directions.

"My lord." Lady Harriet's soft, urgent tone intruded on his thoughts. "I must speak to you privately."

But a servant came into the room just then, and she moved away to speak to the man.

Elias surveyed the room. Gibbs was flushed from the wine. Mrs. Tanksley was fanning herself rapidly. There seemed to be an awkward tension between the squire and Lady Harriet's friend — perhaps owing to Gibbs's denunciation of Eustace's views. Eustace himself looked thoroughly bored and not the least interested, incidentally, in pursuing a suit with Lady Harriet, no matter how much his parent might wish it.

Strangely, when Eustace saw Elias studying him, he grinned and, with a conspiratorial air, left his pose near the mantel and walked toward him.

"I have noticed the way you study Lady Harriet," he said in a low tone. "I can see you wish a moment alone with her. I will suggest that the three of us take a turn in the garden, and then I will leave you. I weary of the company and it will serve as my exit. Not a moment too soon, I might add."

Damned if he needed a half-fledged lad to tell him how to get a woman alone. Still, the idea had merit. Elias could think of no other solution that would foster intimate conversation without sending Mrs. Tanksley further into the doldrums.

Good as his word, Eustace approached Lady Harriet moments later.

"Will you favor me with a turn in the garden?" he asked.

Mrs. Tanksley perked up at that, and beamed, that is until Eustace's next words: "And Lord Westwood, as well. I would welcome a tutorial on the spice business, sir."

Elias was forced to concede that the youth possessed an aplomb well beyond his years. Moreover, he was obviously sensible of his mother's matchmaking scheme, knowing that she would look favorably on just such a nocturnal walk as he proposed.

Eustace offered his arm to a slightly puzzled

Lady Harriet, and Elias quickly fell into step beside them as they exited the room, leaving Gibbs and Mrs. Tanksley to their various moods. But as soon as they reached the garden, Eustace apologized to Lady Harriet for his early end to the evening and, with a quick bow and a knowing wink at Elias, headed swiftly out the garden gate.

Lady Harriet stared after him. "I do not know what has got into Eustace."

Elias knew he would not get a better opportunity. He cleared his throat. "Lady Harriet, I wish to say —"

"One moment, my lord," she interjected. "We are quite alone here and may speak privately, but I feel the need for some false courage. For an idea has come to me, and I own that it wants fortifying."

After that very strange remark — and to Elias's surprise — she led him back into the house through a different door, one that opened into a short corridor, and then into a study. There, she made straightaway to a table that held a decanter and glasses. She filled two of them. Elias waited politely for her to offer him one.

Instead, she drank a large amount from her own glass in one quick gulp. Her instant sputtering told him she was not familiar with strong drink. In fact, it was some moments before she could speak. At last she looked up with a stricken expression. "Oh dear! Where are my manners?" Belatedly, she offered him the other glass.

Cautiously, Elias took a sip. Brandy — French, if

he did not miss his guess. He wondered how she came by it. Ah, but Freddy would have insisted on the best.

Elias had not noticed until now that her green gown was the precise color of an exotic apple he had once found growing, rather incongruously, on an island in the lower Caribbean. It was lovely against her auburn hair, which was coiled beguilingly into a single long curl that drifted over her shoulder. Still, this was no time for distractions. He would not get a better chance to speak to her.

"Lady Harriet," he began in a formal tone. "I am sensible that your friend made untoward assumptions after seeing us earlier today in such close…congress. For that I take full responsibility. I should have taken more care to avoid —"

Her giggle halted him mid-sentence. Then she covered her mouth. Quickly, she poured another measure of brandy into her glass.

"It is not my wish to dishonor you," he continued, determined to get through the thing. "As a widow, you have your reputation to think of, and it is a gentleman's responsibility to be mindful as well. May I offer you my deepest apology for my conduct?"

"Come, my lord," she said. "There can be no dishonor. I am no green girl. I have been married, with all of the sordid knowledge and regret that comes with that state."

Her candor startled him. "I, er, nevertheless —"

"Besides — you merely comforted me. I see no breach in that. Rather, I should have expressed my gratitude. Allow me to do so now. Thank you, sir." She smiled at him.

Elias thought perhaps he had not fully appreciated the appealing sparkle in her blue eyes, nor the way her lips curved upward like a rosy bow when she smiled. "Still, I would like to rectify matters," he said.

She regarded him with a puzzled expression. "Oh? How?"

That was the rub, wasn't it? "The cursed truth of the matter is that I have no idea. Perhaps I have embarrassed you even by mentioning it." Elias took a sip of his own brandy, feeling tongue-tied and foolish.

She responded with a crooked smile. "I should have permitted you to flee when you had a mind to this afternoon instead of forcing you to play nursemaid to me."

"I was not fleeing —"

"Anyway, widows are not expected to comport themselves as virgins. Oh, dear! I am certain I should not say that word in mixed company." She then drank another quantity of brandy.

"To return to my point," he continued resolutely. "Our…closeness was in easy view of anyone who might happen by. Although I have little use for society's strictures, I am sensible that others might well follow them."

She studied him. "I suppose we are back to the question of what you intend to propose."

This was a disaster beyond saving. "I am no good at these parlor games," he growled. "Is there something else you wish for? By all means name it. Short of claiming the rest of my business, that is. Which will be worth precious little if your current course continues." With that, Elias drained the rest of his glass.

Her smile caught him unawares. "Why, yes, my lord. There is something." She took another sip of brandy, then eyed the decanter. "I do believe I could come to tolerate this." She refilled her own glass, then his.

Elias savored the brandy's bracing burn as he waited, unable to imagine what service she would compel from him.

Finally, Lady Harriet leveled her clear blue gaze at him. "We should not suit, so let us stipulate that straightaway. There is nothing between us by way of personal regard, no matter what Monica thought she saw. Do you agree?"

The conversation had taken an ominous turn, Elias thought. "Yes. Certainly."

"Still, I find that I need you just now," she continued. "And so, I am in the unenviable position of proposing to you, my lord. Marriage, that is."

Elias's shock must have been evident, for she quickly added, "We would not really marry, of course, merely pretend for a short while to be engaged."

"Pretend," he echoed, dazed.

She nodded. "If you agree, I will give you my shares of your business."

It was what he wanted. And not.

Not, not, not.

CHAPTER FIVE

THE BRANDY HAD made her slightly dizzy, but Harriet had no trouble perceiving that she had stunned Lord Westwood speechless. She felt somewhat guilty. After all, there was no real need for him to make amends. She should have reassured him on that score, but instead she found his awkward, determined apology intriguing, even appealing. But Monica was no gossip. She would not have spread word of their odd embrace.

And though it mortified Harriet that her weakness had caused her to seek comfort in his nearness, that unexpected interlude had also been strangely stimulating. The scent of sandalwood amid the robust woolen of Lord Westwood's tailcoat had been almost intoxicating. She had not been that close to a man since Freddy. Even with Freddy, Harriet did not recall feeling quite so...aware.

Part of her wished that Lord Westwood had not greeted her proposal with such shock and dismay. Did he loathe her so very much? Was there another woman with whom he had an understanding? She hadn't thought of that complication. Surely, he would mention such a fact — though speech seemed well beyond him at the moment.

"I am sorry to have shocked you," she said, pouring more brandy into his glass. "I would like to give you time to think about my proposal, but I am compelled to mention that I remove to London in a fortnight. I would expect you to do likewise — in the interest of recovering your shares, of course."

Lord Westwood eyed her over the rim of his glass. "In the interest of recovering my shares," he said slowly, "I would do a great many things."

"But marrying me had not been one of those, had it, my lord? Still, you need only pretend to be my betrothed for a bit," Harriet assured him. "I will cry off by Season's end. If you wish, I will put that in writing."

He regarded her warily. "A sworn statement?"

"In the presence of our solicitors," she affirmed.

His assessing gaze held hers. His inspection was such that Harriet felt the need to look away but found, oddly, that she could not. What must he think of her? But it did not matter. Having found the perfect solution to her fears — and she was honest enough to acknowledge to herself that she was weak to need such a crutch — she now felt positively giddy. It was a very good bargain for him as well. By the end of their masquerade, he would be in full possession of his shares.

And yet, he did not look happy — rather, the opposite. His brows met like thunderclouds. His dark eyes narrowed. A muscle clenched in his jaw. Harriet faltered in the face of his obvious displeasure. She took another sip of the bracing brandy and found the courage to meet his gaze again.

"Why?" he asked.

Why indeed? It was difficult to explain to a man like Lord Westwood, who exuded such confidence and self-awareness.

"To be clear," Harriet said. "I do not depend upon masculine appreciation for my worth. Indeed, my life is very nearly perfect."

He arched a brow but said nothing.

"I surround myself with good food and scintillating company," she said. "I am content to go on like this, happily enjoying my independence. I do not need a man."

"So you have said. And yet, it would seem you have need of me."

Harriet looked away. "I have not been to town since Freddy's death," she said, thankful for the brandy's false courage. "People will make a to-do over my return. I feel strangely reticent to face them, especially since I bear some blame for his death. I want to move on with my life, but I find that just now I need fortification, a suit of armor." She eyed him apologetically. "That would be you, my lord. I hope you do not mind."

There was a long silence. Then: "Balderdash."

Harriet eyed him in confusion. "I do not understand."

His gaze narrowed. "You need no buffer against the world. That is at odds with everything you have declared to be the case in our brief, albeit turbulent, acquaintance. Do not ask me to believe such nonsense."

Harriet was silent for a moment. "Perhaps I have not been completely frank," she conceded. "I have omitted something."

Lord Westwood ran a finger over the rim of his glass, but his gaze never left her face. "What?"

She took a deep breath. "The truth is, my lord, I would like to learn to overcome my deficiencies. I would like to learn how the game between men and women is played."

"Good God." He set his glass on the table with a thump.

"I told myself that it did not matter that Freddy did not want me." The words came out in a rush. "But it did matter. Because of me, he fell into unhealthful pursuits. In some way that I do not understand, I must do penance for that, my lord. I must learn to overcome my deficiency. And then I will be able to move on with my life. Otherwise, this marriage that Freddy and I had stands as meaningless. One must learn from one's failures. 'Tis all for naught, otherwise."

"Lady Harriet —"

"But I do not have the slightest idea how to go about it." Harriet turned away from his penetrating gaze. "I feel helpless. I have never felt helpless before."

"I am quite certain of that" was his brusque response.

"It is not that I wish to attract another husband," she said. "I am done with all of that. I will never marry again. I only want to know how this thing between men and women is done. I went about it all wrong, you see. I had not the least understanding of desire."

There was a prolonged silence. Harriet ventured a look at him. She had expected to see ridicule or even embarrassment in his eyes, but she was not prepared to see steel.

"Just how do you expect me to earn my shares?" he asked in a dangerous tone.

Harriet eyed him blankly. "I do not understand."

"What, exactly, must I do to win them?"

"Merely pretend to be my betrothed," she said. "Escort me to parties, dance with me. The things that betrothed couples do."

"How does that help you overcome this alleged deficiency of yours?"

Harriet could see he was intent on making a point, but it eluded her. "I still do not understand."

"You wish to know 'how it is done.' A kiss — that must be worth a dozen or so shares." His lips thinned disdainfully. "But at that rate, it will take an age to win them all back."

"I —"

"Thus it will be necessary to speed up the pace," he said, cutting her off. "Perhaps a tumble in the carriage — might that be worth as much as fifty shares?" He stroked his chin as if pondering the matter. "Would that teach you about desire?"

Harriet paled.

"I thought only whores put a price on their services," he growled. "Little did I realize I would be compelled to become one."

"I meant no insult," she said, horrified. "You

need only spend time in my company in public. I do not expect you to...to make love to me, my lord. I never — *ever* — meant to suggest that."

"I see." His brows arched contemptuously. "You wish to dance around the edges of desire — not put desire into practice."

Harriet stared at him. "My lord, I fear you have misunderstood."

"I think not."

Her face grew warm. "I know little of such things — edges or no edges."

His sharp laugh surprised her. Was he mocking her? She took a deep breath. "I wish to know enough to be sufficiently forearmed against any unscrupulous gentleman or fortune-hunter who would attempt to take advantage of a widow such as myself..."

"As if one would dare," he muttered darkly.

"...and to avoid making a fool of myself in the future, or ruining someone else's life. Do you not see?" she insisted, trying to keep her voice steady. "I fell into marriage with Freddy with no notion of what it would bring. And it was a disaster." She hesitated. "By that, I did not mean to imply that it was his fault. I did not know how to meet his needs. Even now, I do not know the remedy. I only know it is not within my reach."

"Then why not stay here in the country, away from all of that?"

Harriet raised her chin. "I will not hide. I am not a coward. I will face my mistakes and learn from them."

"But not face them alone," he said pointedly.

"You wish me to be your shield. Does that not strike you as contradictory?"

She stared at him. "Yes. You are right. I was wrong to suggest it." He had as good as called her a coward, and he was correct. How could she have come up with such an outlandish proposition? Was it the brandy talking?

The heavy silence stretched into minutes. Such was her mortification that she could not bear to look at him. Harriet put her glass on the table and squared her shoulders. She would calmly bid him goodnight and walk out of the room as if she had not just exposed herself as a great fraud. Lord Westwood would be glad to see the last of her, and who could blame him? She had made an utter fool of herself.

He cleared his throat. But Harriet could not bear to hear another denunciation. "Goodnight, my lord," she said quickly, moving to the door, not meeting his gaze. She could think of nothing else to say, no words that would erase the damage. She had insulted him and revealed herself to be the veriest fool. Her face was hot with embarrassment. "Please do me the very great favor of forgetting I spoke."

"It would be a mistake," he said gruffly.

Harriet halted. Slowly, she turned to him. "It — it would only be a temporary arrangement," she ventured. "I would never wish to feel helpless for any length of time."

"Helpless," he echoed and shook his head in disbelief.

Harriet searched his face. "My lord, do you mean to suggest that you will do this?"

"Do I have a choice, madam?"

"One always has a choice, Lord Westwood."

He grimaced. "Until I met you, I was foolish enough to think that was true."

Harriet waited, bracing herself for the finality of his rejection. "It is an outlandish notion," she conceded.

"Yes," he agreed.

"Quite unthinkable," she added.

"Yes."

Harriet frowned. "Yes, it is outlandish and unthinkable? Or yes, you will do it?"

"Both."

Harriet gasped.

"I will have it in writing," he said before she could speak.

"Of course —"

"And understand this, madam: I dance to your tune because it is the only one available at the moment." He strode to the door, then turned. His dark eyes were hard. "But I should not like to be in your shoes when the music changes."

In the end, she did sign a statement. Swearing on a Bible before Mr. Stevens, her astonished solicitor, and Lord Westwood's solicitor, Mr. Wilson, on her very first day in London, Harriet promised to break her engagement to Lord Elias Westwood by August 12, the scheduled date of Parliament's adjournment. She also directed Mr.

Stevens to permit Lord Westwood to inspect the transactions that involved the sale of her shares, a prospect that her solicitor appeared to regard with some alarm, until she firmly told him she would brook no objection. The papers sealing their bargain were signed as their betrothal announcement was sent to the *Gazette.*

Removing to town had been surprisingly easy. Nervous at the prospect of entertaining Lord Westwood on her own in London, Harriet had prevailed upon Monica and Eustace to accompany her and remain for the Season. She confessed to her friend the truth about her betrothal as they were alone in the carriage bound for London. Eustace rode alongside the carriage. Monica was delighted that Eustace would have an opportunity to acquire some town polish, though she heartily disapproved of Harriet's betrothal scheme and had not entirely given up on attaching Eustace to Harriet in the future.

"Eustace deserves a woman like you, Harriet," Monica had said. "You would be the making of him."

"He deserves a girl nearer his own age."

"He is twenty. There are five years between you."

"There is a lifetime between us, Monica. I have already buried a husband."

"He has no title, so it is not essential for him to marry a virgin," Monica replied frankly. "What I most want for him is a woman of worth. Like you, dear."

Harriet eyed her friend in amusement. "Nonsense. You only want me for a daughter-in-law so that you can be sure he is in good hands."

Monica sighed. "When you put it thus, I suppose you are right. But I want him to choose well. I don't want him blinded by some lightskirt."

"Cut the leading strings, dear," Harriet said. "Eustace must find his own future, not fall into one you have fashioned for him. Besides, the prospect of me marrying your son strikes me as unseemly. He would doubtless recoil at the prospect."

"I suppose the heart goes where it will," Monica said wearily. "I learned that when Francis ran off with my maid, curse his lecherous soul. How fitting that he died on that ship to the Colonies. A cold, watery grave suits him."

Harriet patted her hand. "What Francis did was regrettable, and I do not mean to diminish your pain, but that was years ago. You must bury the past. Perhaps in London you will meet someone to catch your fancy."

"I would rather see how Lord Westwood catches yours," her friend replied archly.

Harriet frowned. "I do not know what you mean."

"Do you not?" Monica made a tsk-tsking sound. "You cannot deny that he is a fine figure of a man."

Harriet refused to acknowledge that point. "It is a business arrangement between us, nothing more."

"My dear, I fear you are headed for disaster. This masquerade is the most ridiculous — nay, dangerous — notion you have ever devised."

"Not at all," Harriet replied. "It is a perfect solution. Lord Westwood will recover his shares. And I will learn what I did wrong with Freddy."

"You did nothing wrong. Freddy was a scapegrace. As was my Francis. Gentlemen of conscience and quality do exist, dear. Lord Westwood may be such a one."

Harriet shook her head. "I seek only a better understanding of my own deficiencies."

"You have no deficiencies," Monica retorted.

"I hope Lord Westwood will be an adequate teacher," Harriet said in a musing tone. "He can be rather gruff at times."

"An adequate teacher? Oh, I suspect so." Monica eyed her pityingly. "You may be a widow, Harriet, but you are the merest lamb."

Harriet laughed. "I have been a married woman, remember?"

"Marriage to Freddy cannot have prepared you for this deep game with a man like Lord Westwood," Monica warned.

"It is not a game," Harriet insisted. "It is a business arrangement."

"Business." Monica arched a brow. "Of course."

Heavenly and Celestial, who had not been told of the fraudulent nature of her betrothal, accepted the news of Harriet's engagement with astonishment, then glee. Even Horace had unbent sufficiently to allow himself a congratulatory smile.

But now, standing in the kitchen of her London townhouse, preparing to supervise preparation of a meal for fifty guests, Harriet could not stop thinking about something Lord Westwood had said before he left Worthington. He had stopped at the bakery for meat pies to take on his drive to town. Harriet was there, along with several of the ladies who would run the shop in her absence. He had not looked altogether pleased to see her. When she tried to explain her bread-making process, he showed a grudging curiosity in how the simple combination of flour and water could turn into such a foul-smelling mixture as that which she had flung at him and the squire.

"'Tis the wild yeast," she explained. "It causes the mixture to bubble and take on a life of its own. I pour some of it off, add more flour and water, and it ferments further. When the mixture is at its most lively, I mix the dough. I keep containers of it at different stages of the process. That way some is always available."

"Deuced lot of trouble, isn't it?"

"The effort to achieve something extraordinary is worth it," Harriet said. "Those spices of yours require some coaxing before they are ready, do they not?"

He seemed surprised at the question, but appeared to consider it. "To be sure, it can take weeks to dry the pimento berry to the precise, shriveled state and color that indicates the flavor is sufficiently concentrated —" He broke off.

"Very well," he added as she tried to suppress a smile. "Point taken. But you shall never persuade me that foul substance of yours has redeeming qualities."

The ladies had insisted on giving him a basket of assorted pastries to accompany the meat pies, but when he searched his pockets for payment, Harriet stayed his hand.

"We do not accept money here."

He frowned. "Ever?"

"The bakery is for the benefit of all."

"You give away your goods?" He eyed her incredulously. "The shop's losses must be astonishing. Why, the price of bread alone these days is substantial."

Harriet nodded. "Exactly. No one can afford to buy it. With all the rain, wheat crops have been failing. We give our bread away to all who need it. In exchange, they put in a few hours each week making more bread. It is the same with the mill. Farmers use it without cost and donate a portion of their flour to the bakery."

"That system —"

"Works quite well," she insisted. "I have heard no complaints other than from Squire Gibbs, and only because his income has been greatly reduced. He is not a bad sort, only a man with eight children and no helpmeet. I have a job for him, if he would but listen to me. But his pride has prevented him from doing so."

"You would employ the man who assaulted you?" Lord Westwood was appalled.

"Sometimes one's dearest friends come from

the ranks of former enemies — do you not think so, my lord?"

"What I think is that you live in a world of fairy tales." With those parting words, Lord Westwood had tucked the basket under his arm and departed for town.

Lord Westwood was mistaken, Harriet thought as she eyed the ingredients for the almond cheesecakes she planned to serve tonight. She did not live in a world of fairy tales. Her feet were planted firmly in reality. A woman on her own must be prepared. A wealthy widow would be fair game to seducers — Squire Gibbs had shown her that, bless his misguided soul. It was time she learned to protect herself. She had certainly known little of men when she married.

Had she loved Freddy? She'd thought so at the time. But his straying made her doubt her love and, ultimately, her own worth. Would Freddy have been unfaithful to a woman more skilled in the feminine arts? The question was unanswerable. And yet the more he had strayed, the more Harriet's doubts had consumed her.

That was the root of the secret she had told no one — not Monica, certainly not Lord Westwood. She intended to triumph over the forces between the sexes that had caused her to give her heart to a man who had not wanted it. She would learn how to keep her heart whole in a world ruled by men.

And then she would never, ever, be hurt by a man again.

CHAPTER SIX

"I'VE SEEN YOU face combat in a happier state."

Elias glowered at his batman. "As always, Henry, your views are inescapable." The news of his betrothal had left Henry uncharacteristically silent for a full thirty seconds, but he had quickly recovered to state his opinion in blunt terms.

Elias saw no need to disclose the exact nature of the betrothal. More than once he wished for someone to tell him that he had not lost his mind in agreeing to Lady Harriet's outlandish plan, but Henry would not have been the one to turn to. At forty, he was more than a decade older than Elias and even more confirmed in his bachelorhood. And while Elias had once come within a hair's breadth of marriage — disastrously so — Henry had never been tempted by the institution and thought it an altogether ruinous state. Indeed, Henry had barely contained his relief when Miss Zephyr Payne left Elias standing at the altar, a white rose in his lapel and humiliation on his face.

Not that Henry wished him unhappiness. The man was loyal and devoted. But his loyalty was that of a fellow comrade in arms. Women might be a necessary evil upon occasion, but they did not belong permanently in a man's life.

Come to think of it, that was a fair summation of his own philosophy, Elias thought grimly. It made him deeply uneasy that he had entered into a betrothal, even a fraudulent one. To be sure, it was in the service of acquiring the shares, without which he could not rest easy at night, knowing that Lady Harriet was dedicated to throwing their worth away on every cause she could find.

Elias stared at his reflection in the mirror. Lines of disapproval etched his forehead just above his nose. His jaw tensed forbiddingly. Henry was right. He looked as if he were headed for his doom.

"Do not wait for me tonight," Elias said. "I do not know when I will return." That was because he had no idea what Lady Harriet expected of him on this, the first night after the *Gazette* officially proclaimed them betrothed. Did she wish him to stay by her side like a fawning supplicant, to linger adoringly after the guests had departed?

The role of paid paramour did not suit him. Elias would rather take on Napoleon and all his eagles than attend this one eccentric, unpredictable widow tonight.

Sometime later, as his coachman maneuvered through packed streets to Berkeley Square, Elias's mood grew darker and darker. Part of him wished mightily he had simply turned the whole matter over to his solicitor and taken her to court, no matter how long the process might take. Yet the plan she offered could be achieved in a matter of weeks. Logic and his finances demanded he do as she wished so that his company would be his again as quickly as possible.

And so he would allow himself to be paraded before her friends like a circus animal so that she could improve her knowledge on the subject of desire and therefore fend off an entire gender and triumph with her prized independence intact.

Since the disaster of his own previous engagement, Elias had determinedly steered clear of those members of the fair sex who might consider him an eligible *parti*. He preferred a different sort of female, one who understood that intimate congress between the sexes was a capricious pursuit — and certainly not one that led to permanence. It was meant to be enjoyed wholeheartedly, but with the heart left entirely whole.

Yes, Elias much preferred to keep the game between the sexes as just that: a game. Lady Harriet's unorthodox proposal had merely provided a new playing field.

He pondered that. He thought about her eyes, blue as a tropical sea on a cloudless day. Her errant auburn curls, dusted with flour. That apple green gown — or any gown that wasn't dreary bombazine.

For the first time since arriving in London, Elias felt the beginnings of a smile. If Lady Harriet wished to learn about desire, perhaps she would get more than she bargained for. In the interest of the game, of course.

"Corruption. All around. In this very room, if I may be frank." With a smile, Oliver Hunt met Harriet's gaze, then turned to those gathered around him. "Beware the rich aristocrats in Parliament who profess to be in sympathy with the plight of the downtrodden."

As many of those same aristocrats now stood in Harriet's parlor, a few nervous titters echoed around the room. Harriet frowned. She did not mind Mr. Hunt's radical oratory; her parlor had seen its share over the years. What disturbed her was the portentous smile he had bestowed upon her all evening. And though he had offered felicitations over her betrothal, he had eyed Lord Westwood with ill-concealed disdain.

Mr. Hunt's visage was normally stern, as befitted a revolutionary. He was a man with a cause, and his cause — just or no — consumed him. He ought not to be smiling at his hostess in quite that way, as if they shared something special. Harriet had seen him a time or two since Freddy's death. Once he had even come to visit her in Worthington on his way to a political gathering. But nothing had transpired sufficient to generate that very odd warmth in his eyes.

Perhaps, Harriet thought, she was reading too much into his behavior. The man did have a compelling presence, which was necessary in his work. He bore a shock of fiery red hair and a wide brow that might have been modeled on sculpture of a Roman emperor. His eyes gleamed with the passion of one who believed his cause was not only just, but divinely inspired. As he spoke, he made eye contact with every member of his audience and, in the way of skilled orators, used his smooth, rumbling baritone to mesmerizing effect.

It was likely, Harriet thought, that she was mistaking the effort Mr. Hunt put forth to captivate an audience for something more personal aimed at her. That was one more example of her utter ignorance of masculine ways.

"What is the cause of the want of employment?" he demanded, lifting his voice heavenward, as if her townhouse were the vast vaulted nave of Westminster. "What is the reason our streets are filled with idle, able-bodied men?"

He paused dramatically, then pointed his finger at his audience. "Taxation! Taxation is the cause of the country's decay."

Mr. Hunt's energetic fervor doubtless accounted for his appeal to young men like Eustace, who had been eyeing him worshipfully all evening. But Mr. Hunt commanded the attention of older men as well. His audience included Tories and Whigs, along with some of the leading opinion writers of the day. Though most were accustomed to inflammatory rhetoric and absorbed his words equally, Eustace seemed truly affected.

As did Lord Westwood. But while Eustace regarded Mr. Hunt with open adoration, the earl could barely contain his irritation. He stood by her side, rigid and stern as Mr. Hunt spoke.

Her betrothal had caused quite a stir, and everyone had been eager to meet the earl. He accepted the many congratulations graciously enough, though somewhat stiffly. And while he had pronounced her almond cheesecakes excellent, he nevertheless held himself a bit apart from her. Truth be told, Harriet was not at ease around him, either. They were nearly strangers, after all. Pretending to be betrothed cast an artificiality between them that served to make their interactions all the more awkward. Strangely, Harriet was also acutely aware of another undercurrent, this one generated by a deeply masculine force in him that made it difficult for her to concentrate on her hostess duties.

She could not but admire his commanding appearance. He wore a close-fitting dark blue jacket, cut in the military style, over a plain waistcoat and black trousers that elongated his already considerable height and underscored his dark eyes and hair. The overall effect was severe, if forceful.

"And what is the cause of taxation?" Mr. Hunt continued, his voice swelling. "Corruption. The same corruption that enabled our leaders to wage expensive wars against Napoleon."

Beside her, Lord Westwood tensed. She saw him gather himself, as if for battle.

"If Napoleon had ridden up to Whitehall," Lord Westwood said in an icy tone that knifed through the room and brought instant silence, "doubtless you would have kindly held his horse for the dismount."

Mr. Hunt's startled gaze flew to the earl. The man's oratory skills were such that only the intrepid dared to challenge him. Even as Harriet watched, a slow smile spread over his features. It was the smile of a man who has spied an easy prey. He nodded in Lord Westwood's direction.

"A former military man," he said in a knowing tone, winking at the audience. "They tend to take offense when I challenge the cause that sent them into the devil's arms. Some are simply barbarians, of course. But others — poor fellows — never realized they were pawns in a rich man's game."

Lord Westwood leveled an unflinching gaze at his attacker. "Not pawns. They chose to fight to save England."

"Hear, hear!" came the approving cries. People moved closer, sensing a rousing debate.

"Save England?" Mr. Hunt regarded him in mock surprise. "Why, I wonder? So that the royalty can fatten itself on the backs of the people? Did you know that the Prince has just asked for another fifty thousand pounds to pay his debts? That Parliament, in its infinite wisdom has just expanded Princess Charlotte's allowance to sixty thousand pounds to support her lavish spending and that of her husband? And that if Leopold should outlive his amiable consort, he may even still draw from our taxes fifty thousand pounds a year?"

Lord Westwood remained silent. Mr. Hunt's lips curled cynically. "Tell me, sir: Are we to have the pleasure of forever footing the royals' outlandish bills?"

People shifted nervously. Though harsh, Mr. Hunt's accusations were nothing more than truth. Even the most conservative among them thought the Prince's debts excessive.

"We did not fight for the royals," Lord Westwood replied quietly. "We fought so that our mothers and fathers and children could retain their freedom."

"Freedom?" Mr. Hunt scoffed. "The freedom to subject ourselves to forced taxation!"

"No," Lord Westwood replied calmly. "The freedom that allows you to stand here tonight and spout such nonsense without having your head removed from your shoulders for treason."

The room erupted in laughter. Someone applauded. Others joined in. The tension immediately dissipated as the audience regarded Lord Westwood approvingly. Mr. Hunt looked decidedly nonplussed.

"It seems that Lady Harriet's betrothed disagrees with me." His mouth pulled into an expression of mock dismay as he tried to salvage his position. "I hope that does not mean that my presence here will be unwelcome in the future." He shot Harriet an ingratiating smile.

Harriet opened her mouth to assure him that it did not, but Lord Westwood spoke first. "Lady Harriet's friends will always be welcome," he said. "Indeed, they will receive my undivided attention."

It was a clear warning. Hunt's face reddened. Without another word, he turned to address some of his youthful admirers. For the moment, at least, a crisis had been averted.

Still, by the time her guests took their leave, Harriet was more than ready for them to go. Her head throbbed from the tension of the evening. She realized she had been on edge all night, burdened by the artificiality this arrangement imposed on her and the earl.

"You can relax now."

Harriet nearly jumped. Lord Westwood had barely spoken since the exchange with Mr. Hunt, and now he stood next to her, watching the last of her guests depart.

"I am perfectly relaxed," she insisted. "I enjoy these evenings immensely."

"That is why your head aches like the devil."

Harriet closed her eyes, unable to deny the obvious. Her head *was* pounding. She had not realized her tension showed.

"Did I disappoint, madam? Perhaps I should have upended the furniture or smashed Mr. Hunt's overactive jaw. Is that what you expected?" His sardonic tone added to the painful drumbeat in her head.

"Certainly not," Harriet said, regarding him warily. "Indeed, I should have been most displeased."

"Despite what your Mr. Hunt insinuates, I am not a barbarian."

"I never thought so, my lord."

"No?" His gaze narrowed. "How else do you regard a man you hired to try to seduce you?"

She flushed. "You know that is not true!"

"And yet, consider that our masquerade is a pecuniary bargain aimed at persuading the world that we are, or will soon be, lovers. Consider, moreover, that it has as its goal enhancing your knowledge of the amorous arts." His dark eyes bored into her. "Do you know another means to achieve such an end?"

"My lord, you are exceedingly blunt," Harriet said faintly. "I would never have described our arrangement in such crass terms. Indeed, I hope you may be persuaded that my intentions are not so mercenary or scandalous."

He bent toward her from his very great height, and Harriet felt a sense of alarm. But he merely spoke in a low voice into her ear. "Had you considered, madam, that it is not wise to toy with desire?"

Harriet eyed him uneasily. "That was not my intention. I regret that you have such a low impression of me, my lord."

"Ah. Then my opinion does matter?" His dark gaze was unreadable. "I would not have thought that part of our bargain."

Harriet clenched her hands at her sides. "You are twisting everything. Please believe me when I say I seek only to move on with my life without duplicating my past mistakes."

Lord Westwood crossed his arms over his chest. "Do not direct your anger at me. It is more properly laid at Freddy's door. He is the one who used you ill. You ought to have thrown the bounder out."

His words, along with the cumulative strains of

the evening, filled her with anguish. "I bear my husband no anger," she said. "He is not here to defend himself, at all events. Besides, you know nothing of my marriage, of the cost —"

"The precise root of the matter," he said.

Harriet looked up at him in confusion.

"'Tis obvious that your marriage cost you dearly. And that you are determined not to admit that."

Harriet shook her head in denial. But tears threatened and she turned away from him. She would not let him see the effect of his words.

Dimly, she was aware that he was holding something out to her. It was a folded napkin that had lain unused on one of the serving tables. "And you are still paying the price, are you not?" he asked softly.

Harriet took the cloth and dabbed at her eyes. "I do not know what is wrong with me." She tried to keep her voice steady. "I am never overset." She took a calming breath. Finally she met his gaze — with equanimity, she thought with some satisfaction.

But her composure vanished in the next instant as he reached out and captured a tendril of her hair and coiled it around his fingertip. He studied it for a moment, then returned his gaze to hers.

She wanted to look away, but those dark, compelling eyes would not permit it. And so she stood there, mesmerized, as his gaze drifted lower, to her mouth. Harriet was suddenly aware that they stood all alone in the foyer and that their closeness was such that his toying with her hair was the least of the personal intimacies to which he might avail himself. The thought did not alarm her so much as render her immobile. The air between them felt charged.

Lord Westwood released her hair, but his hand did not retreat. Instead, his fingertip trailed lightly along her jawline before withdrawing. So intently was she focused on his touch that Harriet could scarcely breathe. She felt herself lean toward him.

His mouth curved upward in a slow smile that betrayed the beginnings of a dimple before vanishing into something infinitely more sensual. He bent toward her, and Harriet felt his warm breath on her neck.

"Primrose," he murmured.

It took her a moment to understand. "I…mix it with a few crushed thyme leaves and distill the essence into an oil for fragrance," she stammered. "It is —"

"A flower that grows by the side of the road," he said softly, "wild and free, daring anyone to pick it."

Abruptly, he stepped back, severing their connection, leaving her suddenly — foolishly — bereft.

Harriet tried to recover her poise. "I regret my outburst, my lord. I am not ordinarily given to tears or excessive displays of emotion."

"Perhaps that is the difficulty."

"I do not take your meaning."

He did not respond, merely studied her in that unnerving way. Harriet lifted her chin. "I did not engage you in this charade with seduction in mind," she insisted.

"No?" Was that amusement in his gaze?

"Certainly not." She felt her face flame.

"Does that mean I should not try?"

She frowned. "Try?"

"To seduce you."

With a sudden sinking feeling, Harriet wondered whether she had made a very bad bargain in her arrangement with Lord Westwood.

"I-I simply ask that you make yourself amiable," she managed. "And endeavor not to look as though it is the worst sort of torment. We should simply keep our focus on the primary goal, which —"

Whatever else she would have said was silenced as he abruptly closed the distance between them once more. His mouth brushed hers ever so lightly, just the slightest touch for the merest of moments, the space of time it took her to inhale.

And then he was gone — out the door, into the night.

Harriet stood there, motionless for a moment. She took a deep, steadying breath. And felt something lingering in the space around her, wrapping itself around her insides like a vise. Something deeply and intoxicatingly masculine.

"Spying again?"

Celestial stepped quickly back from the dining room door. Horace stood there, his gray eyes full of disapproval. "Lady Harriet sounded distressed," she said. "I thought she might need assistance."

"And did she?"

"She was with Lord Westwood. I did not want to intrude."

"Quite right. Not your concern." His voice, normally a quiet baritone, was dry with discontent.

Not for the first time, Celestial thought how much more approachable the man would be if he did not take his position in the household with such starch. It had been that way from the moment she and Heavenly had arrived after Lady Harriet's marriage to Lord Worthington, disrupting Horace's orderly rule over what had been a wholly-masculine household.

In the years since, he'd redoubled his efforts at maintaining decorum, as much to set himself apart from Celestial and her sister as to avoid offending Lady Harriet's sensibilities. But, as Celestial and Heavenly well knew, having served their mistress for a decade longer than Horace, Lady Harriet cared little for order and decorum and even less for society's notion of the proper treatment of a duke's daughter. She much preferred mucking about in flour and cared not who saw her thus.

Horace never understood that, but then he did not appear to have the slightest understanding of women. Which was unfortunate, since he had quite a number of appealing attributes, if he would simply let go of all those fussy notions. He was a fine figure of a man, with quite a nice shade of brown hair graying slightly at the temples, which gave him a distinguished air. His eyes, so disapproving now, could be quite earnest and open in unguarded moments. Unfortunately, almost all of Horace's moments were guarded.

"I will prepare a sleeping potion in the event she is too overset to sleep," Celestial said. "I brought some freshly harvested valerian from Worthington."

Horace eyed her skeptically. "Lady Harriet is never overset."

"That is why I thought she needed help."

Horace's expression was censorious. "Our employer's discussions with Lord Westwood are none of our concern. If I catch you spying on them again, I will —"

"Stop it, Horace," Celestial snapped. "You are just as curious as Heavenly and me about matters between them. I have seen you studying the two of them."

He reddened. "I only wish for Lady Harriet's happiness." He looked as if he would say something else, but hesitated.

"But?" she prodded.

"But I wonder —" He broke off.

"Whether the earl can bring her that?" Celestial finished for him.

"I did not say that," he said quickly.

"You were thinking it," she said.

He did not deny it. Perhaps Horace was beginning to unbend, she thought. That would be all to the good. Celestial studied him with new interest — and no small amount of hope.

"You know, Horace," she said, taking a step

toward him, "I would not object to hearing your views."

He eyed her blankly. "Views?"

Celestial gave a low laugh. "Why, yes. On what might make Lady Harriet — or any woman, for that matter — happy. "

The butler eyed her in alarm. He turned on his heel and retreated through the dining room door.

Alone in the darkened dining room, Celestial stared after him and emitted a long-suffering sigh.

CHAPTER SEVEN

"SO YOU SEE, Stevens, I have enough evidence to warrant a thorough investigation." Elias towered over Freddy's solicitor, in whose presence two days ago he had watched Lady Harriet sign her pledge to terminate their betrothal by the Season's end.

Winston Stevens removed his spectacles and cleaned them carefully and deliberately. But Elias had seen trapped men before, and this one bore all the signs. His pupils were dilated, and a thin film of sweat covered his brow. His hands trembled slightly as he rubbed the lenses, buying time.

As well he might. Westwood Imports was a valuable commodity. For years Elias's friends and associates had besieged him to sell them stock, but he preferred to keep the business in his control. Only he and Freddy held shares. The shares Stevens had sold for Lady Harriet would have been snapped up, and at a hefty price. Yet the mill repairs, sheep, cows, and other improvements she had made amounted to only a few thousand pounds. Stevens must have pocketed the difference, and perhaps even sold other shares without her knowledge.

"Since I have made you a rich man, however inadvertently, it seems only fitting that I be the one to remedy that fact," Elias continued.

Stevens put his spectacles on his nose. "You have no proof."

"Proof," Elias echoed in a musing tone. "Perhaps you are right. I will get an accounting from Lady Harriet as to the precise sums she received from you."

He walked around the edge of the man's desk. "And since I have a very good notion as to who in London would have leapt at the chance to buy into Westwood Imports, it will be a simple matter to track down the purchasers and ask them to produce the bills of sale. Any discrepancy between the sums Lady Harriet received and their purchase price will produce a trail that leads directly to you, Stevens. The proof, you see, can be had."

Stevens was no idiot. He knew when he was beaten. A sickly pallor swept his features.

"I did not intend to hurt Lady Harriet," he began, mopping his brow with his handkerchief. The little weasel looked ready to crawl under the desk, Elias thought.

"Lady Harriet will not press charges — provided you cooperate." Elias did not mention that his betrothed did not know he had discovered Stevens's nefarious scheme. Nor did he think it necessary to tell her, at least for now. First, he would determine whether the man was of a mind to avoid prison.

Stevens sighed in relief, but a wary look crept

into his eyes. "Cooperate? Then you will want restitution? Unfortunately, my lord, the money has already been spent. I had a large number of expenses. Debts, that is." He shot Elias an apologetic smile.

"Perhaps I neglected to mention that Miss Marigold Bennett is prepared to give evidence as to the nature of some of those expenses. I imagine your wife will be very interested to hear her testimony. As will your other clients, who may find that they, too, have funds due them."

"Marigold? Oh, no, my lord, you cannot!" Stevens slumped in his chair.

Watching a man's disintegration was not pleasant, but Winston Stevens more than deserved his fate. According to Elias's own solicitor, Jeremy Wilson, Stevens had often bragged to colleagues about his talented mistress. It had been reasonable to assume that he had also bragged to his mistress about his embezzlement schemes. When Miss Bennett had met them at Wilson's office this morning, she confirmed his theory — and pocketed a hundred pounds for her trouble, having realized that she could no longer count on Stevens for her financial support.

"Enough," Elias commanded coldly. Stevens did not deserve his pity. Greed had brought about the man's ruin. "The only way to avoid prison is to make restitution."

"B-b-but I have no money," Stevens stammered.

"Perhaps there are other means by which you can make amends," Elias said.

"Anything!" Stevens said fervently. "My lord, you have no idea how I regret my actions."

Elias rolled his eyes. The man was coming it a bit too brown, but at least he was willing. "I will require a complete list of the purchasers and the precise number of shares sold to each. I will also require an accounting of how many shares Lady Harriet still owns."

Stevens nodded eagerly. "I have kept good records." He unlocked a drawer, pulled out a sheaf of papers, and thrust them into Elias's hands.

Elias perused the documents. Many of the names were familiar to him. Some were not, but his solicitor would track them down and buy their shares back. Unlike Winston Stevens, Jeremy Wilson was a diligent, dedicated, and honest man.

There was one surprise on the list. "Oliver Hunt?" Elias scowled, the memory of last night's encounter with the demagogue still fresh. "I thought his interest was in politics, not business."

"I, ah, sent letters to many of Lady Harriet's acquaintances to gauge their interest in purchasing shares," Stevens said. "Mr. Hunt responded eagerly. Perhaps he is hedging his bets against the vagaries of a political career."

Hedging his bets? Yes, that was possible. But not against the failure of his politics. Hunt was so convinced of his own brilliance that he would never consider the possibility of failure. No, if Hunt was hedging his bets, it had something to do with Lady Harriet. Elias had not failed to notice the warmth in Hunt's gaze last night as he regarded her. That would bear watching.

For now, Elias tucked the list into his pocket. The information about Hunt was vaguely disquieting, but what Stevens's files revealed was more so. Lady Harriet's solicitor had sold off nearly half of Freddy's shares, more than Elias had expected. It would cost a pretty penny to buy them back. He wondered when he would break the news to her.

Unsummoned, an image came to mind of the scene last night in Lady Harriet's foyer. She had lost her composure, something he suspected did not happen often. For a moment or two Elias had wondered about his own composure. That brief, parting kiss had been sheer impulse, something he ordinarily was not given to.

As he strode out of Winston Stevens's office, Elias banished the stench of the man's dishonesty with thoughts of primroses.

***

"I have been wishing to try spelt for ages." Harriet regarded the lump of dough resting comfortably in a large bowl in her kitchen. Celestial and the other servants had vanished, knowing she often was happiest working on her own.

"Eustace did not come home until dawn," Monica said glumly. She sat at the long worktable, her hands absently clutching a towel that Harriet had placed there.

"See how the dough is soft, almost satiny, and requires little kneading?" Harriet marveled, oblivious to her friend's worried features. "It is lovely."

"London is ruining him. He looks like a Cossack with those voluminous trousers and high collars. Why, he can scarcely manage to turn his head."

"Spelt has been used for thousands of years," Harriet added. "It was good of Lady Hester to send it to me. 'Tis more authentic than that grown in England."

"He has no money to while away the night gambling, so he must have spent his time with a woman. Of the worst sort, no doubt. My poor Eustace!" Monica began to weep.

Startled, Harriet looked up from her worktable. "Oh, dear, I am afraid I have not been attending. You are worried about Eustace?"

Monica blew her nose on the towel. "Harriet, sometimes it is maddening to have you as a friend."

"I am sorry." Harriet abandoned her dough and moved to sit next to her. Monica was often given to fits of emotion, never more when her Eustace was involved. But Harriet could not imagine what had sent her friend into such a state. "Now, what is this new catastrophe?"

"Eustace did not come home last night. He strolled in just as the servants were stirring this morning, still in his evening clothes."

"Surely, it would have been worse had he not been in them," Harriet offered with an encouraging smile.

Monica sniffed. "He does not know how to conduct himself among these sophisticated people. It was a mistake for us to come to London. He is being exposed to all manner of creatures, like that odious Mr. Hunt."

"Oliver Hunt?" Harriet looked surprised. "He may be a rabble-rouser, but he is harmless."

"Harmless? What do you know, Harriet? You think it delightful to have all of these strange people in your parlor, fomenting rebellion —"

"Mr. Hunt was not fomenting rebellion," Harriet said. "The man likes to practice his rhetoric, but I do not think four out of five people hold with his views."

"Ah, but the one — the one in five caught in Mr. Hunt's net...I fear that is Eustace!"

Harriet tilted her head consideringly. "He did seem rather enthralled last night when Mr. Hunt was speaking, but he is of an age when new ideas and people catch his fancy."

"Sometimes you have your head in the clouds, Harriet," Monica said, shaking her head. "You blind yourself to the truth. It was the same with Freddy, and now, Lord Westwood."

"Freddy?" Harriet frowned. "Whatever do you mean?"

"The way you turned a blind eye to his philandering. I hated to see you so degraded. It was not my place to say anything but now that the man is gone, surely you must see the situation more clearly."

Harriet paled. "My eyes were open then, Monica. Do not condemn my behavior because you do not understand it."

Monica thought about that for a moment. "You tolerated his womanizing. What is there to understand?"

"That I am not wedded to anyone else's notions of what my behavior should be," Harriet said sharply. "That I did not wish to stifle Freddy's happiness. His activities did not hurt me in the slightest."

Monica's expression was so dubious that Harriet felt compelled to continue. "Marriage should not stifle either party's unique nature," she said.

"I see." The older woman arched a skeptical brow. "Then may I assume you had affairs as well?"

Harriet blinked. "Certainly not!"

"So it was only Freddy's unique nature that required no stifling?" Her friend regarded her blandly.

Harriet stared at her. "Why do you say these things?"

"Because I wish you to see that you walk through the world with blinders on when it comes to men. That not every man has your best interests in mind when he whispers pretty words in your ear."

"Lord Westwood did not whisper pretty words in my ear," Harriet insisted.

Monica blinked. "I thought we were discussing Freddy."

"Actually, we were discussing Eustace." Harriet rose and snatched the towel from the table. She had no wish to continue the conversation. Monica had a jaundiced attitude toward men, owing to her husband's defection. She tended to paint all of them with the same brush.

"Yes, well, Eustace is an innocent, just like you, my dear." Monica eyed her sorrowfully. "I know you wish I had not spoken, and perhaps I should not have, but for all that you have been married, Harriet, you do not know the least about men. Eustace will be victimized, just as you were. I live in terror that my only son will have his heart broken — just as you did."

Harriet stood very still. "Monica Tanksley, I have never had my heart broken. And I never will."

Monica regarded her for a long moment. Then she sighed. "Very well. Tell me more about this... spelt, is it?"

For the first time since being caught in Lady Harriet's unsettling orbit, Elias regarded the whirl of activity around him with the knowledge that it was entirely normal.

Lady Symington's ball was just like every other London ball during the height of the Season. The hostess and her husband greeted an interminable line of guests as an orchestra tuned its instruments and a flurry of servants prepared for the late-night supper that would send them all home stuffed and satiated until they could rise at midday and prepare to do it all over again.

Thank God that sort of life was behind him. He had almost become part of it permanently, when Zephyr Payne accepted his marriage proposal.

The daughter of Lord Ellwood Payne, one of Lord Castlereagh's intimates, Zephyr had been tending the wounded at the London hospital where Elias was recovering after being invalided home. In his weakened state he had taken one look at her delicate, heart-shaped face and sparkling green eyes and been utterly lost.

How silly that seemed now. If he had married Zephyr, he would not have been free to roam the world in search of unusual spices with which to build his fortune. He would be shackled to a wife and children, reduced to dressing in evening attire every night and attending boring events like this one. He should be eternally grateful that Zephyr had chosen not to present herself that morning at St. Paul's and elected to run off with Pembroke instead.

Elias had not felt especially grateful at the time. Even now, when he thanked his stars that his life was very different from the one he would have had with Zephyr, the chagrin hadn't entirely dissipated.

The entire *ton* had assembled to witness their wedding — Zephyr was Lord Payne's beautiful elder daughter and Elias himself had been considered something of a catch, the newspapers having blown his war exploits entirely out of proportion. Though he had distinguished himself no more than any other soldier at Salamanca, it pleased them to paint him as a hero.

But it had required all of Elias's military discipline to stand for three-quarters of an hour before staring, whispering guests who wondered why Lord Westwood's bride had chosen to be late to her own wedding. The music went on interminably as the orchestra worked to fill the time.

At last a red-faced Lord Payne had drawn him aside, clutching a missive from his wayward daughter explaining that she was likely enjoying Lord Pembroke's husbandly embrace by now. Elias had bowed stiffly and, without a backward look, walked calmly out into the blazing sunshine.

Humiliation did not sit well with him, and having his suit repudiated in such a public fashion before society's elite was humiliating in the extreme. He had been angry, even enraged. But he had gone on to fashion another life for himself. Still, he had not entered a church since. And he had never allowed himself to form another serious liaison.

Elias's gaze narrowed as he watched Lady Harriet leave the dance floor with one of her many partners. Her salmon-colored gown — the fabric was a crisp silk, stiff enough nearly to stand on its own and walk away from all this nonsense — made him think of that first delicious meal she had prepared for him. Indeed, she looked good enough to devour tonight. He wondered whether the men who danced with her thought so. Oddly, they were not the usual dandies and tulips who cared more for the state of their leg padding than a lady's comfort. Lord Castlereagh had danced with her, and Lord Holland, too. Sir Thomas Lawrence, lately knighted, had sought her out.

Her most recent partner was an older gentleman who looked as out of place among Lady Symington's glittering lamplight and tinsel as a humble pigeon at Michaelmas. Elias could not place the man, though he looked familiar. He was holding forth on some topic with great energy, and Lady Harriet was listening intently and with obvious respect.

None of her partners were the sort to rouse in him the least bit of jealousy — though if Lady Harriet had truly been his betrothed, her obvious popularity might have given him pause. Even a man so advanced in years as the earnest gentleman she was now entertaining might harbor designs on so lovely a woman.

She *was* lovely. That thought caught him unawares. In fact, Elias reflected as it gained momentum, he had been drawn to her from the first time he saw her in her shop, covered in flour.

He reminded himself that Lady Harriet was not his type. The females he preferred to entertain did not deny desire. They did not disavow any acquaintance with feminine arts. Most certainly, they did not dump foul-smelling muck on his head or force him to barter his person in exchange for the shares of his own business.

The sort of female who appealed to him understood the nature of lust and did not view it as anything more complicated. Rather like the woman who now stood at his elbow, regarding him from exotic, deep-set eyes.

"Good evening, Lord Westwood." She did not lower her lashes or flutter them in a silly fashion like the debutantes. She did not show him a virgin's pretty blushes. She looked straight at him, her velvet brown gaze meeting his without betraying a hint of coarseness even as they sparkled with invitation.

A portrait of sophistication in a lemon yellow gown with daring but not scandalous décolletage, the woman had piled her glossy chestnut hair high on her head, leaving one tantalizing tendril free to grace her bare shoulder, the better to call attention to the magnificent emerald necklace that was the only other ornament gracing that swanlike swath of flesh.

"You have the advantage of me, madam," he said with a bow.

"I am Lady Caroline Forth, a friend of your late associate, Lord Worthington."

Though he had never laid eyes on the woman, something in her familiar manner immediately told him that this delectable creature had been Freddy's mistress.

"I was surprised to learn that Lady Harriet planned to remarry," she said easily. "She seems so much more comfortable on her own. You must have charmed her, my lord. I imagine you are very good at it."

Her eyes were wide with seeming innocence, but a challenge lurked within them.

Yes, this was just the sort of female he preferred, Elias reflected, one who would not excite him to rage or rashness, but to simple, uncomplicated lust.

CHAPTER EIGHT

HARRIET GREATLY RESPECTED William Wilberforce. A tireless advocate of reform, he had helped win passage of the bill abolishing the slave trade. Since he did not care for social gatherings, she had been surprised and delighted to find him at Lady Symington's ball. He ought to have had her undivided attention. Instead, it was riveted on two figures across the room: Lord Westwood and Caroline Forth.

"The bill was a step," Mr. Wilberforce was saying, "but I will not rest until slavery itself is abolished —"

"Nor should you," Harriet agreed, her gaze straying over Mr. Wilberforce's shoulder to lock with Lord Westwood's half a room away. Her fiancé nodded absently at her, then returned his attention to the ravishing Caroline.

"Nor should we *all*," Mr. Wilberforce corrected. "Anyone who values the sanctity of human life should stand with me. I hope I may count on you, Lady Harriet, to use your influence with the members of Parliament now that you have resumed your salons."

As Caroline placed her hand on Lord

Westwood's sleeve, Harriet forced herself to meet Mr. Wilberforce's gaze. "You have always had my support," she assured him. "Indeed, sir, I have repeatedly offered you the opportunity to address our little gatherings, but you have always declined."

"I know." He sighed wearily. "Most of my evenings are spent in writing and, I confess, resting from the demands of my days. All this traveling is a bit fatiguing at my age. Sometimes I despair of living to see slavery abolished, but just as I reach my lowest point, I realize there is more I can do." He hesitated. "I understand that Lord Castlereagh has consented to attend your salon on Thursday next." To Harriet's amazement, he blushed.

"My dear Mr. Wilberforce," she said with a smile, "if you are trying to wangle an invitation, say no more. I will send one round in the morning. It would be my very great honor."

"You are too kind, Lady Harriet, though I have handled this awkwardly." He gave her an apologetic smile, then bowed. I fear I am not at my best at society balls. If you will excuse me —"

"Even your worst is a delight, sir," Harriet replied gallantly. "I look forward to seeing you next week." She smiled as he took his leave. Her next salon was shaping up to be a lively and important event.

It was what she enjoyed most — bringing together influential leaders with disparate views in the exchange of stimulating ideas. Her salons had come about gradually, perhaps in tandem with the decline — for that is how she had come to view it — of her marriage with Freddy. Harriet saw no use in sitting at home waiting for him to return when most likely he would not. Instead, she had redoubled her own social schedule, and discovered a number of philanthropic causes that awaited her assistance.

That had been rewarding, but at the same time it had been impossible to escape the realization that for many in power, society's ills suited them perfectly. Indeed, they saw nothing wrong with the way things were — happily for them, they had been born on the right side of the banquet table — and viewed change as unnecessary. But those locked in the past were incapable of crafting a vision for the future. Harriet's salons aimed to foster open-mindedness and tolerance.

Harriet did not feel tolerant at the moment. That is because she had just registered the sudden disappearance from the party of her betrothed and Freddy's former mistress.

If Lord Westwood wished to take the air with Caroline, it should not disturb her in the least, Harriet told herself. Nevertheless, as she stared at the spot where they had stood in such a friendly fashion not moments ago, it disturbed her a great deal.

And before she could truly examine the reason, Harriet found herself crossing the ballroom, ignoring the greetings and stares that came her way as her gaze fixed on the large double doors that led out onto Lady Symington's secluded terrace.

Her pulse pounded in her ears, blocking out

everything but those beckoning doors and the black night beyond.

Elias was lazily contemplating the front of Lady Forth's gown. She had a way of toying with the bodice that made the neckline gape provocatively. All the while, she regarded him with wide-eyed innocence, as if she thought he would find the combination of superficial virtue and sincere seduction irresistible.

Clearly, Lady Forth had marked him as her next conquest. Normally, Elias did not mind that sort of game. He wondered why this one irritated him.

"I find the night air most stimulating," Lady Forth said in a husky tone as she studied a potted rubber tree near them on the terrace. Her fingers played with the emeralds that dipped into the shadow between her breasts.

"Do you?" Elias tried for a neutral tone. No need to be openly contemptuous, although something told him she would scarcely notice.

As Lady Forth turned to him, she ran a tip of her finger around the trim of her bodice, which afforded him an even closer view of her charms. She pulled a dainty lace handkerchief from her décolletage and brought it to her lips. "Most stimulating," she affirmed. "I am a notoriously poor sleeper, my lord. I fear I am at my best long after others have retired."

The woman might as well wear a sign advertising

her services. "And is Lord Forth a night owl as well?" Elias asked blandly.

Lady Forth sighed in mock fatigue. "My husband prefers to keep to the country, where he rises with the chickens and goes to bed at an obscenely early hour. The country does not suit me. We have therefore come to an accommodation. I keep my own hours in town, while he remains in the country. It is an equitable arrangement, do you not think?"

"Certainly a convenient one."

Smiling, she nodded. "One does grow lonely. As a man who travels, you must find that to be true."

"One compensates with various amusements."

"Yes."

She moved closer. The front of her gown brushed his lapel. She did not try to make the contact appear accidental. Instead, she inclined her face upward, a clear invitation in her eyes. He felt her hand on his tailcoat. Her lashes fluttered shut as she waited — it was abundantly clear — for his kiss.

Lady Forth was a beautiful woman, Elias thought. Her lips were lush and ripe, ready for the taking. No doubt she bestowed a cornucopia of sensual delights on her beyond-willing paramours during those illicit, late-night hours. And though she did not make the blood run to his head in a dizzying rush, it was certainly flowing to another, more responsive part of his anatomy.

Her lips parted with the assurance of one at the pinnacle of her allure. While Elias did not find her charms irresistible, there was little doubt they were sufficiently diverting. He lowered his mouth to hers.

And in that moment, sultry with promise, something heavy and unpleasant struck Elias's leg with the force of a dead weight. With a little shriek, Lady Forth jumped backward — even as a large, shiny object thrust itself into the rapidly enlarging space between them.

It was a rubber leaf, heralding the fall of the tree itself. The large potted plant toppled to the ground, landing at Elias's feet with a resounding crash. His gaze shot to the place where it had stood. To his amazement, Lady Harriet now occupied that very spot.

"Oh, dear!" His faux fiancée looked stricken. "I did not see that shrub. I'm afraid that I — I tripped and knocked it over."

Elias eyed the unwieldy tree at his feet. "An unobtrusive little bush, to be sure."

Lady Forth, to her credit, looked only a bit rattled. "Harriet, dear," she managed, recovering quickly. "How good it is to see you again. My felicitations on your betrothal."

"Thank you, Caroline." Lady Harriet's gaze moved from Elias to Lady Forth and back to him.

An awkward silence descended. Curious as to how Lady Harriet intended the scene to play out, Elias elected to remain silent.

"Well," Lady Forth said quickly, "you will excuse me for not lingering to chat, Harriet. Lord Westwood was kind enough to escort me out here to take the air, but I believe the night has taken a chilly turn."

With a perfunctory smile, she walked inside the house, apparently not the least disconcerted at being caught in a provocative position with another woman's fiancé. Clearly, it would take more than a rubber tree to faze Lady Forth.

Standing in the shadows, Lady Harriet wore an unreadable expression. Elias cleared his throat. "I expect I should apologize."

She bent over the tree, busying herself with the task of trying to set the pot upright. "There is no need."

"I was on the point of kissing the woman," he pointed out unnecessarily.

"That is your concern, not mine." She pulled hard on the plant, but its weight and bulk prone was more than she could manage. She bit her lip.

Elias reached down, lifted the tree with one hand, and set it upright. "Many women would object to finding their betrothed in such a circumstance."

She looked up at him. "I suppose so. But ours is not a real betrothal. You owe me no special loyalty."

That was exactly the thought that had run through Elias's head when he had strolled outside with Lady Forth — and what he would have told Lady Harriet if she had challenged him. The fact that she did not was oddly disturbing.

"You did not mind that Lady Forth and I conducted ourselves in a manner that could have made you the object of public ridicule?" He eyed her curiously. Their betrothal might be a sham, but all of London thought it real. Had his *tête-à-tête* with Lady Forth progressed, Lady Harriet would have been humiliated. Elias knew he should have thought that through before accompanying Lady Forth outside. His brain, however, had not been the part of him in control at the time.

"I do not set myself up as judge of other people's behavior," Lady Harriet said tightly.

"You merely throw trees at them."

She flushed. "That was an accident. I would never do such a thing intentionally."

"Of course not," he agreed easily. "As you have said, you are not given to displays of excessive emotion. Was she Freddy's mistress?"

Shock registered on her face but she did not answer.

"He wouldn't have made the effort to disguise it," Elias said. "You knew all along."

Her chin rose defiantly. "What does that matter? Many men have interests outside of marriage."

"Fox-hunting or boxing, perhaps."

She eyed him coldly. "I see no point in discussing it."

"And, since you do not judge others," Elias said, studying her, "I assume you bear the lady no ill will."

There was a moment's silence.

"That is not quite true," she said at last. Her candor surprised him. "I was glad she made him happy, but I do wish she had not been quite so... insistent in her efforts to please him."

Elias frowned. "I do not take your meaning."

"Freddy was not well. He would have done better to come home that night, instead of going to her. She should have seen that."

"That night?" Elias stared at her. "Do you mean that Lady Forth was —"

"The last person to see Freddy alive," she confirmed. "He died in her arms. I suppose he died pleasurably, but I have never been able to look at Caroline in quite the same way since then."

It was a miracle that Lady Harriet had not thrown ten rubber trees at them. "I am sorry." The phrase sounded empty, even to his ears.

Her too-bright smile almost made Elias cringe. "Thank you, my lord. And now, perhaps you would care to return to the party. I believe Caroline was right. The night has grown chilly."

"I will take you home."

She eyed him in surprise. "We have not had supper yet. And I do not want her to think —" She broke off, embarrassed.

"You do not want to give Lady Forth — or anyone else who might have noticed — the satisfaction of knowing that she has caused you distress. That is understandable. But the fact is she did cause you pain. I see no need for you to remain."

"I am not the sort of woman to leave a party early claiming a headache," she insisted. "I do not give in to such weakness."

"Perhaps it is time you did." Elias put his arm lightly at her back and steered her toward the house. "I will make our excuses."

"I did not give you leave to order me about, my lord," she protested.

Elias did not respond. Lady Harriet had some devilish queer ideas, but he was not about to prolong her suffering. He propelled her through the ballroom toward the exit. For her own good, someone needed to take the woman in hand. It would have to be him.

As it turned out, she made very little protest in the end. By the time the carriage rolled away from Lady Symington's, she had lapsed into silence. But the stubborn set of her chin and the tightness of her features told him that while she had assented to leaving, she was by no means signaling any charity toward him. Given Lady Forth's role in Freddy's downfall, Elias could scarcely blame her.

Had she really shoved that rubber tree at them? It was possible that she had tripped and sent it sprawling, but the pot and tree together must have weighed nearly four stone. It would have taken a determined push to move it.

Elias wondered why Lady Harriet was so insistent on disavowing her anger. To be sure, he sometimes struggled with his own temper, but he had never denied its existence, as she seemed intent on doing.

Had her marriage proved so very disappointing that she must hide her anger beneath platitudes about not judging others? Elias could well imagine that Freddy had been a trial. The man had been a scamp and a gambler with no business sense. Westwood Imports succeeded because

Freddy had been content to permit Elias to make the decisions. But Freddy's detachment, which worked for their business partnership, would have been disastrous in a marriage.

Elias did not understand why Freddy had felt the urge to stray. Lady Harriet was infinitely more interesting than the manipulative Lady Forth. Even as a young bride, she must have been captivating. Elias hadn't attended the wedding — he'd been in Jamaica at the time — but he suspected that even then Lady Harriet possessed an intriguing combination of innocence and intellect. Clearly, Freddy was not the man to appreciate such gifts.

Something gnawed at Elias, now that he thought on it. Six years ago, at the time of Freddy's wedding, Elias had been overseeing the small property they had purchased to start their business. He had never questioned Freddy's sudden infusion of funds a few months after the wedding, assuming they derived from the man's gambling successes. That money had enabled Elias to expand the business, purchasing more farmland and dramatically increasing the quantity and quality of spices Westwood Imports offered, which in turn increased the company's profits and scope.

Freddy, however, rarely had gambling successes. That night at White's, when they agreed to take his winnings and start a business, had been an isolated event. Until Freddy's wedding, in fact, the business had struggled.

Now Elias understood what bothered him: The

money that rescued his business must have come from Lady Harriet's dowry.

Lady Harriet, not Freddy, had made the expansion of Westwood Imports possible, however unwittingly. And while Elias had reaped handsome profits, the return on her investment had been a faithless husband.

"I will take some brandy, thank you."

Harriet did not recall offering Lord Westwood brandy. Indeed, all she wanted was to retire to her room in peace and try to forget about the hellish evening. She had felt the stares on her all evening, but that was perhaps to be expected at her first formal ball since Freddy's death. Then there was the presence of Caroline, undoubtedly giving rise to more curious gazes. That she had disappeared with Lord Westwood would have only fueled wagging tongues. All in all, it had been a trying few hours.

Lord Westwood was probably famished, since they had missed Lady Symington's late supper. But Harriet could offer him little in the way of a proper meal. Celestial had the night off, and Heavenly had gone to Kensington to visit a friend. Horace was probably around somewhere, but he was of little use in the kitchen.

"I regret depriving you of your dinner, my lord." Harriet's thoughts were a jumble. The image of Lady Forth's lovely face turned up to Lord Westwood's, awaiting his kiss, lingered.

She shook her head, trying to banish those

thoughts. Lord Westwood was not Freddy. He wasn't even her betrothed. There was no need to deprive him of drink and dinner, especially when he had cut short the evening because of her. Harriet poured him a glass of brandy from the decanter on the sideboard, and made for the kitchen. To her surprise, he followed her.

Harriet had never held with the fashionable practice of relegating the kitchen to the basement. The food from such a kitchen never arrived hot to the table. A damp, airless basement was not the place for culinary inspiration. Remodeling Freddy's townhouse so that the kitchen and dining room were but steps apart had been one of her first acts as his wife. Perhaps that fact spoke volumes about their marriage, Harriet thought ruefully.

Tonight she was grateful for her airy, cheerful kitchen and its modern conveniences. The iron stove had long since cooled, but the cold chamber, filled with ice from the adjacent icehouse, kept milk, meat, and other perishables properly chilled so they did not spoil. The wine-roasted gammon, fruit, and baguettes left from last night's meal would make a perfect cold buffet.

She felt Lord Westwood watching her as she set the meat on a platter and prepared to carve the joint.

"Allow me," he said, taking the knife from her. He proceeded to cut the meat into neat, perfect slices and arrayed them on the platter.

He noticed the basket of persimmons on the table and picked up each one and inspected it, inhaling deeply. "This will not disappoint," he said, placing one red-orange specimen on the tray. Deftly, he removed the top leaf and broke the fruit in half, offering one piece to her.

Harriet eyed him in surprise. He handled food — and knives — as if they were second nature. Perhaps in the West Indies, customs were different from those in England, where men did not exert themselves in the preparation of food, only its consumption.

"The persimmon is not normally grown here," he observed, biting into the soft, fibrous fruit. "Indeed, I know of none grown beyond Asia — other than in the Valencia region of Spain. How came you by these?"

"You are a wonder, sir," Harriet said, shaking her head in amazement. "Are you an expert on every manner of food?"

"You have not answered my question."

"Nor you mine," she said teasingly, surprised at the companionable air between them. "They are indeed from Spain. Horace bought them for me down by the Surrey Docks. He knows I am always in search of imports from the Continent."

They ate at the long worktable, where the servants usually took their meals. Lord Westwood did not look out of place here, even in his elegant double-breasted corbeau coat and cream breeches, but Harriet felt awkward in her stiff ball gown, which rustled audibly whenever she shifted in her chair.

"Wine-roasted," he observed, savoring the meat. "Madeira?"

Harriet smiled. "You have quite a talent, my lord."

"I have a talent for clumsiness."

His blunt comment startled her, but she did not have to wait long for him to clarify. "I did not know about Lady Forth's connection to Freddy, or to his death," he said. "Please forgive my behavior."

Harriet did not want to talk about that. "Your apology is unnecessary," she said stiffly. "I do not set myself up as judge of others' behavior. Indeed, I am quite tolerant."

"Excessively so, it seems."

"You imply that tolerance is a flaw," Harriet rejoined. "The truth is, there is far too much intolerance these days."

Lord Westwood speared another piece of meat. "Handing over your husband — or your betrothed — to another woman is tolerance in the extreme, is it not?"

"I have never handed any man to Lady Forth," she said indignantly. "It pleases her to take them."

"Oh, I daresay that after tonight she might think twice," he said. "I'll warrant you never tossed a rubber tree at her and Freddy."

"That was an accident. Why do you not believe me?"

"What I believe is that you are a woman of some complexity who is blissfully unaware of the contradictions in her nature."

Harriet stared at him. "Whatever do you mean?"

"You profess tolerance," he said, "yet in a jealous pique fling potted plants —"

"Such hubris! May I remind you, my lord, that we are nothing to one another? I have no cause to be jealous."

He gave her a long look. "And yet, even you must acknowledge that for a moment tonight you lost control."

"I have never in my life lost control," she insisted.

"I imagine that is what makes it so difficult to own up to it."

Harriet looked away, but she felt him watching her.

"Control is a worthy objective, to be sure," he said. "I confess that for many years, my temper got the best of me. I cannot remember what provoked it — no, I do remember, of course. It was my father. Always. We disagreed on almost everything."

Curious, Harriet turned to him.

"I was given to smashing things in my rage, generally making a fool of myself," he continued. "I could put it off on youth, but that is no excuse."

"And yet, I have seen no such excess from you, sir," Harriet said.

"That is because in the military I learned that to give in to anger, to lose control, is to risk death," he said. "Only cool heads prevail in war. And so I taught myself to control my temper. But that sometimes comes at a cost."

"I see no cost to equanimity, my lord," she said. "Indeed, it is a state to be sought above all."

"In many endeavors," he agreed. "Business decisions certainly must be made dispassionately. But it is perhaps no coincidence that I spend my days searching for the spices of life." He regarded her steadily. "Without that passion, I suspect I would be royally bored."

And then, suddenly, his mouth curved upward in a grin — dear Lord, there *was* a dimple, there in his left cheek.

Oh my, Harriet thought.

"The problem you face is somewhat different," he said.

Harriet found herself staring at his mouth, remembering that fleeting kiss he had given her in her foyer the night of her salon, wondering what it would be like if he kissed her in earnest. "It is?" she said absently.

"Yes. I have given the matter some thought," he said. "I recognized my anger, but channeled it into other passions. You, on the other hand, deny the very existence of yours. That is why you tolerate such blathering idiots in your house —"

"I beg your pardon?"

"— and why you smile so brightly as another woman tries to seduce your betrothed, and perhaps why you ceded your husband to her without so much as a struggle."

"I did not — "

"And, why you care so much about that bakery —"

"Stop!"

"— but fear any genuine passion for a member of the opposite sex." He sat back in his chair, looking, Harriet thought, rather pleased with himself. "Perhaps one day you will come to feel that there are passions worth fighting for."

Harriet was aware of an odd ringing in her ears; it eclipsed her annoyance at his hubris. *Passions worth fighting for* — she did not know what that meant. But his words catapulted her back to the early days of her marriage, when her love for Freddy had soared, only to fall to earth as his perfidy became apparent. Whatever passions she'd felt for him had evaporated. Instead, she found comfort in the routine she had set for herself, uncluttered by any craving for something as extreme and unattainable as a grand passion.

But perhaps she had not succeeded in expunging all sentiment. Had she felt anger at Freddy for the manner in which he had conducted their marriage and the ungraceful way he had departed this earth? But no, the man was who he was. The blame was hers, for expecting loyalty and affection that were foreign to Freddy's nature and for not being an adequate wife. Or so she had told herself.

And yet, here was this odd ringing, perhaps the sound of a carefully constructed world unraveling. Here was this man who scarcely knew her challenging the very principles she had taken as truth.

"My lord, I fear I must ask you to leave," she said in a constricted voice. "My head aches and —"

"Not yet," he said. "As it happens, I have

discovered that I am obliged to you. It is a debt I intend to satisfy."

"I do not understand," she said.

He reached across the table and took her hand, so suddenly that Harriet nearly jumped. "I had not realized that your dowry provided a significant portion of Freddy's investment in Westwood Imports, particularly that which enabled the company to expand after your wedding."

"Oh." Neither her father nor Freddy had ever informed her about any matter involving finances. Her father thought such things unseemly for a woman's ears, and Freddy never troubled himself to explain anything.

"You did not know?" he asked.

Harriet shook her head.

"No matter," he said. "It is clear that Westwood Imports would not have thrived without those funds. That fact does not alleviate my desire to stop the erosion of its worth caused by your selling off shares and distributing the proceeds to benefit your neighbors. Nevertheless, I am obliged to offer you an arrangement by which you retain some ownership, provided you refrain from such sales in the future."

Harriet stared at him. "I would not accept a restraint upon my use of the shares."

He frowned. "You wish to keep to our original bargain?"

"Yes." Harriet massaged her temples. "Forgive me, my lord. This night has posed too many challenges. I wish to retire."

"Of course." He studied her. "Perhaps I may be of service in another way."

Harriet eyed him warily. "How?"

"Your life is filled with too many distractions. 'Tis a case of the tail wagging the dog. I can remedy that."

Harriet rose abruptly. "Setting aside that unflattering comparison, I feel compelled to state that the only trying distraction I face at the moment is you, my lord. I believe your hat is in the foyer."

She whisked his plate away, although he managed to snare a last piece of meat with admirable quickness. "Your life is in shambles, madam," he continued. "It is my duty as your putative betrothed and as a man in your debt to set things aright."

She glared at him. "What things?"

"The salons. They are unnecessarily agitating. Henceforth, I will review the guest list before the invitations are sent."

Was it only a moment ago she'd been contemplating the curve of his mouth? Now, Harriet yearned to stuff a towel in it.

"Lord Westwood?"

"Yes?" He eyed her benignly.

"Please leave my house."

The kitchen stood empty, silent, and dark.

Celestial emerged from behind the pantry door, where she had slipped when the voices of Lady Harriet and Lord Westwood had drifted toward the kitchen. Then Horace stepped out, rubbing his arms stiffly. He pulled a deck of cards from his pocket.

"I had a good hand," he groused. "I don't know why we had to hide like common criminals. For damned near three quarters of an hour, too. I'm so stiff I can hardly move."

"We were in the way. They wished to be alone."

"Hmmph! As if that's going to accomplish anything. They were at each other's throats."

"Not the entire time," Celestial put in.

"Time enough," he retorted, straightening his collar and brushing off his sleeve. "Don't see how they have a prayer of marrying. I give the betrothal three weeks."

Celestial regarded him thoughtfully. "He is drawn to her."

"Of course," Horace replied impatiently. "Lady Harriet is a fine woman. Don't mean they ought to marry."

"I think Lady Harriet is drawn to him, too." Celestial smiled. "Imagine! She threw a tree at him and Lady Forth."

"Means nothing. Women want only what they can't have."

Celestial's smile faded. "What makes you say such?"

"A lifetime of learning, that's what. Women can't be trusted." Horace wiped some crumbs off the table.

"You think all women are like that?"

Horace shot her a wary gaze. "Not all, I suppose. You're a right enough one. But we've known each other for a few years. And there ain't no funny stuff between us."

"No," Celestial agreed.

During the silence that followed, Celestial studied him as he straightened the chairs. The man was a mystery. He had always held himself a bit apart from the others in the household and adhered to his particular ideas as to what was and was not proper behavior in the service ranks.

Sometimes, Celestial felt his eyes on her, watching her, and she wondered whether he was merely inspecting the way she did her work or whether his interest went beyond his purview as head of the staff.

"It was rather close behind the door all that time, wasn't it?" she ventured.

Horace ran his finger around the inside of his collar. "Hardly enough room to breathe."

"I am sorry you were uncomfortable," she said.

Horace did not respond, merely picked up the cards again and sat down at the table. He tapped the deck on its edge so that it formed a neat, perfectly aligned rectangle.

"I did not mind it as much as you." Celestial joined him at the table.

He tapped the deck again and began to deal out the cards. He did not look at her.

Celestial took a deep breath. "I find your presence comforting, Horace. Even…stimulating."

A card fluttered to the floor. Quickly, Horace bent down to retrieve it.

But as he bent upright again, Celestial plucked

it from his hand. As their fingers touched, Horace froze.

Celestial placed the card on the table.

Quickly, Horace rose. "'Tis late for another game. Past time to retire." But his feet did not move.

"Do you think you could bring yourself to like me, Horace?" Celestial asked softly.

"What? Why, I like you well enough, I suppose," he said. "Don't know why you'd think otherwise."

"That is not what I meant," Celestial said. She stood as well, and now there was very little space between them. "Could you bring yourself to kiss me, Horace?"

Horace's eyes widened. "That wouldn't be proper. Why, we have never —"

"No, we haven't," she agreed. "Could you?"

"Could I what?"

"Kiss me." She looked up at him. Her lips parted.

Horace swallowed hard. "Damn it, Celestial. Ain't proper. I don't think — "

"That's right, Horace." She put her arms around his neck. "Don't think."

CHAPTER NINE

"**B**EGGIN' YOUR PARDON, my lord, but you never did learn to tie a cravat properly." Henry eyed the pile of rumpled muslin at Elias's feet.

With a sound of disgust, Elias threw his latest effort on the floor. "Spare me the lecture, Henry. I grew tired of waiting."

"I was only gone for a moment," Henry grumped.

"A moment to press the coat, half an hour to gossip with the footmen. I ought to hire a housekeeper. She would get far more work out of those two. And you, for that matter."

Henry drew himself up. "The day a female has free rein in this household —"

"Enough." Elias waved a dismissive hand. "See if you can discipline this into something presentable." He handed Henry another length of muslin and absently began to hum.

Casting Elias a speaking look, Henry proceeded to fashion the fabric into a proper emblem of his employer's rank. Henry had been with him for so long that Elias did not know what he would do without the man — even though he occasionally put his nose where it did not belong.

Last night, for example, Henry had been very curious as to why Elias had returned early from Lady Symington's ball, especially since the countess was known to set a very fine dinner table. Being Henry, he had not hesitated to remark upon the subject.

"Not like you to turn down a chance at lobster patties," Henry had pointed out. "And she probably had Gunter's prepare a special dessert —"

"I had a perfectly adequate meal." Elias was not about to confess that he had taken cold gammon and fruit in Lady Harriet's kitchen and considered it a meal beyond price.

Nor could he say why he felt like humming this morning, especially since she had all but thrown him out of her house last night.

He should have realized from the outset that hurt was at the bottom of Lady Harriet's singular way of looking at things. After all, it was a subject with which he had more than passing familiarity, thanks to Zephyr. But whereas he had acknowledged his pain — if not to the world, at least to himself — Lady Harriet buried hers, denying its cost. Elias hoped Freddy was being charred to a crisp in some eternal fire for causing her such misery.

Interestingly, their "betrothal" had taken on a new light for Elias last night. Despite her denial, nothing less than jealousy and anger could have prompted her to roll that tree at them. He understood her lingering anger at Lady Forth, but why jealousy? As Lady Harriet had said, they were nothing to one another. That thought would bear exploring.

"I found this in your pocket, my lord." Henry held out a paper.

Elias glanced at it. It was the list Winston Stevens had provided of the people to whom he'd sold Lady Harriet's shares. "That is for Jeremy. I have charged him with buying back those shares in Westwood Imports. Shouldn't be too difficult, since I will pay a good price. Except for that Hunt fellow. The man plays a deep game."

"Oliver Hunt?" Henry brushed a speck from the back of Elias's jacket. "I've seen him holding forth in the park. Draws a crowd."

"I cannot like his manner," Elias said. "He is too familiar by half with Lady Harriet."

"Found this, too," Henry added, holding out a lace handkerchief. "Has some letters sewn on it. One's an F, looks like."

Elias frowned. He had not known that Lady Forth had slipped her handkerchief into his tailcoat pocket. "You may return it to Lady Forth," he said. "No, on second thought, do not. She will only take that as an invitation."

Henry knew of Lady Forth. All of London did. She'd been Lord Worthington's mistress. Perhaps she was in the hunt for a new protector. If Lord Westwood was in some intrigue with Worthington's former mistress, that might be all to the good. But Henry only nodded and put the handkerchief into his own pocket.

Elias eyed his batman's handiwork. "No one will fault you for my appearance, Henry. The cravat is perfection." With an uncharacteristic grin, Elias nodded at Henry and left.

Frowning, Henry stared after him. His lordship had been humming. That was a bad sign. Lord Westwood never hummed — except when there was a woman. An image of Miss Zephyr Payne sprang unbidden to Henry's mind. Miss Payne had made Lord Westwood hum.

He ought to have taken his lordship's betrothal to Lady Harriet more seriously. Henry had assumed it was part of his employer's scheme to regain control of his business, for the earl was a practical man and would do what was necessary to achieve his goal. But humming was not good. Humming meant that Henry's life might very well change, and not for the better.

He was not about to take the chance that this betrothal might turn into a wedding or that he, Henry Milton, would end up in a house ruled by a woman.

Action was called for.

"I have had a letter from Squire Gibbs," Monica told her as they took tea in the drawing room. "Oh, Harriet, I wish I were back in Worthington. London is too busy. Eustace has not been home three nights in a row. What does he do with himself, I wonder?"

"What all young men his age do," Harriet replied. "Do not worry. Eustace has more than his share of common sense. He has grown into a man."

Monica sighed. "I shall have to accept that fact, I suppose, but it is hard. For years I have done nothing but fuss over Eustace. I do not know what I shall do now."

Harriet eyed the missive lying in her friend's lap. "What does Cedric have to say?"

"He implores me to try to persuade you to sell the mill." She paused. "And he allows that the country is very thin of company. I think he misses you."

"Me?" Harriet laughed. "Not likely."

"He wanted to marry you, Harriet."

"He wanted to possess my mill," Harriet corrected. "In Cedric's universe, marriage is the only way to bend a recalcitrant female to his will. It is a very masculine way of looking at things."

"Clearly he has abandoned that strategy, since he believes you betrothed to Lord Westwood. But you are too hard on him. He needs a mother for all those children." Monica shook her head. "Poor things."

Harriet slanted an assessing gaze at her friend. "I have thought about employing Cedric to oversee the mill and the crops. He knows the mill better than anyone, but I do not know whether his pride would let him accept the job, and on my terms, by which I mean a fair price, or no price at all for those who cannot afford it."

"He is a proud man," Monica conceded. "The children are driving him to distraction, and he sometimes drowns his troubles in drink. But beneath it all, Mr. Gibbs is a worthy man. I do believe he is honest."

"His temper —"

"All men have a temper, dear. It is because they wish to control things and cannot."

"Dear me, Monica. How did you come by such a view?" Harriet asked.

"Life, dearest." Monica sighed.

Harriet regarded her friend closely. Monica's life had been lonely after her husband's abandonment, and she had filled it with devotion to Eustace. Her friend was never happier than when nurturing someone who needed her. Unfortunately, her efforts were not paid back in kind. Her husband had run off, and her son had grown up.

"If only I could be certain that Cedric would abide by my wishes," Harriet said. "I will not have him forcing prices up again. The mill is for everyone, regardless of their ability to pay."

"His family ran the mill for generations," Monica pointed out. "Perhaps he is not to be blamed for expecting things to continue in the same fashion."

"Do I gather that you have been corresponding frequently with Cedric?"

Monica flushed. "I do not think he writes me for any reason other than he knows I have your ear."

"There is one way to find out." Abruptly, Harriet sat down at her writing table and began to compose a letter.

"What are you doing?"

"I am writing to offer him the position we

discussed. I will ask him to visit me in London to discuss my proposal. I shall invite him to stay here. Should you mind?"

Monica looked startled. "Why should I mind?"

"No reason." Harriet smiled.

"Eustace will be pleased," Monica quickly added. "He enjoys Mr. Gibbs's company."

Harriet tactfully refrained from pointing out Eustace and Cedric had never had two words to say to each other. But if it pleased her friend to construct such a fantasy, it was none of her concern.

"This is a list of rabble-rousers and ne'er-do-wells." Lord Westwood regarded the guest list in disapproval.

"Mr. Wilberforce is not a ne'er-do-well," Harriet said. "Or do you hold with slavery, my lord? I imagine those plantations of yours are worked —"

"By paid laborers. I abolished slavery on all of my properties."

That surprised her, but Harriet pressed on. "And pray, into which category does Lord Castlereagh fall, rabble-rouser or ne'er-do-well?"

He shrugged. "A statesman or two does not mask the fact that they will sit cheek and jowl with radicals and bedlamites."

"Mr. Hazlitt is a very respected critic," Harriet said, "and Mr. Shelley —"

"Is a radical thinker who fancies himself a poet."

"There is nothing wrong with that."

"More to the point," he said, "how can you think of having Hunt here after the scene he caused on the last occasion?"

Harriet regarded him. "It's Mr. Hunt who is the root of your difficulty, isn't it, my lord? You did not like the way he challenged you."

"Nonsense. I simply dislike how you turn your house over to him —"

"You think to bully me into acquiescing, sir." Harriet ignored his darkening expression. "But I shall not rescind my invitations simply because you do not wish to submit yourself to an evening of lively discourse."

"More like the rantings of lunatics."

Harriet sighed. Lord Westwood had sent her a note this morning announcing that he would present himself at two o'clock to review the list for tomorrow night's salon — a privilege she did not intend to grant him. Nevertheless, he had appeared precisely at that hour, and they had spent the better part of the time since arguing over the guest list.

"My lord, I wish to disabuse you of the notion that your critique of my guest list is at all helpful," Harriet said finally. "Although you may not agree with all that is said during my salons, the free exchange of views is precisely the object. How would it be if everyone agreed with everyone else? Change would never occur, and we would all be the poorer for it."

He regarded her. "So it is change you desire. Tell me, madam: Does that apply to your own life as well? For it seems to me that you have constructed a very narrow box for yourself that permits no alteration."

Harriet stared at him. "Whatever do you mean?"

"You are determined to get on with your life — a commendable goal, to be sure — but you intend it to be exactly the same life you have always known."

"The life I knew included a husband," she said tartly.

"Granted. But in picking up the pieces of what previously defined you, perhaps it is wise to ask yourself whether they still fit."

Harriet stared at him. There it was again, that strange disquiet, portending something she did not care to examine, a crack in her carefully ordered world. But she was content with the life she had constructed for herself. Who was he to try to change it?

"You are free to go elsewhere tomorrow night," she said crossly, "although in that event I will assume you do not want your shares badly enough to continue the masquerade."

He stared at her. "I find you impossible, madam."

"Likewise, my lord."

Suddenly, he caught her hand and pulled her to her feet.

"My lord?" Harriet eyed him in confusion.

"Come," he said. "I fancy a drive."

"I — where?" she stammered. "Now?"

Though he provided no answer, that was clearly his intent, for he took her arm and propelled her to the door, his hand a firm presence at her back.

And before Harriet could recover her astonishment, Lord Westwood swept her down the front steps to his waiting curricle. He handed her onto the seat, then jumped up beside her. With a crack of his whip, the horses shot out of the drive.

What sort of persuasion worked with a woman as stubborn as Lady Harriet? Perhaps he should have asked himself that question before he decided to make off with her in an open curricle ill-suited for such a purpose, but Elias had run out of patience in the exact moment she told him he was free to go elsewhere. Elsewhere was where he suddenly wanted to be — beyond the confines of Lady Harriet's parlor and her intractable notions about those dashed salons.

The clip-clop of the horses' hooves set the rhythm as he drove them past Grosvenor Square, up to Oxford and then west, past the street traders, over remnants of stones laid by Romans. His passenger made no objection but was scarcely in a position to do so, as she sat with her hands clutching the edge of her seat, her hair flying loose from its pins. And so he drove on.

It was a lovely day, Elias thought, drinking in the sunshine and the wind on his face. Sometimes a man simply had to head to the country. It had been too long since he'd worked outdoors in Jamaica with the sun beating down on his shoulders, warming him in a way London never could. As much as he had tried to bring bits and pieces of the island back to London, they mostly served to remind him of what he was missing. The dasheen bushes he'd planted behind his townhouse were but shadows of their Caribbean cousins.

His nose picked up the heady scent of wildflowers as brick and stone gave way to oak and heather. They must be halfway to Uxbridge by now, he realized. Elias glanced at Lady Harriet, who had given up trying to shield her hair from the wind. Their swift departure had not permitted her the luxury of fetching a hat, and now her hair was a tangled mess. She had not even taken her shawl, and her arms were bare up to the point of the small pieces of fabric that served as the sleeves of her frock and which could not possibly have provided any warmth. He had once found such unkemptness off-putting. Now he eyed that tangled auburn hair and found himself thinking that it would look just that way were she lying in bed gazing up at...well, someone.

Certainly not him.

Elias reflected on that. Had Freddy not corked up his toes, saddling him with a spendthrift business partner, he and Lady Harriet never would have inhabited the same universe. They had little in common, and while he could imagine her locked in a lover's embrace — that tousled hair falling over her naked shoulders, the cool expanse of bare skin slowly warming to white-hot heat — he was not meant to be that man. Theirs was a contrived arrangement. He would do well to remember that.

Pulling back on the reins, Elias directed his

pair into a clearing just off the road. What had he been thinking to embark on this mad, impulsive dash out of town? He took a deep breath, trying to regain his equilibrium, as the curricle rolled to a stop under the shade of a stout oak tree. A meadow stretched out before them, filled with cornflowers and marigold, their purple and yellow hues vibrant against the plum and pear trees that rose in silhouette in the distance.

Elias stepped down from the curricle and secured the reins. He glanced at Lady Harriet. She had begun to smooth her hair into place, though she still appeared somewhat stunned — justifiably, to be sure. He had given no thought to her comfort and safety, merely sent them galloping west in pursuit of something that did not reek of city rabble-rousers and intellectual pretense. She had doubtless been frightened half to death.

"I should apologize," he said, unable to muster much enthusiasm for that task as he drank in the pastoral scene and inhaled the scents around him with a pleasure that went bone-deep. Here was air and land untouched by the bustle and crudeness of town.

"Pray, do not, my lord," she replied easily. "That would spoil things." She caught the hem of her frock, draped it over her arm, and eased herself over the leather seat — brushing aside Elias's quickly extended hand. Placing her free hand on the dasher, she disembarked, albeit unsteadily. As her foot touched the ground, she shot him a triumphant glance.

"There! You thought to save me from a tumble, did you not? But I did not need —" She stumbled then, but caught herself at the last moment. "Oh, dear! Pride does indeed goeth before a fall. Or is that before destruction? Either way, I am well-paid for my conceit." She laughed merrily.

That laugh — wholehearted, unabashed, infectious — struck Elias like a mortal blow.

It was as if he had not seen her clearly until this moment. Her windswept hair fell free over her shoulders; the corners of her eyes crinkled in mirth. Their blue sparkle dazzled like Caribbean seas under the blazing sun. And her mouth — no half-measures there, no modest upturn that signaled restrained, ladylike amusement. No, her lips parted in a full-on laugh at her own vanity that was perhaps the most wonderful sound Elias had ever heard.

And then he picked up the heady scent of primrose. She had worn it again.

Elias took a steadying breath. "You did not object to the drive?" he heard himself say.

"Oh, goodness, no," she said. "Well, I did wonder where you meant to take us, but after a bit I stopped caring. It was most stimulating."

She did, indeed, look most stimulated. Her lips curved upward, their dusky pink reminiscent of a shade of orchid that grew wild on trees in Jamaica. "You do not mind the country, then?" he asked.

She hesitated. "That is a more complicated question. I grew up in Cornwall. The cliffs and the moors were cold and forbidding — desolate, really. Sometimes I despaired of anything growing there, least of all me." She looked around, her eyes taking in the fields of wildflowers and, in the distance, a windmill. "This, however, is quite lovely."

Elias offered his arm and this time, with perfect charity, she took it and allowed him to lead her away from the curricle. "I sense that you do not much like London," she said.

He slanted her a gaze. "I find there is much artificiality in town."

"That is why you do not like my salons." When he made no response, she pressed his arm. "That night in my kitchen, you mentioned your father. Tell me about him."

Elias shook his head. "That's in the past."

"Everything before this moment is in the past, so that is no excuse." She smiled. "I fear I must insist."

He found that he was powerless to refuse her. "There is little to tell. I was raised in the manner of the heir to an earldom — Eton, Oxford. Latin, boxing, fencing, the like. They did not hold my interest. Then my father sent me to the West Indies to learn my way around his properties there." He hesitated. "It was a revelation."

"In what way?"

"In every way. I discovered the pleasure of working the land — and discovered spices. There was nothing for it after that." He smiled a bit sheepishly.

Her answering smile ignited a warmth inside

him. What the devil was wrong with him? Elias wondered.

"My father had other ideas," he continued. "He wanted me to learn to be a proper gentleman, whereas I preferred to explore my new interests. We were not able to discuss those differences without mutual anger. I have come to regret that."

"I am sorry," she said.

"After he died, I discovered that the West Indies property had been sold to pay his debts," Elias said. "There was little left in the estate. He had never disclosed his financial difficulties to me. Had I known, perhaps I would have made different choices."

"Such as?"

Elias regarded her. "This is a very odd conversation. I cannot think you wish to hear about my regrets."

She pressed his arm again, her gaze troubled. "My wish to hear about them is clearly exceeded by your reluctance to speak of them. I did not intend to embarrass you. My inquisitiveness was unpardonably rude."

"Not unpardonable, surely." Elias found he could not take his eyes from hers. "'Tis only that regret is an odd business. It has led me around to the view that while honesty must always be honored, candor need not be."

Her sudden, answering smile nearly took his breath away. "And yet, you have been quite candid with me, sir, in stating your case against my use of those shares."

"Some truths must be stated." Elias left it at that.

He found he had no wish to introduce acrimony.

Neither, apparently, did she, for she took his arm again quite companionably. She was nearly a head shorter than he, but her pace matched his and Elias found he quite liked the way her hand nestled into the crook of his elbow. In this manner they resumed their walk toward the meadow.

"I suppose," she ventured after a moment, "that it would be intrusive to ask what you did after discovering your estate had no funds. Do forgive me, sir, but I own that I am curious as to how you brought all to right again."

"I joined the military," he responded. "There was no money to buy my colors, but I was strangely happy as a penniless soldier. Afterward, I ran into Freddy, and our business was born."

Lady Harriet pondered this. "It would seem that Freddy was perhaps the making of both of us."

"I cannot agree."

"Why not?" She eyed him curiously.

He hesitated. "It does not seem that your marriage was a happy one, whereas I have been supremely happy in my business."

She looked away. "Assessment of one's happiness is a subjective matter, I suppose. I find that I am not eager to dwell on it. And now I find myself in sympathy with you, my lord, for I agree that this discussion suddenly seems rather intimate."

"Perhaps not for two people who are betrothed," he replied lightly.

She stopped and looked up at him. "We are not well-suited, are we, my lord? And yet despite your dislike of our arrangement, you have been quite sporting."

"I find it less onerous by the day," Elias said.

Lady Harriet looked startled. "But we were at such loggerheads earlier."

"And will be again, no doubt."

Her gaze searched his. "No doubt."

"Should you like to walk for a bit more?"

She nodded, her eyes not leaving his face as she took his arm once more. Elias led her into the field of wildflowers. He spotted some primroses, and reached down and plucked one. The flower was banded in pink, its bright yellow center giving way to cream. Its scent was reminiscent of sweet olive, and Elias instantly associated it with her and the night he kissed her. Not really a kiss, he mentally corrected, only a fleeting brush of lips in her foyer as she battled a headache. Quite inadequate, now that he thought on it.

He held the flower out for her inspection.

"That does not look like the specimen Celestial grows," Lady Harriet said. "She uses it to make a potion to treat some illness. I cannot remember what."

"There are many varieties," Elias responded. But floral specimens were not uppermost in his mind. Instead, he —

"Why is it that Caroline Forth can capture a man's fancy with merely a look?" she asked suddenly.

Elias stared at her, stunned by her abrupt change of subject.

"I will grant that she is lovely," she added, "but I confess I do not understand her appeal."

He had no wish to disrupt a pleasant outing with a discussion of Lady Forth and her various attributes. Perhaps Lady Harriet's question was merely rhetorical. But no, she was eyeing him expectantly.

"Come now, sir," she prodded. "In the spirit of our agreement I call upon you to enlighten me. It is not a trivial matter for me, I assure you." He thought her voice wobbled slightly.

"She is beautiful, I suppose —" he began.

"Let us not even debate that," Lady Harriet interjected. "Pray, do not be evasive, my lord. This is a woman I have spent much time contemplating, and you are the only person to whom I have acknowledged that very lowering fact. She gave Freddy something I could not, and I have no notion what it is. I only know that it makes me feel less of a woman, somehow."

Freddy had been out of his blasted mind, Elias thought grimly. "Her beauty is on the surface only," he said. "Like a mirror. Each man sees in her a reflection of his own worth."

She frowned. "I do not understand."

This discussion was deuced awkward. "I suspect she thrives on constant adoration," he said. "Many beautiful women do."

"Yes, but if beauty is the measure of one's worth, one must always need to be beautiful," she said.

"Exactly," he said. "And that fact must be affirmed again and again. Each man who succumbs to her charms affirms her power anew."

"But what does the man gain?"

Elias shifted uncomfortably. "Aside from the obvious?"

"'Tis not obvious to me, sir," she said. "What does he gain?"

"His opinion of himself must only be enhanced by the fact that she chooses him as the one on whom she bestows her, er, favors."

An appealing blush spread over her features. "Yes, I see. She is his conquest and he is hers." She hesitated. "It is something of a mercenary transaction, is it not?"

"Of that there can be little doubt."

"I do not understand why Freddy needed to have his opinion of himself enhanced by Caroline Forth. Or by any of the others."

"Nor do I," Elias said. Not when he'd had Harriet Worthington in his bed.

"Have you never thought to marry?"

That surprised him. "Once," he said. "Fortunately, circumstances intervened."

She eyed him curiously, and Elias was relieved when she did not pursue that further. "Marriage is difficult," she said, her expression wistful. "I was certainly not good at it. And while I do not admire Caroline, I sometimes wish I could be like her a little. If only I could have —"

"Damnation!"

She eyed him in surprise. "My lord?"

"There is naught for you to envy," he growled. "You have no need to borrow from Lady Forth's bag of tricks." He held out the primrose. "See this flower? It grows wild in the field on its own. Yet I defy anyone to improve upon it."

She reached for it, but Elias deftly swept it out of her reach and instead tucked the bloom into the tangles in her hair. Then he discovered his fingers had no wish to retreat. They lingered to ensnare a curl, and as he brushed it back from her face, his fingertip grazed her cheek.

Elias heard her quick intake of breath, saw her eyes widen. Their gazes locked. The primrose in her hair beckoned him.

He had no choice but to kiss her.

As his mouth met hers, her lips parted on a little gasp — the perfect invitation, whether or not she intended it as such. He kissed her lightly, just the merest touch, which nevertheless set his blood afire. As he brushed her lips — once, then again — he felt her answering shiver and discovered he would not be satisfied with a chaste, fleeting kiss. Her lips were soft, full, and inviting. They begged to be ravaged.

Elias caught himself before that thought could blossom. It would be folly to venture down that road. But just as he marshaled his discipline to sever their connection, she reached up and placed her fingertips lightly on the top of his shoulders. Standing nearly on her toes, she returned his kiss in rather greater measure, her mouth pressing against his with unmistakable enthusiasm.

Instantly, his arms went around her. His senses awash in the intoxicating perfume of primrose and desire, Elias deepened the kiss beyond anything he had contemplated only moments before. Her lips, made for plundering, readily yielded.

It was not enough.

Elias's restless, seeking hands moved to her arms, savoring the silky smoothness of her bare skin, sliding down them and then upward again until those tiny sleeves barred further exploration. His fingers threaded through her hair, burying themselves in the thick tangles, savoring their disarray. But that was not enough, either. So he caught her about the waist and drew her hard against him.

She did not resist. Instead, she leaned into him, pliant and willing, as if their bodies were joined by more than the simple connection of their lips and his rude embrace.

No good could come of this, he realized. It was excessively unwise. But his brain had ceded authority to another part of his anatomy. He kissed her urgently, violently, his lips demanding her secrets. She did not pull away, and it might not have registered if she had, for by now his body burned with need.

Her hands clutched the edges of his coat as Elias trailed kisses down the smooth expanse of her neck to the base of her throat, where the skin was pale, translucent, almost virginal. Shamelessly, his hand snaked up her side and, after a moment's hesitation — not enough to count, really — found the soft, perfect roundness of her breast.

When she answered with a low moan, Elias's knees nearly buckled.

He lifted her off her feet, raising her up to his

full height, holding her against the length of his body without a shred of space between them. Her lithe form was as light as gossamer, and it fit perfectly against his. The scent of primrose banished whatever caution he might have salvaged. It was hers, her essence. He wanted — *needed* — to possess her. Here. Now. To lie with her amid the wildflowers and see her hair fanning out from her flushed face, her eyes reflecting the glory of her passion.

They were a heartbeat away.

She opened her eyes to look at him, and Elias saw the heat there. But there was something else in that blue gaze — shock, bewilderment, and perhaps uncertainty.

Good God. What was he thinking? Mustering what was left of his control, Elias eased his grip on her, suffering sweet torture as her body slid down the length of his before he set her firmly on her feet. Then he released her.

For a long moment their gazes held. She looked as dazed as he felt.

"Well," she said at last. "I, that is — Oh, my."

Elias thought her voice was not quite steady. Her cheeks were flushed — was that from desire or embarrassment? Her lips trembled, but whether with longing or confusion he could not tell.

The primrose was still in her hair. Its scent would ever after be hers, exotic and free. Her breasts rose rapidly with her breathing, and a sheen of perspiration clung to her skin. Her lips were swollen from his kisses.

Elias took it all in and knew, suddenly, that there were worse things than failing to win back his shares, than enduring Lady Harriet's salons, than denying himself this delicious passion.

What was worse than all of that was the knowledge that he might, if he were not very careful, lose his heart.

Silently, and more shaken than he could ever admit, he took her hand and led her back to the curricle.

She said not a word as he handed her in, then climbed in beside her. Elias turned the vehicle around, toward London. Regret followed them all the way back.

CHAPTER TEN

SUCH A THING had never happened to Harriet. Though she had known the intimacies of married life, her wildest dreams could not have imagined anything like the drive with Lord Westwood yesterday afternoon. His passion. Her boldness.

Harriet was quite aware she had breached all bounds of polite behavior. And with Lord Westwood, of all people, the very man who had sought to dictate her guest list. The very man to whom she clung so tightly as to leave no doubt about the ease of his conquest. It had seemed the most natural thing in the world when he kissed her. Then she brazenly returned that kiss, inviting so very much more.

She had not foreseen that his kiss would leave her weak in the knees. Most assuredly, she had not expected to find herself breathless and locked in an intimate embrace that eloquently revealed Lord Westwood's burgeoning enthusiasm for the task.

"Too much cream," Celestial declared.

Harriet stared at her blankly.

"Too much cream in the filling. It won't

hold together." Celestial's look said she knew exactly why Harriet's mind was wandering. Lord Westwood had created quite a stir in the household when he had taken her off with him in such an abrupt fashion.

His return had been much less conspicuous. When Horace opened the front door, she and Lord Westwood had stood there in a strange, still silence. The earl had turned and left without a word. Harriet had walked blindly to her room, not looking back. She had not appeared for supper. Sleep had not come for many hours.

"Now, Celestial," Harriet admonished wearily, "I know whether a filling will come together or no. It only wants beating. It is supposed to be rich."

Celestial shrugged. "Rich is one thing. Killing a man with wretched excess is another."

Harriet stiffened. "Is there something you wish to say, Celestial?"

"Only that it's clear that something happened between you and Lord Westwood. I've never seen you concoct such a decadent thing. The man inspired you, I'm guessing." Celestial shot her a knowing gaze.

Harriet flushed. "That is enough. It is time to work. We have dozens of these to make."

The inspiration for the little puff pastries had come to her overnight. Her restless sleep had brought dreams filled with a churning fire that licked at her insides and sparked wild fantasies. In one of them, she had been in the kitchen, creating decadent dishes for Lord Westwood's pleasure. As he watched her pile layer after layer of brittle pastry and soft filling, his turbulent gaze hinted of savage appetites. Harriet had awakened trembling, thinking his hands were caressing her.

And though it had only been a dream, what he aroused within her was no dream. Harriet had spent most of her waking hours since yesterday trying to understand what had happened between them. She did not have an answer, but she did have her Napoleons.

That is what she had decided to call them, for they had all the qualities of a coddled tyrant: rich and hard on the surface, pandering to greed and lust within. It was a tricky pastry, with layers of dough interspersed with butter held at just the right temperature to create the brittle "leaves" that helped it stand up to the decadent cream filling, itself thick enough to insist on its own reckoning. It was a pastry that promised the world — and delivered it in the lusty cream designed to make a man greedy for more.

Harriet wanted Lord Westwood to like her Napoleons, for he, too, could be rigid and inflexible on the outside, yet his lips had been soft as silk on hers. They had spawned strange forces within her, made her bold and brazen.

To be sure, she had wanted to learn about desire. But this overwhelming need he had awakened within her bore no resemblance to what she had experienced with Freddy. It had swamped her, left her shaken and helpless, unable to deny the startling fact that she had wanted Lord Westwood more than she had ever desired her own husband. And the feeling lingered still.

Rather than showing her how to guard against desire, Lord Westwood had opened the door into a world she had not known existed. And yet, her own body had somehow known, betraying her with its wanton need. The afternoon had ended strangely, in silence, as if neither of them knew what to make of it.

For although their betrothal was a sham, something between them was not a sham, something tantalizing and dangerous, something that wished — nay, demanded — to be pursued. She had waded into the swirling waters of that world, and Lord Westwood had played the gentleman and returned her to safety.

But what about the next time? Would there be a next time? Did she wish there to be?

Yes. Dear Lord, yes.

Monica was right, Harriet realized. She *was* ignorant of the world. She had been married, but Freddy's kisses had never affected her the way Lord Westwood's had. Poor Freddy! She had given him so little.

Her salon was tonight. Part of her could not wait until Lord Westwood arrived. The rest of her was filled with uncertainty and wished for the end of this strange masquerade. For the first time she wondered whether this course she had set them on was wise — and whether she would be able to end it. Thank goodness for the document they had both signed that would severe their connection.

A few hours later, Heavenly stood over Harriet like a martinet. "Sit still! I will never get these combs in. I wish I knew what was going on around here. Strange comings and goings. Ain't seemly."

"For the seventh time, Heavenly, there is naught to tell," Harriet said. "We drove out to the country and drove back. The scenery was lovely."

"Hmmph. Things aren't right in this household," she grumbled. "With Celestial and Horace smelling of April and May and you making a fool of yourself over that lord —"

"Celestial and Horace?" Harriet was astonished. "Do you mean —"

For an answer, Heavenly sighed heavily.

"Celestial is entitled to her own life," Harriet said gently. "I know you must wish for her happiness."

"What about my happiness? If she leaves, I'm all alone."

"Why should she leave? She and Horace can remain in my employ."

Heavenly shook her head. "Won't be the same. Already, she hardly confides in me anymore. All she wants is to be with Horace."

She dabbed at her eyes, then regarded Harriet critically. "You look beautiful tonight, Miss Harriet. If that earl isn't nice to you, I'll come after him with my knitting needles. Oh, I almost forgot. This came. A gentleman's gentleman it was who brought it, from the looks of him. A dapper sort."

The image of Lord Westwood dodging

Heavenly's knitting needles almost made Harriet laugh — until she saw the note Heavenly thrust at her.

Dearest Lady Harriet,
You have been constantly in my thoughts since last we conversed. Perhaps I ought not to speak of this, since you are betrothed to another, but I long to spend a private moment in your presence so that I can persuade you of my feelings. Please grant me that small request tonight. I remain truly yours, etc.
Oliver Hunt

Dear heavens! Mr. Hunt had never led her to believe he possessed any fondness for her, much less such strong feelings. Perhaps she should not have taken that warmth in his eyes so lightly. But with all the turmoil between her and Lord Westwood, Harriet had no wish to speak to Mr. Hunt privately about his feelings, whatever they might be.

Her carefully planned salon suddenly appeared to be a disaster in the making.

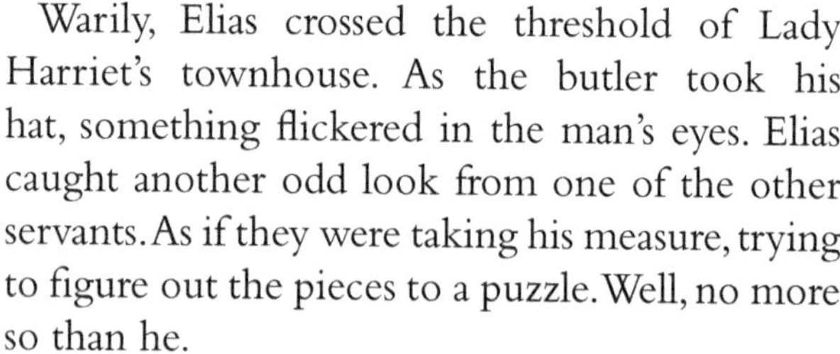

Warily, Elias crossed the threshold of Lady Harriet's townhouse. As the butler took his hat, something flickered in the man's eyes. Elias caught another odd look from one of the other servants. As if they were taking his measure, trying to figure out the pieces to a puzzle. Well, no more so than he.

Lady Harriet stood to the rear of the entrance,

positioned to greet her guests. Seeing him, she flushed and quickly looked away.

Elias recognized the same uncertainty within himself. Like a green youth, he found himself gauging her reaction, trying to read in those blushes the truth of her thoughts.

The awkwardness, he suspected, would continue until they put it to rest, either by pretending nothing untoward had happened between them — or by becoming lovers in earnest. That last was a prospect with a myriad of complications, and he refused to entertain it. Retrieving his shares did not include succumbing to lust for the woman who was spending down his company's worth. Oh, perhaps they would dance around the edges of it — there was that bargain between them, after all. They certainly had gone a long way toward fulfilling its terms yesterday. More than he bargained for.

There was the rub. Lady Harriet wished to learn about desire, but it was he who had learned something — that Lady Harriet Worthington had more passion in the tip of her finger than any woman he had known. He had been within a whisker of losing all control.

And now what? He could scarcely keep his distance. Their agreement called for him to stay at her side, playing the dutiful fiancé. They could pretend that yesterday hadn't occurred, which was about as likely as wishing down the sun. Even now, Elias could not take his eyes from her.

Still, lust was manageable, as long as one was forearmed. Love, of course, was something else.

That had brought him nothing but a very public heartache and lifelong distrust of the thing poets penned odes to. He had not expected to feel unbridled lust for Lady Harriet, and while that was disturbing, it could have been far worse. Thank God, his heart was whole.

As he reached her side, he caught the faint scent of wildflowers. It stirred his blood, instantly recalled him to that meadow yesterday. Her emerald silk gown brought out the fire in her hair, and he imagined himself removing the combs, entangling his fingers in that auburn mass once more. Perhaps she would rise on tiptoes to kiss him again, and he would lose himself in that kiss, in the feel of her body against his.

When she turned to him, however, the smile pasted on her lips was as remote as an iceberg.

Clearly she had made her choice — to pretend that yesterday had not happened. Elias decided to follow along and see where that led. Denial, after all, could run both ways.

As Elias took his place in the receiving line beside her, a resonant baritone voice brought him up short.

"Lady Harriet," the man said, bowing deeply.

It was that fool Hunt, fawning over her hand as if it were the Holy Grail. He brought it to his lips, lingering over it — excessively, Elias thought.

"M-Mr. Hunt," she stammered.

Elias frowned. What in Hunt's greeting had made her lose her composure?

"We have much to discuss," Hunt said in a low tone.

"Perhaps later." She flushed.

If his ears were not mistaken, Oliver Hunt had just set the stage for an assignation with his fiancée. Hunt nodded at Elias by way of greeting and quickly moved away.

Throughout the evening, Elias watched the man and grew certain he was up to something. Hunt held forth in small groups with his usual arrogance, but his gaze often strayed to Lady Harriet.

Young Eustace was among those hanging onto Hunt's every word. Elias tried to recall whether he had gone through such a worshipful phase in his youth but was quite certain he had not. Indeed, at Eustace's age, Elias had already worked the fields of his father's Jamaica property and seen battle on the Continent. In neither case had there been time for idle pursuits such as hero worship. Then again, Elias had a dim memory of following one of his commanders around like a shadow, drinking in his every utterance on the strategies of war. Perhaps he had not behaved so very differently after all.

Belatedly, Elias noticed that something of a dispute had broken out in one corner of the parlor between Hunt and another man — William Hazlitt, if he did not miss his guess. Elias knew him only by reputation as a bit of a gadfly, with strong beliefs and opinions about a variety of literary and political topics. It appeared that Hazlitt had taken offense at something Hunt said. Elias drew nearer, determined to keep abreast of Mr. Hunt's every activity this night.

"I live to my own self, sir," Hazlitt was saying. "I take a thoughtful interest in what is passing in the world, but I do not feel the slightest inclination to meddle in it. If any man be influenced by my essays, that is perhaps to the good, but it is not a result that I seek."

"A man with your credentials would do better to turn your acclaim to good use," Hunt admonished. "How sad it is to see a man who wastes his celebrity in the cause of no one but himself when he could, if he wished, serve the public good. As I do."

"Rubbish!" Hazlitt retorted. "There is not a more mean, stupid, dastardly, pitiful, selfish, spiteful, envious, ungrateful animal than the public. It is the greatest of cowards, for it is afraid of itself."

By now, the other conversations had stopped. Everyone gathered around the two men, one an acclaimed man of letters, the other noted for his revolutionary zeal. Wilberforce, the man Elias had seen conversing with Lady Harriet at Lady Symington's ball, spoke up.

"It is true that people are customarily afraid of change," Wilberforce said in a conciliatory tone. "And not all change is for the best, of course. But sometimes the public must be led to change because it will result in the greater happiness of others."

Hazlitt scoffed. "How little security we have when we trust our happiness to others!"

"My point exactly," Hunt snapped. "Many people have no security at all. Are you so blind, man, that you do not see? They must be taught to see their future and seize it."

Studying Hunt's florid features, Elias found it hard to believe that this was the man who had so calmly skewered him the other night for his loyalty to the Crown. Tonight Hunt lacked the patience for effective debate. He seemed agitated, almost preoccupied, and his attacks were more curt than considered.

"I see well enough that you, Hunt, have a love of power," Hazlitt replied disdainfully, "and therefore a love of yourself that will always take precedence over any charity you profess for that mewling public of yours."

Hunt rounded on Hazlitt, closing to within a whisker's breadth of the man. "You, sir, are an ass!"

"Better an ass than a fraud," Hazlitt spat out.

At Hunt's swift intake of breath, Elias heard fast bets being placed as to whether the two would come to fisticuffs. Ever the peacemaker, Wilberforce tried to intervene, but the two men simply ignored him. They glared at each other like two belligerent bulls.

"Do have a Napoleon, gentlemen!" Lady Harriet darted between Hunt and Hazlitt with a plate.

From his vantage point several feet away, Elias could just make out the plump, enticing pastries. They looked to be made of several layers. He had not seen their like before. He edged closer, but everyone else had the same idea. By the time he reached the platter, nary a one remained.

The argument was quickly forgotten. Everyone

to a man was engaged in the act of polishing off the confections, which looked to have a brittle exterior interspersed with a cream filling.

Brittle on the outside, soft where it mattered. Like Lady Harriet.

Or perhaps not. Perhaps what happened between them yesterday was an aberration. Perhaps she did not harbor any real desire for him, or any man. Perhaps all the attention she lavished on every damned thing that came out of her kitchen was the only real passion that moved her.

And perhaps, Elias thought darkly, she had no idea that she was capable of sending a man to the very limits of his control.

"Mr. Hunt?" Harriet's uncertain gaze swept the shadows of the terrace. Instantly, a figure stepped out of the darkness.

"Harriet," he acknowledged in a velvet voice. "You do not mind that I call you Harriet, I hope?"

Harriet eyed him uneasily. She had been taken aback at receiving his short note a quarter hour ago to meet her here. "What did you wish to see me about, sir?"

"I have thought of nothing else but our *tête-à-tête* since today, when I received your letter." He took her hand. "When you asked me for advice about your late husband's business concerns last fall, I had dared to hope you would turn to me for more counsel, perhaps for companionship. I am not normally a patient man, but now I see that patience does indeed have its reward. I am touched and overwhelmed by your declaration."

"Letter?" Harriet was bewildered. Last fall, when she had decided to sell some of Freddy's shares of Westwood Imports, her solicitor suggested that she mention the fact to her friends and acquaintances to see if they were interested in purchasing them. That did not strike her as seemly, so she ultimately abandoned that course. Perhaps she had said something to Mr. Hunt at the time, though she could not recall. But she was quite certain she had written no letter to him — then or now.

"You write like an angel," Mr. Hunt said, pulling a piece of paper from his pocket, though in truth he had been rather surprised at her faulty grammar. "I shall treasure this missive until the day I die."

"I should very much like to see that paper, sir. I warrant that I sent you no such letter." Harriet reached for it, but he jerked it away and instead caught her about the waist.

"So coy, so playful," he murmured, crushing her against his chest. "So delightful!"

Harriet tried to pull away. "Pray do not, Mr. Hunt! Indeed, you do not appear to be yourself tonight. I daresay you have not been getting your rest, what with all your, er, important activities." To her dismay, his arms locked around her.

"It is true that I have been engaged in important work." His sonorous voice deepened.

"Revolutionary fervor can be unpredictable. Riots all over the country have demanded my attention."

"I can well imagine." Harriet tried to pry his fingers from her waist. "It must be a great deal of work to channel the people's zeal to other areas."

"Oh, I am perfectly happy with their efforts," he said. "Rioting is the only way to get a recalcitrant government's attention. Only by creating mayhem can we accomplish anything. But it must be organized mayhem. It does no good to destroy something insignificant."

"I see," Harriet responded, contemplating whether it would be a breach of etiquette to dig her nails into the man's loathsome fingers. "What do you consider significant?"

"Factories, storehouses, and the like," he said. "It is the only way to get the attention of the rich and put pressure on the government."

Such was Harriet's astonishment that she momentarily forgot about her predicament. "You condone such destruction?"

"I condone anything that leads to change. And I am delighted to have found a perfect helpmeet." He brought his lips to hers.

"Mr. Hunt, you have formed entirely the wrong impress —" But her words were cut off by his kiss.

"Lord Westwood."

Elias turned. He had been watching the door to the kitchen, wondering where Lady Harriet had gone to. Perhaps she was fetching more pastries, he thought hopefully. "Eustace," he acknowledged politely. "I trust you are well."

"Well enough, my lord. Only —" Eustace halted, then stared down at his feet.

Elias almost felt sorry for the lad. He had not missed the troubled look in Eustace's eyes during Hunt's heated dispute with Hazlitt. Though a relentless iconoclast, Hazlitt had held his composure rather more than Hunt, who in Elias's view had revealed himself to be an abusive, irrational bully.

Eustace looked downcast indeed. Had the bloom faded from that particular rose? All to the good, Elias thought. Hunt was not worthy of Eustace's youthful adoration.

"Do not take it so hard, Eustace. A true man does not need to belittle others to prove himself a man."

"Yes, sir. That is, I —" Eustace broke off in obvious discomfiture.

Elias eyed him in alarm. He fervently hoped that Eustace was not about to cry. "Why do we not go out to the terrace?" he said quickly. Lady Harriet's pastries could wait.

"Yes, the terrace." Eustace nodded vigorously and with apparent relief. "That is just where we should go. I think it is best if you see for yourself." To Elias's surprise, Eustace flushed a deep red.

"What the devil are you talking about?" Elias demanded, as Eustace pulled him through the parlor toward the terrace.

"Shhh!" Eustace admonished. "It would not do to attract attention. Come, my lord. Please hurry, or I fear it will be too late."

"Too late? For what?"

"Just hurry."

When they reached the terrace doors, Eustace fairly pushed him out into the night air.

At first, Elias thought they were alone. Then he picked out a muffled conversation in the vicinity of what he assumed was a normally silent bush.

"My dear, I will treasure this moment until I die," said a familiar baritone.

"And that moment, sirrah, is now!" Eustace shouted triumphantly in the direction of the tall shrubbery. He looked expectantly at Elias.

A figure — Hunt, if Elias did not miss his guess — peered from around the bush, followed by another figure — that of his fiancée.

"Eustace! Lord Westwood!" Lady Harriet's eyes were wide.

Elias registered her rather disheveled appearance and Hunt's proprietary air. Then he glanced at Eustace.

"This is what I was trying to tell you, sir," Eustace replied, regarding Hunt with the look of a vengeful angel. "Do you wish to kill him now, or shall I have the honor of acting as your second?"

Elias's gaze returned to Hunt and Lady Harriet, who was smoothing the fabric of her gown and looking anywhere but at him. Hunt, to his amazement, began to laugh.

"Go away, Eustace. You are bothering me.

Rather like a pesky fly on the corn pudding. This is a matter between two men, not a mere pup."

"Yes, do leave us, Eustace." Lady Harriet said in a wobbly voice. "I do not think you too young, but you must see that this is most embarrassing for me —"

"Embarrassing?" Hunt frowned. "My dear —"

"I am *not* your dear," Lady Harriet interjected. "Not in the slightest. If you could see past your inflated self-regard, you would have realized that instantly. I had no wish for such fondness between us. Indeed, rather the opposite."

"Now, Harriet, why deny what is perfectly plain to me, as it must be to this fellow here," Hunt demanded.

"This 'fellow'," Elias said evenly, "is engaged to the lady whom you have, by her own admission, embarrassed." He took a measure of pride in the fact that he had not lost his composure — though even as that thought formed, his fists curled at his sides.

Hunt laughed. "That is rich! Can you not see that I am everything you are not? Learned, compelling, a galvanizer of men —"

"No!" Eustace said suddenly. "That is not true."

Hunt merely shrugged. "Why should I care for the opinion of a green youth?"

"Eustace is correct." Lady Harriet stepped forward, eyes flashing. "You are quite the fraud. This past quarter-hour in your company has persuaded me of that. I must ask you to leave, Mr. Hunt."

"Nonsense, madam. There are a dozen men

inside who will hang on my every word. I cannot disappoint them."

"Then perhaps they will follow you outside," she responded coolly.

Hunt scowled at her. "Nonsense. You wrote me a letter. You led me to believe that my attention was more than welcome — indeed, warmly sought."

Lady Harriet flushed. "I did no such thing!"

"What sort of tease is this?" Hunt demanded.

Lady Harriet looked stricken. "Mr. Hunt," she protested, "I did not —"

"You lie, madam!"

And that is when Elias's fist connected with Hunt's jaw. In the next instant, Hunt lay prone at her feet.

"Oh, my!" Lady Harriet cried. "Was that necessary, my lord?"

Elias regarded her for a long moment, then turned away. He had not been able to control his temper after all. That was disappointing, though not quite as disappointing as Lady Harriet's behavior. Indeed, he did not know what to believe.

He thought it best to leave. Eustace was more than capable of showing Mr. Hunt to the door, especially now that Lady Harriet's butler had arrived on the terrace, looking quite appalled at the scene before him.

Elias sighed heavily. He had not gotten even one of those pastries. But that was not the problem. No, it was very much worse than that. He regarded his fiancée. She still looked lovely in that green gown, though its bodice was scandalously awry. Her eyes held dismay — that much was clear — but there was something else there as well. Something, his brain told him, very like perfidy.

In the last twenty-four hours, he had learned a great deal about her. Now, he knew something else: That she was as counterfeit as their betrothal.

CHAPTER ELEVEN

"YOU CANNOT GO to his house!" Monica looked horrified.

"I must." Harriet picked up her reticule and walked past Horace, who had finally abandoned his effort to appear uninterested in matters involving his employer and Lord Westwood. "I cannot allow him to think I threw myself at Mr. Hunt."

"Mr. Hunt has apologized — quite prettily, I thought." Monica had rather enjoyed the spectacle of the proud Mr. Hunt groveling before them in the parlor this morning.

"Perhaps he will even muster the courage to apologize to Lord Westwood, although I doubt it," Harriet said. "The man seems to have little in the way of honor."

Monica shook her head. "What does it matter, anyway? The betrothal is a sham. Why not let things be?"

"A *sham*?" Horace stared at them. No sooner were the words out than he clapped his hand over his mouth in mortification. "I beg your pardon, madam," he said, his face red. "I should not have spoken. I do not know what has come over me lately."

Harriet frowned. The normally reticent Horace had been turned inside out trying to satisfy Celestial's thirst for information. "Your concern — everyone's concern — is gratifying," she said crisply, "but I am leaving now."

Before Monica could protest further, Harriet swept out the door. Determination gave her courage, but truth be told, she was as nervous as a cat. Lord Westwood had not responded to her note. He had not come round to escort her to the party they had been engaged to attend last night. Harriet could not abide his silence. Disapproval, perhaps. Even his anger. But not his silence.

Silence meant that she did not exist.

She and Freddy had had too much silence between them, and it had created an even greater gulf. Harriet had never broached the subject of their marriage to him; likely he would have been surprised to learn that she felt solitary and isolated. She was certain that Freddy had never felt isolated or alone. He led an unencumbered life, and emotions were not part of it. Diversion, not reflection, was his way.

Harriet had prided herself on being neither a cloying nor a demanding wife. Then again, she had only a vague notion of what a marriage should be. As her mother had died birthing her, Harriet had no opportunity to witness her parents together. Her father had been remote and cold. Harriet knew he blamed her for her mother's death.

Knowing nothing about marriage, Harriet had nevertheless assumed that she and Freddy would find their own way. But something was missing. Harriet had not known how to articulate what that was. Sometimes she thought the problem existed only in her own mind. Why was she not satisfied with a state that other women enjoyed? Was there something wrong with her? The longer she and Freddy lived as two islands in the same household, the more confused she had become.

Marriage to a man incapable of fidelity proved a trap: Always, she hoped that things between them would improve, but each day presented new opportunities for realizing that they would not. Her disappointment had turned inward, making her doubt her worth. And so she tried to find a path through the world on her own terms. Her salons and her cooking brought her a measure of fulfillment. And independence, of course.

But what was independence, anyway? The freedom she had in her marriage proved an empty consolation. Freedom did not make up for the sense of failure that haunted her.

Still, if she had learned anything from her time with Freddy, it was that silence did not erase problems; it only made them worse. Perhaps if she had found her voice, Freddy would not have strayed.

Lord Westwood was not Freddy. He was not even her fiancé. But his silence wounded her in a way that was profoundly disturbing. And she meant to deal with it forthrightly. She resolved to be silent no more.

Harriet had never visited a gentleman at his house. It was not done, even by independent women, unless one wished to be taken for a lightskirt. Harriet did not care about her reputation. She only knew she was finished with silence.

Eustace, who had adopted Lord Westwood as his new hero, said the earl was often home in the afternoons. Eustace had been very helpful since that night. He readily believed her assertion that she had sent no missive to Mr. Hunt. She did not know what Lord Westwood believed, but his silence led her to suspect the worst.

Harriet stood nervously on Lord Westwood's front steps. It occurred to her that for form's sake she should have asked Eustace to accompany her here, or even Monica. But it was too late now. Besides, her errand was too personal, too private to be witnessed by a third party.

The manservant who answered Harriet's knock was stiff and unfriendly. He disappeared, and after what seemed like an eternity, returned with word that Lord Westwood was available for a few minutes. Harriet did not know what to make of that dismissive statement, but she followed the man through a long corridor. At the far end of it she spied a pair of muddy boots large enough to be Lord Westwood's and a gardening shovel and trowel propped near an exterior door. Other than that, there were few clues about the man who resided here.

Indeed, the house itself looked only occasionally lived in. Harriet knew that Lord Westwood spent extensive time in the West Indies, but surely someone could have set out a vase or two of flowers when he was in residence. Much of the furniture was draped in Holland covers, adding to the air of disuse. Only the study into which Harriet was ushered lacked that stale, uninhabited atmosphere. A fire blazed in the hearth, and a blue and brown mosaic-patterned carpet covered the floor.

Lord Westwood presided at a massive oak desk, his hands resting lightly on a sheaf of papers. An open ledger book lay off to the side. His slightly distracted expression vanished the moment she crossed the threshold, to be replaced by something infinitely more wooden. Harriet smiled brightly, but received no answering smile.

"How may I assist you?" His tone was cool.

Harriet told herself not to be daunted. Her visit was out of the ordinary; he was bound to think it strange. She closed the door behind her. She did not sit but faced him, standing before his desk.

"I wish you to understand about the other night," she said. "About Mr. Hunt, that is. I fear you formed a misimpression."

He offered no response.

"Mr. Hunt indicated he wished to speak to me, so I met him out on the terrace," she continued.

Lord Westwood merely regarded her, his expression unreadable.

"You see, Mr. Hunt thought I had sent him a letter suggesting that I had formed a particular affection for him." Harriet told herself not to be intimidated by his forbidding demeanor. "But I did not send him a letter, nor do I hold him in any particular regard."

She paused, giving him an opportunity to respond, willing him to say something, at least.

His gaze narrowed. "You insist, I suppose, that the two of you were not engaged in any untoward behavior," he said at last.

"I insist only on the truth," Harriet said. "And the truth is not what Mr. Hunt spoke but what you know of me and my character, regardless of what you think you saw."

Skepticism was written on his features. "I fear I know little of you, madam, after all. And you less of me. Indeed, I fail to see the point of this conversation. What is it you wish me to do?"

"I wish for no more silence," she said firmly. "And you have been nothing but silent since you left my house. What am I to make of the fact that you did not escort me to Lady Newcomb's party last night? You sent no word."

"Perhaps I had nothing to say."

"That may be. But if there is one thing I have learned about you, Lord Westwood, it is that you are a man who takes his obligations seriously. And you had an obligation to escort me, in your role as my fiancé."

She thought he winced. He took a deep breath. "You are correct. It will not happen again."

Harriet stared at him. "Is that is all you care to say? No word of explanation?"

"Yes."

"That is disappointing. Perhaps it will interest you to know that Mr. Hunt paid me a call this morning. He apologized for his behavior and said he had only acted after receiving my letter — which I did not write, as I have said." She leaned forward and placed her hands on the desk. "I believe him. So you see, someone tricked us both."

He looked dubious. "Who?"

"I do not know. Nor do I know why. But I will not have you think the worst of me, my lord. I will *not.*"

Lord Westwood regarded her for a long moment. "Does it matter what I think?"

"Yes," she said. "Deeply so. I am not sure why."

"Deeply, you say?" He studied her.

Harriet flushed. To her great dismay, she felt her eyes grow moist.

He rose, then, and Harriet steeled herself. She could hardly blame him if he did think the worst of her. To her surprise, he came around the desk. They stood facing each other. His expression softened slightly. "I have the devil's own temper, Harriet. Sometimes it is best that I do not share that with the world."

Harriet. He had used her given name. A little thrill shot through her. Still, she held to her resolve. "I am not the 'world,' my lord," she said. "I am your fiancée."

"No," he corrected. "You are not. Or have I missed something?"

That is when Harriet remembered. She opened her reticule. "Here," she said. "I brought this for you. It is not as fresh as it was two days ago, when

I made it." She held out the Napoleon, which she had wrapped in a linen handkerchief.

His gaze flicked over it, then returned to her. "Orange blossoms," he murmured.

She was surprised that his excellent sense of smell had failed him. "No, I used only cream and caster sugar, egg whites, and a few shavings from a vanilla bean."

"I was not referring to the pastry."

Harriet's eyes widened with sudden understanding. Her face grew warm. "I did splash on some orange water for fragrance."

"No primrose oil?"

"I...I thought the orange a pleasant change."

"I prefer primrose. Perhaps you will wear that in the future." He took the Napoleon and placed it on the desk, all the while regarding her steadily. "I could not abide the notion that you were so free with your favors."

Harriet's face flamed. "I am not, sir."

"And yet, on our drive..." His voice trailed off, but his gaze remained locked with hers.

Harriet cleared her throat. "I am not normally given to such displays, my lord. I believe I was carried away by the, er, moment."

"Ah," he murmured. "The moment."

Harriet felt something hovering in the air between them, something thick with possibilities. He gestured to the chair behind her. "Sit, please."

She sank into the chair. Lord Westwood leaned back against the desk and regarded her from a hooded gaze. "This is a lark to you, is it not?"

"What?" She frowned.

"This 'betrothal.' It is a game, an adventure, an amusement."

Harriet shook her head. "It is no game, my lord. There is much I must learn."

"And yet, I cannot think of an area in which you need instruction," he said. "You are a skilled hostess, an excellent cook, a deflector of revolutionaries, a devotee of aging reformers. There is seemingly no area that can be improved upon. I have been thinking about that this past day and more. And now I put it to you: What is it you attempt to gain by this false liaison?"

"I have explained my reasons at great cost, sir, to my own dignity," Harriet said with asperity. "It is cruel of you to make me explain again why I seek to protect myself from unwise associations and…desires."

"So do we all, madam," he growled. "So do we all."

"I do not understand."

He opened a desk drawer, took out what appeared to be a page from a newspaper, and handed it to her. "This account greatly exaggerates my military exploits. The rest, however, may be of interest."

Harriet looked the page. It was from the *Times*:

> *The Prince Regent, the Dukes of Clarence and Kent, the Duchess of York, and Lord Castlereagh were among those in attendance for the solemnization of the wedding vows between Miss Zephyr Payne, daughter*

*of Lord Ellwood Payne and Lady Clarissa
Payne, and the celebrated war hero, Lord
Elias Westwood. Indeed, it was the year's
most anticipated wedding.*

Harriet looked at the date — five years ago
— then at the earl, whose features now appeared
made of stone.

*Lord Westwood is celebrated for his daring
service at Salamanca, when Wellington sent
him behind French lines to gain intelligence,
even as the Duke was forced to withdraw
when superior French numbers threatened his
supply line. Wellington reversed his decision
after learning that Marmont had erred by
separating his left flank from the main army,
intelligence brought to him by Lord Westwood
under the direst of conditions that left the
earl with a severe chest wound. The Duke
immediately moved to attack the French left
wing, using heavy cavalry and Pakenham's
Third. The Duke credited the earl's heroism
for that key Coalition victory.*

*The entire ton had assembled at St.
Paul's to witness the union of Lord Payne's
daughter and the earl. But it became clear,
after an especially lengthy performance by
the Cathedral orchestra, that something was
amiss. At last, Lord Payne was seen speaking
urgently with Lord Westwood, and shortly
thereafter, Lord Payne announced to the*

congregation that no wedding would occur this day. Later, it was revealed that Miss Payne had eloped with Lord Marcus Pembroke.

As for Lord Westwood, he was observed to walk calmly out of the church without any word of explanation or regard. Indeed, no response to such a situation can be imagined.

Harriet looked up at him, aghast. "How very dreadful for you."

"On the contrary. I was well-served by Miss Payne's decision to elope with Marcus. She spared me the parson's noose, for which I have no talent or inclination. I am eternally grateful. Marriage is not for me."

"But you must have loved her," Harriet said.

"Love? 'Tis an illusion created to make people feel better about signing their lives over to the institution of marriage," he said. "I distrust the state myself. After your own marriage, I suspect you might as well."

But Harriet was focused on the yellowed page. "When I cry off at the end of our bargain," she said slowly, "it will be seen as history repeating itself. It will be a public embarrassment for you."

The earl shrugged. "Irrelevant. I agreed to the terms of our contract and will abide by them."

"If it is irrelevant, why did you wish me to know about it?" Harriet asked.

"To show you that actions have consequences. That pretense leaves no one unscathed. That one must be honest before it is too late. And so I put it to you thus: Am I anything to you other than Freddy's business partner, the man you have ensnared in this humbling masquerade? Is it, in fact, all a masquerade?"

Harriet's heart was thundering in her chest. "I — I do not know how to respond."

"That is honesty in itself, I suppose." He returned the newspaper to its drawer. "And now I find I must be honest with you."

Did he mean to terminate their agreement? Trepidation filled her as Lord Westwood crossed his arms and regarded her from eyes dark with purpose.

"Let us stipulate that you have better taste than to willingly cavort with Oliver Hunt in the shrubbery," he said.

He believed her, Harriet realized. But her relief faded at his next words.

"Nevertheless, I have discovered something this week that affects our agreement."

Harriet's heart sank. "What, my lord? Tell me — please."

"It is this: This is no lark for me. I warn you now that if we continue this masquerade, this pretend courtship, I cannot answer for the consequences. I have forged a strong will and even stronger defenses over the years — thanks, in part, to the madness with Zephyr — but I have acquired precious little nobility in the process."

"Nobility?" Harriet frowned. "I do not understand."

He sighed. "How can you be so innocent? And yet, I sense that you have not the least idea of what you have done."

"What have I done, my lord?" Harriet eyed him in alarm. "Tell me and I will make it right. I did not intend for our arrangement to be a burden."

"You cannot make this right," he growled. "It has gone too far."

His gaze slammed into hers, and Harriet nearly recoiled from the darkness there. "What I am saying, madam, is that you are not safe with me," he said in a low, silken voice. "I cannot promise to escort you to routs and parties and then take my leave on your doorstep. I cannot pledge to drive with you into the country and refrain from kissing you, or touching you, or making you mine."

He took a step toward her. "It is no longer pretend for me. I warned you once about toying with desire. You have opened a Pandora's box that will not be sealed. I want you, Harriet. And if you give me the slightest opportunity, I will have you."

Harriet stared at him as he closed the space between them and pulled her to her feet.

"Even now," he said, lowering his mouth to hers, "I fear you are in very grave danger."

So stunned was Harriet that she might have fallen had his arms not encircled her. His lips plundered hers, and, after a moment's shock, Harriet gave herself over to the force of that kiss. Trying to keep her balance, she grabbed the lapels of his waistcoat and held on for dear life as abruptly he turned them around and backed her against his desk — not gently.

Surely she must die from this rough, terrifying

magic, Harriet thought. She clung to him, her pulse pounding as his mouth bruised hers. She had never been kissed like this. It was beyond all imagining. It was terrifying. And she wanted it to go on and on.

When at last he relinquished her mouth, it was to trail slow kisses down her neck, his rough chin scraping over her skin in delicious torment. The desk at her back blocked any escape — not that she wished to be anywhere but here, under his savage spell — so Harriet simply closed her eyes and savored the rawness of his flesh on hers. Then all thought fled as his mouth returned to ravage hers anew. This time, she answered him. She met him with equal force, pressing her body against his, powerless to curb her own wantonness, knowing only that she wanted more of this sweet torture.

Her intimate encounters with Freddy had been brief, impersonal, almost polite. But there was nothing polite in Lord Westwood's primitive response. His knee nudged between her legs, brooking no resistance. In the next instant his thigh was against the most intimate part of her. For a fleeting moment, Harriet froze. Then instinct took over. She arched against him and heard his low, answering groan. Wherever he meant to take her, she had no wish to stop.

His hands roamed over her, claiming her. They caressed her waist and dipped lower, to her hips, as his mouth found an excruciatingly sensitive spot on her earlobe. When his tongue invaded the outer curve of her ear, Harriet thought she would perish from sheer, wicked delight. Her every nerve tingled; every place he touched burned with desire. When his hand closed over her breast, she gasped — not so much in shock as for the unholy thrill.

She wrapped her arms around him in wild, glorious abandon. Her body felt acutely attuned to his, her every sense focused on the mesmerizing power of his touch. His hands slid down her backside and in one swift motion, he lifted her onto the desk, facing him. Then he stepped between her legs and pulled her closer still. His hands slid under her thighs as he kissed her breast through the fabric of her gown, his mouth hot, insistent. Harriet's skin burned through the muslin barrier between them. Her fingers coiled in his hair as she pressed against him, full of shameless longing.

Something fell to the floor, something small and insignificant. Engulfed in a sensual fog, Harriet paid little heed. But then she realized that it was not insignificant at all. It was, perhaps, the best of her.

"The Napoleon," she murmured. "Can you save it?"

He shook his head, denying her. Instead, he caught her hand and slowly turned it over, then kissed each fingertip, one by one.

Harriet forgot about the pastry. Her answering, yearning sigh seemed to come from her very soul. The force between them eviscerated her defenses, made her forget everything except for the pursuit of some wild reckoning. Her arms locked around him, pulling him tighter.

She wanted more. *All.*

Instantly, he understood. His hands moved to her ankles, warming them through the plain cotton of her stockings. She heard her leather slippers fall to the floor. Then his hands roamed slowly — tantalizingly — upward over her calves, then down again in a slow caress that created rivers of desire deep in her belly. Again and again they caressed her limbs, and Harriet lost herself in his ministrations, glorying in his touch. Finally he untied the laces of her stockings and slipped his fingers under the fabric, easing it down her legs, slowly uncovering her bare skin to his touch. He slipped each stocking over her foot, discarding it on the floor between them.

Now his hand was on her bare thigh, and Harriet had no thought of denying him. When at last he touched her intimately, she gasped, her entire world contained in his touch. It was as if nothing else existed, only his hand on her, stroking and finding places unknown until now. Helpless against this new, raw urgency, Harriet buried her face in the soft lawn of his shirt and lost herself in his touch.

He seemed to see deep into the heart of her need, guiding her body to its perfect rhythm. All rational thought had vanished; she was ruled only by the gathering storm. She heard herself whimper — a desperate, shameless plea — and when at last he touched her chin, tilting her face upward, she tried to turn away from his inspection.

But his mouth descended to hers, capturing her lips in the precise instant his hand unleashed waves of pleasure within her. Harriet cried out as the torrent of sensation claimed her, and he took her passion and returned it in hot, searing kisses.

Until finally, when she was spent, he did not take his own pleasure but merely brushed his lips against her forehead.

"Lady Harriet," he said softly, "you are a complete and utter fraud."

Lust was manageable. Had he actually told himself that?

Well, and the tables had turned, hadn't they? Far from being a woman who needed schooling, Harriet Worthington possessed enough raw magnetism to wreck all the compasses on His Majesty's royal fleet. Apparently she had no idea of her power.

Elias had escorted her back to her house; that she had come to him alone spoke volumes about her lack of acumen in such matters, though she more than made up for that with her other gifts. Indeed, there was more sensuality in her than in any woman he had known, including the likes of Lady Caroline Forth.

It astonished him that the woman who had professed to know nothing of desire was capable of enjoying such unabashed pleasure from a man's touch.

Had she found such pleasure with Freddy? Elias suspected his late business partner had not looked beyond the satisfaction of his own immediate needs. If so, that was another reason the man ought to have been thrashed for his wasted opportunities. Fate had given him a woman ready to have her sensual nature awakened in all its glory. Instead, Freddy had sent her into widowhood uncertain and insecure.

Elias did not delude himself about his own role: He had merely been the instrument of her awakening. Anyway, there had been no choice in the matter. The moment her arms wrapped around him, urging him onward, the thing had been decided. At least he'd been honest. He had not, would not, safeguard her from the consequences.

Contrary to his warning, however, he had walked her to her doorstep and left her there. A man could be noble once.

Besides, she deserved time to consider where this dangerous masquerade had taken them.

Lady Harriet frowned at the contents of the bowl. The dough had been sitting in it for several days, and save for a bubble or two along its surface, had showed little sign of life. "Lady Hester did not mention a long rise," she said.

Celestial peered at the inert, shapeless mass. "If you ask me, that dough is a lost cause."

"I did not," Lady Harriet said irritably. "Ask you."

Celestial's eyes widened. Lady Harriet had not been the same since she arrived home after paying a call on Lord Westwood yesterday afternoon. And a scandalous call it was, what with her employer venturing to his house by herself. Mrs. Tanksley had fretted over that for more than an hour after Lady Harriet left. Such was her alarm that she had been ready to send Horace to fetch her when Lady Harriet herself appeared, looking far and away like a woman who most definitely ought to have had a chaperon.

Her sprigged muslin frock was wrinkled and would need to be washed and pressed before it could be worn again. Her mouth was red and swollen, her face flushed, her demeanor distracted. Then there was that trail of reddish marks down her neck. If Celestial had not herself so recently discovered the joys of romantic pleasure with Horace, she might have missed the signs. But since she had, she felt deep in her bones that Lady Harriet and Lord Westwood —

"I will take some of that gammon, if you please," said a deep, masculine voice.

Celestial jumped, as did her mistress, and if Celestial had any doubt as to Lady Harriet's thoughts, the violent blush that overwhelmed her mistress's features at the sight of Lord Westwood said it all.

He stood there, nearly filling the door frame of the kitchen. He carried a large basket of vegetables, including an enormous plant with wide, heart-shaped leaves, some brightly colored peppers, and two large coconuts.

Both women stared at him in stunned silence, Celestial was the first to recover. What had he asked for? *Gammon.* Yes, that was it.

Quickly, Celestial retrieved the meat from the cold chamber. She set it on the worktable and then fled without a word, leaving Lady Harriet and Lord Westwood quite alone in the kitchen.

Harriet stared at him, her heart thundering in her breast. "What is this, my lord?"

"Callaloo. A Caribbean dish." He set the basket on the table, next to the meat, and rolled up his sleeves nearly to his elbows. "I'll take a large knife. And a basin." At her stunned expression, he added, "that is, if you do not object."

"Object?" she echoed. "To, er, what?"

The hint of a smile hovered about his mouth. "Why, I intend to cook for you, madam. What's more, this dish is a treat I am certain you have not yet experienced."

The intimacy in his tone made her shiver, and when Harriet met his gaze she was not entirely certain he was referring to food. "I-I have no objection," she stammered. "Indeed, I am curious as to what you have planned."

"Oh, very little is planned," he said. "I merely throw what I have into a stewpot. Often the best treats are surprises, don't you think? Do you have one?"

Harriet blinked. "One?"

"A pot. A big one, please." He turned his

attention to the large plant with the heart-shaped leaves and began to separate the leaves from the stems.

Harriet found herself staring at the exposed part of his arms, which looked burnished from the sun and strong enough for any task — in or out of the kitchen. She shook her head, trying to recall herself to the task at hand. She found a pot and offered it to him, only to see him frown.

"'Tis copper," he said. "I am accustomed to clay."

"I find copper exceptional, my lord," she responded, striving for a coherent thought. "It, er, distributes the heat evenly and gives one more control of the cooking process."

"Control. Yes, you would prefer that. Set the thing on the stove, then." He took the leaves and immersed them in the basin, washing each one carefully. He moved easily, as if it was nothing to engage in what even in the West Indies must be women's work. Moreover, he looked utterly composed, as if nothing out of the ordinary had occurred between them.

He must have felt her watching, because abruptly he halted in the act of stripping a stem of its outer covering. "You may help, if you wish."

The gleam in those dark eyes made Harriet's heart flutter alarmingly. "I would gladly do so," she managed, "were you to give me the slightest inkling of what it is you are making."

"Callaloo is like a stew, but not as thick. Like a soup, but with less broth. Mainly, it is green. Rather like the color of your skin at the moment.

Tell me, Harriet: Do I make you unwell? If so, I promise this dish will heal what ails you."

Harriet very much doubted that. She had not felt well since that shocking interlude in his study yesterday, when she had given herself over to him, enslaved herself to the pleasure he conjured so effortlessly. She had not known it was possible to lose herself in such a fashion, heedless of all around her. Later, when she examined her behavior, it had profoundly shocked and embarrassed her to know that she had forgotten herself so completely and engaged in such intimacy with a man who was not even her true fiancé, much less her husband.

Even now, she could not look at him without feeling that intense warmth steal over her. "I am not unwell, Lord Westwood," she insisted.

"Elias better suits the state of things between us, do you not agree?"

Harriet stared at him. "I-I confess I am a bit at sea."

"When at sea," he said, turning back to the greens, "it is essential to give in to it. I find that when one moves with the turbulence, the journey is considerably smoother. Here —" He handed her some leaves. "Tear these into pieces."

Harriet was still not certain what they were discussing, but she took the greens readily, grateful for a task that would occupy her wayward thoughts.

For his part, Lord Westwood — *Elias* — was chopping the stems. "This is dasheen, a bush plant native to Jamaica," he said. "I grow it in my garden here, though it does not flourish as well. To it we will add a little okra for thickening and some onion and herbs. Thyme is traditional, but I also like to add pimento."

"Pimento?" Harriet stared at the brown powder.

"Berries of a shrub that grows on Jamaica. Dried, then ground just before cooking so as not to degrade their potency. Some call it allspice." He glanced around the kitchen. "Rice would be the perfect accompaniment, if you have it."

Harriet found she quite relished shredding the big leaves, then setting the rice on to cook; the chores calmed her nerves and created a companionable silence between them. Yet it was only the illusion of calm, she knew, since she could not imagine feeling composed in his presence ever again.

When she was finished with the leaves, she saw a colorful orange pepper that he had cut in half. She had not seen its like and reached for it. But he caught her hand before she could touch the cut surface.

"It is hotter than you might imagine," he said. "The heat marries with the bitterness of the greens and elevates the dish. However, its heat is tolerable only after the pepper is cooked."

But it was the heat of his hand that Harriet was most aware of, and when he withdrew it she felt strangely bereft. That's what came of being a wanton woman, she decided. One's thoughts went constantly to the pleasures of the flesh, and every touch became disruptive. She did not know how to purge such thoughts.

Even now, as she watched him add the greens, stems, and okra to the big pot, Harriet could not think of anything but the touch of his hands on her.

She hoped he did not notice her distraction. Indeed, his attention appeared to be focused wholly on the copper pot. Into it also went onion, celery, garlic, the orange pepper, a quantity of salt, and the meat. When Harriet raised a mild objection that the gammon itself surely provided sufficient salt, he overruled her, saying the additional salt would bring out the flavor of the greens. She knew better than to argue with the man's unparalleled sense of taste.

Next he produced something resembling a small, stout machete and a tool with a pointed end. The latter he inserted into two of the small spots at the tip of one coconut. Holding the coconut over a bowl, he drained it of the white, milky liquid. Using the machete's blunt edge, he tapped around the girth of the coconut, turning it as he worked. In a moment, it had split into halves. The other coconut was treated in the same fashion. He poured the liquid into the pot with the other ingredients.

"Now, we wait while it cooks down." He scooped some of the coconut meat out of the shell and offered it to her. "Try it."

Harriet took the piece and found it quite delicious.

"It keeps for weeks when dried." He took some for himself, his gaze never leaving hers. "'Tis perfect for a soggy climate like the Caribbean."

Something in those dark eyes told her that the soggy Caribbean climate was not uppermost in his mind. Harriet turned away from his disconcerting inspection. But his hand touched her shoulder, and he drew her back around to face him.

"I will not pretend that things are as before," he said in a low voice. "I imagine that you are embarrassed at seeing me here, invading your kitchen. It may be that you wish me at Jericho."

She forced herself to meet his gaze. "I rather wish myself at Jericho. My behavior of yesterday —"

"Yes," he said. "That."

"Freddy…" she began, then covered her face with her hands.

Gently, he pulled them away. "I confess his is the last name I wish to hear." Then he enfolded her in his arms. His hand stroked her hair with exquisite gentleness, almost as if she were a child.

After a moment, Harriet lifted her head to look at him. "To think that I once thought you a bilious snob." She managed a game smile.

He arched a brow. "And I thoroughly disapproved of you."

"I suspect you still do." She'd meant it playfully, but her smile faded as his brows drew together.

He sighed. "I have never met a woman who so prides herself on her independence, who seeks out opportunities to flout convention and to consort with the many false intellects this city produces. So if that is any measure, I suppose I still do disapprove."

But he caught a strand of her hair and curled it around his fingertip, robbing his words of their sting. "'Tis the same woman who denies all knowledge of passion," he said in a musing tone. "I cannot reconcile her with that woman who was helpless in my arms yesterday. Perhaps neither can you. Perhaps that is the source of your embarrassment."

His lips grazed the tip of her ear. "*That* woman invaded my dreams last night," he murmured. "And I will do all in my power to have her in my arms again."

With that, his mouth claimed hers. Harriet could only lean helplessly into him as he plundered her lips, daring her to deny him. But she needed no persuading. She yielded willingly. When he relinquished her mouth to kiss her earlobe, then the base of her throat, she felt as if she were exposing her innermost secrets to him, without heed as to what he might do with them. But the small frisson of alarm that rippled through her was swiftly silenced by fierce, enveloping passion.

And when his hands slid down her back and crushed her against his length, Harriet thought she would die of longing. As he backed her against the worktable, she put her arms around his neck and clung to him, betraying herself with a breathless sigh.

Suddenly, there was a great clattering sound as he swept the pans and utensils onto the floor. He lifted her onto the table in their stead and eased her backward, onto the wood. As he rose over her, eyes dark with fire, Harriet looked up at him, her heart in her throat.

"Elias." The word was a desperate plea. Need consumed her. She could not fight it.

But he was in no hurry. Slowly, he lowered himself until his lips once more claimed hers — but only just. He held himself above her, brushing her mouth lightly, teasing her, even as he must have known that her lips wanted — *needed* — to be possessed.

Harriet strained toward him, wanting the weight of his body on hers. She tried to pull him closer, but his hand caught her wrists and pinned her arms lightly above her head. Only then did he cover her with his body, settling some of his weight on her as his other hand slipped under her, cushioning her against the wood but also tightening his hold — a captor's embrace. It was a measure of her desperation that she wanted so much more.

"Elias," she pleaded again.

He silenced her with a kiss — this time, the kind she wanted, the fierce, all-consuming joining that marked her as his. Her mouth opened to him, wanting nothing so much as this wild, rough invasion. She yearned to wrap her arms around him, but he still imprisoned her wrists, so she could only wait in helpless longing.

Finally, as if he sensed her hunger, he freed them. But when at last she reached for him, he slid away from her. Instead, his mouth began to trace a lazy, tormenting path from her lips to her ear, then down the length of her neck. His warmth sent shivers through her, but if he felt her trembling he ignored it, for his mouth simply continued its slow, maddening path over her flesh.

When he kissed the rise of her breasts, Harriet buried her hands in his hair, pressing him closer still. She felt the neckline of her frock slip; then his mouth was on her nipple, sculpting lazy circles around and over its tip.

And then, merciful heavens, he moved lower. Through the fabric of her dress he kissed her ribs, her abdomen. Harriet arched into him and her fingers entangled in his hair, instinctively pushing him lower still. His arms went under her, and she felt him shift his weight to support her legs as he pushed her skirts aside. Now the heat of his mouth was on her thigh. But he did not linger there.

When he kissed her intimately through the fabric of her chemise, she froze. Then that barrier was no more, and his tongue flicked over her soft folds, shocking her into helpless, delicious wonder.

Harriet spared a fleeting thought for the extent of her depravity and then could only accede to the swirling sensations gathering within her. She arched upward, silently begging for completion and an end to this sweet torment. But he seemed intent on exploring her secret places, finding new ways to drive her beyond all control. She was powerless to resist. All she could do was entwine her fingers in his hair, her distant lifeline. Lost in pleasure, she gave herself over to him with every shred of her being.

Finally, her body grew rigid until at last there was nothing but wild ecstasy and a cry that came from somewhere, perhaps her very own lips.

And then, silence.

At last, he moved upward and over her once more, letting her feel the hard length of his own desire. His gaze locked with hers, but when she thought he would take her, he simply kissed her mouth, letting her taste herself on his tongue. Harriet ached for him to take his pleasure; when he ended the kiss and raised his head to look at her, she did not hide her longing. She reached for him, but he eased himself away from her, leaving her alone on the table.

But he did not intend to leave her there, it seemed. Instead, his arms went under her, lifting her gently, cradling her against his chest before setting her carefully on her feet once more.

Swaying slightly, Harriet could barely stand. Her knees were weak, her mind befogged, her world disoriented. She forced herself to look at him — she was no coward, she told herself — and saw that he was far more composed than she. Indeed, he stood there calmly, watching her from eyes that betrayed no hint of the turmoil she felt.

Then, his mouth curved upward in a slow, crooked smile — that dimple! — and Harriet's heart turned over in her chest. A spark leapt to his eyes, and it catapulted her back to the moment when he'd claimed her with his kiss.

How, Harriet wondered weakly, did one go on from here? She stood there, paralyzed by the force of her world shifting on his axis.

He had no such paralysis. With an economy of motion, he bent down and picked up a pan, a spoon, a towel, the utensils he'd consigned to the floor. He moved to the stove and stirred the callaloo, inhaling deeply.

Then he turned to her. "'Tis ready," he said in a silken voice that conjured those molten kisses. "Pray, be seated."

Harriet sank unsteadily into a chair as he put some of the callaloo and rice on a plate and placed it before her with a flourish.

CHAPTER TWELVE

ELIAS BOWED POLITELY over his betrothed's hand and led her out for the waltz. Her auburn hair was held in place by a silver comb that his hands longed to remove. Her gown was a soft apricot, with a décolletage that begged to be cast aside to reveal the rosy tips the fabric hid from his view. Her gloved hand, its lithe fingers covered in white kid, rested lightly on his arm as she moved gracefully to the ballroom floor. Her silk skirt rustled, taunting him with the intimate secrets it shielded from his eyes.

Her brilliant blue eyes looked almost feverish as he led her into the figures of the dance, but she fixed them resolutely on a point beyond him. Elias did not think she was ill — unless it was from the same fever that gripped him. As they moved through the motions of the waltz, surrounded by the other dancers in Lord and Lady Blathmore's ballroom, Elias wondered whether it was possible to staunch this blinding desire that gripped him and blazed anew each time their gazes met.

The other guests might see an impeccably attired widow dancing with perfect decorum with her fiancé. Elias saw only the woman beneath him on her kitchen table, a siren urging him to have his way with her.

He'd found her secret places, made love to her with his mouth, his tongue, his hands, daring her to open herself to him, to give herself over to raw pleasure. For all that Freddy had put her through, she deserved that and more. Watching Harriet Worthington discover her feminine passion, awakening to her own sensuality, thrilled him beyond his wildest dreams. Elias wondered if he could ever get his fill.

And there was the rub. By one measure, he had more than fulfilled the terms of their contract, albeit in a manner neither of them could have foreseen. But the truth was, he burned for her. If Lady Blathmore had a secluded terrace with shrubbery, he would have taken her there straight away. He no longer cared where or when he made love to her. Just as long as he did.

But Harriet was aloof tonight, as if she, too, were grappling with the consequences of their actions. Was her much-vaunted independence threatened by the force of her desire? Had it disturbed her to be controlled by passion? She had created an orderly world for herself that helped her survive her marriage and widowhood. It likely did not leave room for enslavement to blind, raw need. Wasn't that what their blasted contract was about? To help her avoid being ruled by passion?

And what of him? Elias had no wish to lose himself in an all-consuming passion. Once he'd almost shackled himself to a wife, but that had brought public disgrace and, ultimately, relief at having been spared that encumbrance. Dalliances with women like Caroline Forth were simpler. They left no scars, no encroaching chains that could not be cast off. He had been perfectly satisfied with his life.

Was he still? Did he mind that the woman he burned for moved through the figures of the dance with a wooden expression, failing to meet his gaze? Did he mind that she displayed more warmth to her other dance partners than to her putative fiancé? Did he mind that she belonged not in this grand ballroom in her fashionable gown but in his bed, writhing on the sheets, waiting for him to claim her?

Elias exhaled shakily as he returned her to the side of her friend, Mrs. Tanksley. No doubt she would be led out momentarily by her next partner, who would have no idea of the sensual woman beneath that façade.

That stopped him — the thought of another man touching her, awakening her to new sensual delights. Another man joining their bodies, perhaps having no care for her needs. Another man touching her intimately.

Any man but him.

His pulse thundering in his ears, Elias bowed formally over Harriet's hand and relinquished her. Then he turned on his heel and sought the comfort of Lord Blathmore's port.

"You know, dear, you do not look at all well."

Harriet eyed Monica, who was regarding her in concern. "I am quite well." But even as she spoke, her attention was on Elias, who looked as if he could not leave her fast enough. Already, he was halfway across the room, headed for other pursuits. Caroline? Someone else? It hardly mattered. Any of those women could offer him far more than she could. She was unschooled and naïve and not in the least capable of meeting a man's needs. Indeed, all she could do was take from him. He had made love to her without a care for his pleasure — surely no man could tolerate such a thing.

He had brought her to ecstasy again and again, but she had done nothing for him. Instead, she had begged shamelessly for his touch, taken her own pleasure. She had not wanted him to see her in such unguarded moments, but he had refused to let her hide her face that first time, almost as if he enjoyed watching her in the moment of release.

Could that be? Freddy had never shown interest in her needs. To be sure, he had touched her intimately, but it had not seemed to gratify him. At times, he had come to her with the scent of another woman on him, and Harriet had tried to turn away but he would not allow it. For all that, he'd not been a cruel man. But it had been manifestly clear to her that she was not woman enough for him.

Elias had not led her to believe that. But what else could he think when she had not made the slightest effort to please him? The fact that she did not even know how filled her with despair. Freddy had always taken what he had wanted. He'd given her no instruction. She had not known there were different ways of lovemaking. Freddy had certainly never made love to her on a desk or on her kitchen table. Nor had he employed his mouth or hands in such a fashion.

This was not how she had envisioned her arrangement with Elias. She had thought perhaps some careful instruction in her drawing room as to the ways of predatory gentlemen, perhaps an exercise in discourse she could put to good use. She envisioned that he would, by his presence, shield her this Season from gossip about Freddy and his women, so that others might say that it was a pity her husband had been unfaithful but how nice that she had moved on to that handsome Lord Westwood.

And he was handsome. His eyes were his most compelling feature, dark and magnetic, capable of igniting her with the slightest glance. They saw straight into a part of her she had not known existed. Harriet loved the feel of his thick, unruly hair in her fingers as he made love to her. His arms were so strong that lifting her onto the table had seemed child's play, and his size such that he could easily crush her with his weight — only he had not, holding himself above her, careful to spare her the full measure of his power.

Harriet had never felt this way toward any man. He was never out of her thoughts. She craved his touch, craved the feel of his body against hers, craved the passion that overtook her when he touched her. She could not control her desire. Once more, she had lost control of her life because of a man.

No, this was not the way she had envisioned this arrangement. She had not expected him to make love to her. She had not wanted that. And now, it seemed she wanted it very much. But one day soon, this would all be over. Their agreement would be at an end. Harriet was very much afraid she would never get over the loss.

"I believe you are woolgathering," Monica said. "And here is that nice Mr. Wilberforce, ready for his dance. You must make an effort, dear. Else people will think you are pining for Lord Westwood. And I am sure that is not the case."

Harriet slanted her friend a sharp gaze, but Monica was all innocence and benign smiles. Harriet gathered her resolve, and forced a smile to her face as she greeted Mr. Wilberforce. Indeed, she was quite fond of him and under other circumstances would have been delighted for a few moments with him.

But Elias was nowhere to be seen, and her much vaunted independence lay in shreds on the dance floor.

His Grace, the Duke of Sidenham, was an imposing figure of a man, if for no other reason than the lines of his face, which etched his visage into craggy cliffs and lowlands not unlike his native — some would say godforsaken — Cornwall.

He eschewed the trappings of his rank. Not for him the ducal robes and regalia, the purple belt and imported taffeta his ancestors had worn, the fur and hammered gold brooches. Instead, he preferred a coarse leather jacket and buckskin pantaloons of the type one might see on tradesmen, though no one would mistake his imposing — not to say arrogant — demeanor for one of low station. In His Grace's view, a man's quality inhered in character alone, and if he had not always found himself on the angel's side of that measure, he had at least recognized when the devil was on his shoulder.

In the matter of his only daughter — his only child, in fact — the duke would, if called to account, acknowledge a lapse or two, chiefly as it pertained to her tender feelings. He had rarely attempted to ascertain whether she possessed any, being too much wrapped up in the bleakness of his own tragedy, which is to say the tragedy of a man who lost his only love far too soon. And so, when word of certain matters reached him — for even in the wilds of Cornwall, the Mail ventured — the duke decided it was past time he saw to these matters himself.

Which is why, when Harriet's party returned from Lady Blathmore's, she found her father sitting in her drawing room, brandy in his glass and impatience on his face. Hovering just outside the room were Celestial, Heavenly, and Horace, anxious not to miss a single ducal request — for while the man did not dress the part of a prince, he fully expected to be treated like one.

"Father!" Harriet exclaimed, her heart sinking. Amid the turmoil of the last few days, it wanted only this.

"You will introduce me," he commanded, eyeing the assemblage, which included Monica — looking as if it were well past her bedtime — and Elias, who regarded the imperial figure before the fire with some interest.

Before Harriet could introduce him, Elias stepped forward. "I am Elias Westwood, sir."

"Ah. The man engaged to marry my daughter — or so the *Gazette* declares." The duke regarded him from deep-set blue eyes under sandy brows that nearly met over his regal nose. "And yet, you did not apply to me. Indeed, this is the first time that I have laid eyes on you. Why is that?"

"Because it is a private matter, Father, between Lord Westwood and myself," Harriet said. "I do not see how it involves you."

Her father regarded her, and then shifted his gaze to the earl. "And you, sir. Is that your view as well? That a father need not be applied to in the matter of his daughter's hand?"

"No," Elias said. "That is not my view."

The duke's brows arched. He turned to Harriet. "It would seem, daughter, that your betrothed disagrees with you. I sense there is more to this than meets the eye. But perhaps tonight is not the time."

"It will be my pleasure to wait upon you tomorrow," Elias said.

Harriet eyed him in alarm. "There is no need." She did not fear that he would willingly disclose the truth of their betrothal to him, only that her father would subject him to merciless inquisition that could force his hand.

Her father studied her. "Perhaps it is best that my daughter and I discuss the matter first," he said. "I will send for you at the proper time."

Elias bowed his assent and bid them goodnight.

It was nearly noon when he received the summons from the duke. Accordingly, Elias dutifully presented himself at the door of Harriet's townhouse without any notion of what to tell her father. Their arrangement was not his to reveal. At the same time, her father had every right to seek the truth.

That did not make facing the duke any easier. His Grace received him in the parlor, a pair of spectacles on his nose, a quill and parchment on the writing table at his elbow. He was a large man, and his graying hair must have once been the color of Harriet's.

Without any preliminaries, the duke fixed his gaze on Elias. His eyes were blue like Harriet's, but harder, at least now. "You were Freddy's business partner. From the looks of it, the only one with any business sense."

Elias opened his mouth to respond, but the duke stopped him. "Do not bother to defend him. Worthington was careless and a scapegrace, and I feared he would not make her happy. But she wanted him, and that I understood." The duke hesitated. "I have learned in my life that when a woman I love wants something, I am hard-pressed to say no. It has been, I fear, the defining fact of my life. Not always for good."

Elias made no response. He knew little of the duke, only that he had broken the entail to secure Harriet's sovereignty over Freddy's estate and made it possible for her to direct her own affairs. Though she had described him as controlling, it appeared to Elias that her father simply intended to protect her.

"Harriet tells me that your engagement is none of my concern," the duke said. "She begs me not to interfere. But I cannot like a man who is not forthright. Do you take my meaning?"

"I do."

The duke waited, but Elias said nothing.

"I am not a patient man, Westwood. I wish to ascertain whether you are good for my daughter."

"Is that not for her to decide?"

"Exactly what my daughter said. But I expect more from you." The duke's gaze was hard. "I wish to know whether you will take care of her. Whether you will do for her what every man in her life has failed to do — and I count myself in that number. In short, I want her protected — and by that I do not mean safeguarding her financial affairs, which I have already seen to. I want her happy, Westwood. I want her loved. Can you promise that?"

Elias met the man's gaze. "I cannot."

The duke blinked. "That is honest. I'll grant you that."

"I cannot say what the future holds," Elias said carefully. "Nor can I break your daughter's confidence, when she has not given me leave. All I can say is that I will try to live up to her expectations."

"Do not make the mistake of taking her for granted, Westwood. Time has a way of destroying that which we most value. My wife was taken from me giving birth to Harriet. It is possible I blamed my daughter for that, to my undying regret. I withheld affection that ought to have been hers in full. I am not proud of that. So you see, I will not rest until I see her happy."

"I would expect no less, sir," Elias said.

"And am I to be satisfied with that paltry response?" the duke demanded.

Elias saw the pain in the man's eyes, but he could do nothing to alleviate it. "I expect not. But my hands are tied, sir."

"Something is amiss here." The duke leaned forward. "Still, here is a question I trust you can answer: What is it about my daughter that entices you?"

Elias blinked in surprise. "Er, her eyes."

The duke arched a brow. "I see nothing special in them. Indeed, they are the same as mine."

Elias shook his head. "Hers are the color of Caribbean seas. Yours are merely blue."

The duke frowned. "I see. What else?"

"Her skill with food, certainly."

His Grace waved a dismissive hand. "Let us stipulate that she is an excellent cook and that the fact is irrelevant."

"Not irrelevant," Elias insisted. "You have not seen her at her worktable, covered with flour, working the dough — just long enough to hold it together, mind you, yet not erode its innate tenderness. Truly, her pastry is magic." He made a sweeping gesture. "It lands on the tongue with the evanescence of air, yet explodes on the palate with a burst of crispness that surpasses any it has been my privilege to enjoy. It is the stuff of gods."

The duke's brow furrowed.

"I have not even begun to describe the filling in her meat pies," Elias continued. "'Tis seasoned prominently with cinnamon but teases the nostrils with a range of other spices — thyme, cloves, perhaps even a small quantity of mustard seed — which manifest themselves as a startling underlayer in the precise moment that the pie enters the mouth…" Belatedly, Elias noticed the duke's thunderstruck expression, and fell silent.

The duke regarded him in astonishment. "You wish me to believe my daughter's chief appeal is…her food?"

"No," Elias said quickly. "Certainly not."

"You are quite eloquent on the subject," His Grace said after a moment, "but I bid you continue. What, beyond my daughter's eyes and culinary skills, makes you wish to marry her?"

It would be fortuitous timing, Elias thought, if one of Harriet's meddling servants would pick this very moment to come in and inquire if the duke required anything. But none did, and so it appeared he would be forced to amplify his response further, though it amounted to tacit agreement that marriage was the goal — when, of course, it was not, for either Harriet or him. "I cannot pretend indifference to her beauty," he offered.

"Beauty fades," the duke snapped.

"Her intelligence is exceptional, although she has a distressing habit of surrounding herself with rabble-rousers and revolutionaries, and I cannot like that," Elias said.

"Quite right." His Grace nodded approvingly.

"She has no appreciation of her true worth," Elias said. "I would endeavor to change that."

"Oh?" The duke looked intrigued. "How would you bring about such a transformation?"

Elias slanted the man a gaze. "If you do not mind, sir, I will keep that to myself."

The duke regarded him assessingly. "Perhaps that is for the best."

"It seems to me that the duke does not look unfavorably on Lord Westwood," Monica said.

Harriet looked startled. "I did not hear him say such a thing."

"Not in so many words, but did you not think he regarded Lord Westwood with a certain amount of respect? And he is already preparing to leave, after only a few days. I do not think he would do so if he did not trust your fiancé."

"He is not my fiancé, as you well know, Monica," Harriet said wearily. "'Tis but a masquerade."

"And yet, I cannot think that your heart is untouched," her friend replied.

"It is not," Harriet insisted. "Besides, Lord Westwood could have no wish to extend our arrangement."

"Do not make the mistake that I did," Monica warned. "I have lived my life alone because one man played me false, but not all men are like Francis and Freddy, Harriet. Please consider that."

Harriet was pensive. "I have not visited Cornwall in a very long time. I begin to think that the further I remove from Lord Westwood, the better."

Monica looked shocked. "You would leave in the middle of the Season? What of your arrangement?"

"Lord Westwood has fulfilled the terms of our agreement rather too well," Harriet said ruefully. "Indeed, I realize now that I knew little about this pull between men and women. I thought of it as an inconvenient distraction, a nuisance to be put in its place so I could carry on unfettered by men who wished to control me. I was wrong."

She felt her face grow warm. "I wanted to arm myself so that I would never be vulnerable again. But I was the merest babe, Monica, the merest babe." Harriet's voice broke. "I have thrown all caution and common sense aside. This is beyond anything I had with Freddy. It is a passion — such a passion! — beyond my control." Seeing

Monica's expression, Harriet halted. "I see I have shocked you."

Her friend fished a lace handkerchief from the folds of her frock and handed it to her. She smiled gently. "Nay, you have but made me envious."

Harriet took the handkerchief gratefully and blew her nose. "Lord Westwood controls me in a way no other man has done. Indeed, he threatens the very foundation of my independence."

"Surely not," her friend murmured.

"Oh, Monica, I am too embarrassed to say more," Harriet said. "You and I have both been married, but this is beyond all imagining. It has shocked me to the core. I have behaved disgracefully, and to my everlasting shame, there is a part of me that wants no rescue. Don't you see that I must save myself? 'Else he will consume me."

Monica was silent for a long moment. "What I see is that you have encountered something most of us do not experience in a lifetime. And that you wish to run away from it because you are afraid of the cost."

Harriet shook her head. "Pray, do not be harsh. I do only what I must."

The next morning, Harriet's father appeared surprised to see her, along with Heavenly, standing on the drive with a trunk and bandboxes as he prepared to depart for Cornwall. But he merely smiled and assisted her into his carriage without any inquisition.

Staring at the receding caravan of carriages,

Monica shook her head in dismay and sank into a chair.

"Do not worry, Mother," Eustace said. "Lady Harriet will right herself. She merely needs time to sort it all out."

She eyed him fondly. Her son, it seemed, had acquired some wisdom beyond his years. "Perhaps you are right. Harriet is confused at the moment. We have Lord Westwood to thank for that. I hope he knows what he has wrought."

"If you had seen him floor Hunt that night, you would have no doubts." Eustace's eyes gleamed. "Fond of her, he is."

"I hope he is more than fond," Monica groused. She was not sure whether she held the earl in charity. On the one hand, he was to blame for Harriet's precarious emotional state. On the other, this bargain Harriet had seen fit to strike with the man had been wrongheaded from the outset. Lord Westwood's behavior had, if nothing else, caused Harriet to recognize that fact. Sometimes one had to destroy the facade before constructing a decent house, Monica reflected. And Harriet had built a more impermeable façade than anyone she knew.

Moreover, for all that Lord Westwood's behavior had chased her friend from London, it had not escaped Monica's attention that Eustace's revered Mr. Hunt was now merely "Hunt." If the earl had accomplished that transformation, Monica decided, she was grateful.

It was not until the next morning that Lord Westwood came to call. He found Monica in the drawing room, where she was writing letters. Truth be told, Monica had intended to send a note round to the earl had he not presented himself today. As the cause of Harriet's flight, he had every right to know what he had wrought — and an obligation, Monica hoped, to repair it.

He seemed shocked to hear of Harriet's departure, a fact that delighted Monica, though she kept that to herself. But when Lord Westwood demanded to know where, precisely, the duke made his home, she hesitated.

"I know nothing of Cornwall, I'm afraid," she said. "I only know the duke lives in a castle on the north coast."

He muttered something she did not catch and strode to the door.

Eustace, who had come into the room in time to see the earl's reaction, hastened after him. "Sir! Might I accompany you?"

Lord Westwood turned. "Your aid is always welcome, Eustace, but I fear my errand is rather personal. And should you not remain to assist your mother? Not the thing to leave in town her alone."

Eustace squared his shoulders. "Quite right. I had forgotten my duty."

Monica eyed her son. Was it her imagination, or did he stand a little taller after Lord Westwood reminded him of his responsibilities?

As for Lord Westwood, she was more heartened than she thought possible at the knowledge that he meant to hasten after Harriet. She would have wished him Godspeed, but the earl was halfway down the front steps before she thought of it. She hurried after him.

Lord Westwood bounded toward his waiting curricle, so intent on his mission that he failed to see another man approaching Lady Harriet's front steps, and collided with him. The man landed in a heap on the cobblestones.

"My apologies." Lord Westwood helped him to his feet. When it became apparent that the man was not injured, the earl was off, not sparing him a second glance.

Monica stared in amazement. The man Lord Westwood had knocked onto his posterior was none other than Cedric Gibbs.

He picked up his hat, shoved it on his head, and climbed the steps.

CHAPTER THIRTEEN

"RUNNING AWAY, AIN'T you?" Heavenly said sourly.

Harriet looked around the room in which she had lived as a child. The little painted vanity still sat next to the matching cheval glass. The window seat still afforded a marvelous view of the sea. The tall shelves that had held so many of her books still flanked the comfortable feather bed. The room had not changed.

And yet, she was a lifetime removed from the lonely girl she had been.

"Sure as fox flees the hound, you are running from Lord Westwood."

"Nonsense," Harriet said. "I merely wished to visit my father's home."

Heavenly hung one of Harriet's gowns in the wardrobe. "You can tell yourself that. Don't make it true."

She turned and looked Harriet up and down. "I've seen you run circles around the likes of Squire Gibbs. I've seen you run that bakery, see to the mill repairs, and hold your own with them haughty swells in London and their outlandish talk. I've never seen you hide."

Harriet sat down on the bed. "I am not running away." But her voice lacked conviction, and Heavenly shook her head.

"Miss Harriet, you've been running away from men all your days, and that father of yours is partly to blame. But that don't mean you have to keep doing it."

"My father? But —"

"The man lives like a hermit. I don't know what he sees in this drafty castle, but I do know that it is no place for you. I think you know it, too. Why, you married the first man who offered for you just to get away from here."

"I loved Freddy!" Harriet protested.

Heavenly nodded. "His lordship was a right charming scamp, but he didn't know how to love a woman any more than His Grace knew how to raise a daughter after the duchess died." Heavenly scowled. "Him and his castle by the sea. A lonelier place I have never seen."

"But it is beautiful here," Harriet said, wondering why the view out the window failed to chase the chill the castle always brought to her bones.

"'Tis only beautiful for them that don't let grief eat them alive," Heavenly retorted. Then her expression softened. "He never saw that his coldness was destroying you. Poor lass."

"I do not know why I permit you to talk to me like this." Harriet rubbed her eyes, willing away the tears.

"Somebody's got to. You've had two cold men in your life, neither one of them capable of giving you what you need. I guess that's why you shriveled up."

Stung, Harriet shook her head in denial.

Heavenly shot her a knowing look. "Lord Westwood knows how to warm a woman's heart, even a shriveled-up one, doesn't he?"

"That is enough!" Harriet cried. "I am nothing to him, and he is nothing to me."

Heavenly made an exasperated sound. "Lord Westwood is everything that Lord Worthington was not, and you know it."

"I will not have this talk," Harriet said fiercely, losing the fight against her tears.

"And here I thought you were a fighter." Heavenly turned away, so that Harriet could not see the moisture in her own eyes.

A man could be forgiven, Elias thought, for thinking Cornwall the farthest end of the earth. Doubtless his view came from having ridden the better part of three days to get here. He had taken his best Arabian, but even so it was necessary to change horses, and the nags available on the road did not have the speed and endurance of his prized horseflesh. The roads themselves were rutted and rough. Elias took some comfort in that fact, because it likely meant that Harriet and her father had made even slower time in their carriage. He had no wish to find his betrothed well-ensconced in the fortress that he imagined the duke's home to be.

In the military, one took a fortress not by

making a direct run on the most fortified gates but by starting with a tactical maneuver, and then storming it on all flanks. Elias intended — what, exactly, *did* he intend?

In truth, Harriet Worthington was not his betrothed, nor did she wish to be, and she had every right to retreat to her father's home. Elias had no standing by which to demand that she return with him. He could not very well tell the duke that he wished to make love to his daughter until she cried out the truth.

That stopped him. What truth? That she belonged to him, that she would never allow another man to claim her? That she would abandon all pretense and own him as hers?

Own him? God.

He had lost his mind. She had done this — with her pastries and her flirtations with revolutionaries, and her repeated claims that she needed no man to complete her. And if he had learned anything from the experience with Zephyr, it was that a man is most a fool when he is ready to accept the parson's noose — which he almost certainly was not.

Why, then, was he here?

The setting certainly held little appeal, beyond a wild beauty that did little to mask the harshness. The north coast was raw and unforgiving. Sheer, high cliffs tumbled hundreds of feet onto beaches dotted with granite sea stacks. Not far away was a castle ruin rumored to have once been King Arthur's stronghold. Elias did not hold with the legend, but he could well imagine that the rocky headlands, with their commanding views of ceaselessly turbulent seas, had given rise to mythic tales of nigh-invincible kings.

The duke's castle was no less evocative a structure, he decided sometime later as he surveyed it from what passed for a road into the compound. The castle might have presided on the clifftop for hundreds of years and, from the look of that rugged granite, would last a few hundred more. Elias tried to imagine Harriet growing up in such a place, isolated and alone. The nearest neighbors looked to be a fishing village some distance away on a rocky beach.

No wonder she had been drawn to Freddy. His lively, irrepressible spirit represented nothing so much as rescue from the bleakness that surrounded her.

The road led him to some great iron gates that, fortunately, were open. Elias passed through them into a rough, deserted courtyard. He looped his nag's reins around the ring of an ancient post and took stock of his surroundings. The castle itself soared more than a hundred feet above him. Two enormous doors pitted with age appeared to serve as the main entrance. Elias sounded a rusty iron doorknocker on one of them, and, after some minutes, the door swung open on its squeaky hinges. A solemn-looking footman stared at him with a slight air of puzzlement, as if the castle did not receive many visitors. The man led him through a darkened corridor illuminated with braces of candles that in no way cast sufficient light.

At last Elias presented himself in the drafty Great Hall that no manner of fire could warm. One wall bore an enormous coat of arms. On it were images of a dozen or more gold coins surrounding a double-headed eagle over an azure blaze. A rusty suit of armor stood in the corner, a shield at the ready, with a twelve-foot lance propped upright and next to it. He wondered why the duke had seen fit to raise his daughter in such a place.

Soon the duke entered the hall. The man did not seem surprised to see him. "So you have come," was all he offered by way of greeting.

Brandy was called for. There was a prolonged silence as each man took the other's measure. The only light was a ring of torches along the wall and a smoky oil lamp on the table between them. It added to the atmosphere of grim otherworldliness, a time out of time in which immortal knights and kings did battle under the watchful eyes of magicians and sorceresses. Harriet's father might have been such a king in another life — or even in this one, for Elias had no trouble imagining the man in that suit of armor in the corner.

It was some time before the duke spoke.

"I prefer my solitary state, but Harriet needs people and life," he said at last, dispensing with preliminary pleasantries. "I could not give her that. One day I looked up and she had become a woman — like her mother."

For a moment he seemed lost in thought. "I had not wanted children. I thought my Julia too frail, too slight for the physical ordeal of childbirth.

But it was what she wanted, so I gave in. It was thus my fault she died, but God help me, I blamed Harriet as well. I have had years to regret that."

Elias said nothing. Privately he thought the duke had taken too much guilt unto himself for what surely had been the vagaries of fate. But the guilt had long festered, and he suspected the man would never be dissuaded.

"I knew she wished for a Season," the duke continued. "She deserved an introduction to society, the opportunity to meet people her own age. God knows, she got none of that here. And so I took her to London, and she met Worthington. She had no experience of men. She did not recognize what he was. She wanted him, and I knew that if I forbade the marriage, she would defy me."

Elias tried to imagine Harriet, six years younger and achingly vulnerable, swept into Freddy's aura without the protective armor she had since spent years devising. He saw a father who wanted desperately to assure her happiness, but did not know how.

"You protected her as best you could," Elias said.

"No, I failed." The duke's brow darkened. "He had other women. I safeguarded her money, but I could do nothing about her heart." He leveled a hard gaze at Elias. "And so you see, Westwood, there is nothing more important to me now than Harriet's happiness. I see that you want her. You have come all this way, after all. But can you be the man she deserves?"

Elias did not immediately respond. Why was he here, if not for the woman who had caused such a strange madness to grow within him? Only one answer presented itself, and it was as good as any.

"As to that, sir, I do not know," he said. "I only know I cannot do without her."

The duke pondered that. "I had you investigated."

Elias eyed him warily. "What did you learn?"

"That you do not fear work, that you have labored on your properties alongside your workers. That you are accorded an expert on spices, and particularly in the matter of appealing to English tastes. I myself enjoy good food, but I have had the benefit of my daughter's skills. Most of England, however, has not. The country is ripe for a culinary adventure. You will do well."

The duke's gaze settled on the coat of arms. "We do not practice primogeniture in Cornwall. One day all of this will be Harriet's. That is another reason I had Freddy's entail broken. My daughter will be a very rich woman and there will be none to lay a claim on any of her property."

"I have no interest in your daughter's money or possessions."

The duke's eyes narrowed assessingly. "Even if that is so, there are other difficulties. You travel for considerable periods of time out of the country. If you had a family, they would doubtless be alone a great deal."

"Yes," Elias said.

"You were engaged once," the duke continued.

"Standing at the altar at St. Paul's, in fact, awaiting your bride."

"Yes. She eloped with someone else."

His Grace looked speculative. "An experience like that can sour a man. Why would you wish to risk marriage again?"

Elias sighed. Agreement or no, honesty compelled him to put a halt to the duke's illusions. "I cannot pretend that I do wish it, sir. Indeed, I must be frank: I have no plans to wed. It cannot come as a surprise to you that your daughter feels likewise. Our betrothal is not what it seems. I cannot say more without her permission."

The duke regarded him for a long moment. Elias knew his response was not what the man wanted to hear.

"I suppose it is no surprise," the duke said at last. "She was hurt by Worthington's betrayal, more deeply than I had imagined. More deeply, perhaps, than she understands. She would not wish to repeat such an experience."

"Whatever happens, I will not betray her," Elias said quietly.

"I would kill you if you did."

In spite of himself, Elias smiled. "I would expect no less."

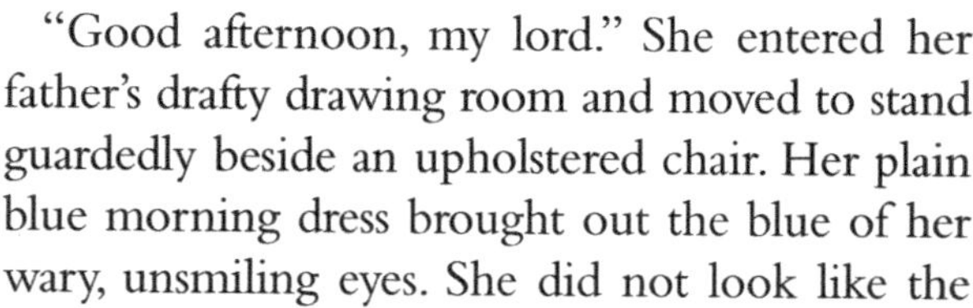

"Good afternoon, my lord." She entered her father's drafty drawing room and moved to stand guardedly beside an upholstered chair. Her plain blue morning dress brought out the blue of her wary, unsmiling eyes. She did not look like the vibrant, confident woman Elias had come to know, the woman who had responded with such abandon when he made love to her.

He took a deep breath. "I will come right to the point, Lady Harriet."

"In London you used my given name." Her tone was flat. She seemed withdrawn, cool. "But that is neither here nor there. Why are you here? I cannot imagine what caused you to undertake such a journey."

"I am here to ask that you release me from our contract now."

Her eyes widened. She placed a hand on the chair, her shock plain.

"My apologies," Elias said quickly. "I spoke too abruptly."

Gathering herself, she faced him. "It is merely that I was not expecting such a request. We agreed to end our engagement in August. I did not know you wished for... for another outcome."

"I do wish it."

She studied him. "Why?"

"I believe the terms have been fulfilled."

A flush stole over her features, and she turned away.

Instantly, Elias moved to her side. He put his hands on her shoulders and turned her around to face him. "Our agreement was wrong-headed from the outset, Harriet. Its premise was flawed. Freddy would have been untrue to any woman. There was nothing about you, no flaw or inadequacies, that drove him into Caroline Forth's arms."

She looked stricken. "You have seen Caroline. She is beautiful —"

"She is a fraud," Elias growled. "There is not one smattering of genuine feeling in her. You are more woman than she will ever be."

She shook her head. "No."

"Look at me, Harriet."

Her chin rose, and she met his gaze squarely. "I know you are merely telling me what you think I wish to hear," she said. "But it is no use. I am aware of my shortcomings. You need not invent excuses or ply me with platitudes."

"'Tis no platitude to say that you are the most desirable woman I have ever known," Elias said softly. His hands slipped to her waist. "I cannot continue our charade. I wish us to start anew, with only honesty between us. Return to London with me. Now."

But she pulled away. "I cannot."

"You are afraid I might hurt you — as Freddy did." He caught her hand. "I would never betray you."

But she held herself stiffly, withholding. "Very well," she said, her voice lifeless. "I will write a letter ending our agreement and authorizing the transfer of my shares to you. That is what you want, is it not? My shares?"

Without waiting for an answer, she left the room.

"This is better news than I could have hoped for," Jeremy Wilson said proudly.

Henry slumped in the hard wooden chair in Wilson's office. He had left a damned good bottle of wine to respond to the solicitor's urgent summons.

"I never thought to have such success, but even that Hunt fellow finally agreed to our terms. Not graciously, but he agreed nevertheless — especially after I explained that Lord Westwood might feel compelled to present his offer in person. Henry, you may go and inform his lordship that I have successfully repurchased all of the shares Lady Harriet sold."

Henry frowned. "The earl is in Cornwall." He had tried all week not to think about the potential import of Lord Westwood's hasty trip to Cornwall. He had never seen the earl go to such extremes over a woman.

The solicitor nodded. "That is why I have summoned you. I know I can count on you to deliver the news to Lord Westwood personally."

"What? To Cornwall?" Henry eyed him in disbelief. "'Tis a three-day ride at best! Days in the saddle, dashing over hill and dale just to have the earl sing your praises while fine wine sits a-wasting in London. Won't do it."

The solicitor's gaze narrowed. "I know you like your comforts, Henry. You live quite well when Lord Westwood is away, don't you? But the earl has made this bit of business his highest priority. He would not look kindly on your refusal to cooperate."

Henry sighed. He had no desire to risk the earl's temper. Scowling, he scraped back his chair. "Very well. Give me the papers."

"Mrs. Tanksley?"

Monica looked up from her knitting. Squire Gibbs sat on the edge of his chair, glowering at the corner of the room where Eustace sat reading a book.

"Yes, Mr. Gibbs?"

"How long must I stay in this house?"

Her spirits sank. She had found the week with Squire Gibbs most companionable. As she had long suspected, he was not the ogre some people thought. Indeed, he seemed to be a changed man since she had last seen him in Worthington. He had shed some weight, and his face had lost its florid appearance.

Since his arrival in London, he had had little to drink, with the result that their evenings had been spent in pleasant conversation, their days in quiet walks. She had assumed that he, too, enjoyed their time together. Now she realized that her loneliness had led her to see friendship where there was only tolerance.

"Until Harriet returns, I suppose," she replied. "She is eager to speak to you about the positon."

"If she is so eager, why isn't she here?" he growled.

Monica bit her lip. "I did not realize that passing time in my company was such an onerous chore." Oh, dear, why had she said that?

Surprise swept his features. "It is not," he quickly assured her. "It is just that —" He broke off.

Monica placed her knitting in her lap. "Yes?" she prodded warily.

"That son of yours," he said in a low voice.

Eustace sat in the corner, reading a book. He did not appear to hear.

"Eustace?" Monica repeated, eyeing her son. "What about him?"

"He has appointed himself your chaperon." He reddened.

Monica had indeed noticed that Eustace rarely left her alone with Mr. Gibbs. Her son was taking his new responsibilities as man of the house very seriously. The knowledge that Mr. Gibbs found Eustace's watchfulness irritating cheered her. Perhaps he was not completely indifferent to her after all. "Does that bother you, sir?" she asked carefully.

He looked away. "I am not a man to spend my days in inaction," he said, ignoring her question. "There are things to be done in Worthington. If the mill is to be properly fitted for the milling season, certain steps have to be taken."

"Then you mean to accept Harriet's offer?" Monica asked, surprised.

"She has been most generous," he said stiffly, "especially given…my past activities. It has taken me time to realize that. But time waits for no man, and I have been in a fair way to wasting much of it these last few years."

"My dear sir!" Monica exclaimed. "Why do you say so?"

He flushed. "My eldest — that's Louisa, as you may remember — she and some of the older children sat me down two months ago, told me their mother would not wish to see me in such a state. Truth is, I was so angry at the world over her death that I neglected the ones who needed me."

Monica eyed him sympathetically. "Acceptance, sometimes, is hard-won."

"That's it, exactly," he said. "I cannot change what happened, but I can do a sight more than I have been doing toward making my children's lives better. That's when Harriet's letter came. And it occurred to me then that if I am going to run the mill, that there are things that must be done, and soon."

Monica absorbed his words. "What things, Mr. Gibbs?" she ventured.

But he was looking at Eustace. As he realized she had spoken, Mr. Gibbs turned back to her and Monica realized what a nice shade of brown his eyes were. "What's that, Mrs. Tanksley?"

"You said steps must be taken before the mill can be fitted for the milling season. I only wondered what they might be."

He seemed surprised at her interest. "Well, since you asked, the chute has to be oiled, the hopper cleaned, and I am convinced that the angle of the shoe is all wrong." He hesitated. "Surely, this must bore you."

"On the contrary, Mr. Gibbs." Monica eyed him encouragingly. "I am riveted."

He beamed. "What most excites me is black lava stone."

"Lava stone?"

"From Coblenz, on the Rhine. More accessible, now that the war is over. Lava rock makes the hardest millstones, and it can be cut and grooved with great precision. An experienced miller can set the stones very close together, so that the meal is ground very fine. Harriet would have the whitest, smoothest flour for miles around." He said this with such enthusiasm that Monica smiled.

"Why, Mr. Gibbs, I do believe you are quite determined."

He regarded her somberly. "I am thinking about my children. Without the mill, I don't mind telling you that our income has been drastically depleted. Harriet has offered me a way out, and I must take it."

"I do hope your children have not suffered." Monica was troubled. She had assumed Mr. Gibbs's finances were not what they were during the years his family controlled the mill, but she had not known his situation was dire.

"Only from the lack of a woman's influence," he said. "We are not destitute, but I have been feeling quite the fool these days. I should be shot for thinking that Harriet — or any woman — would have the likes of me." He shook his head.

Their gazes held. Monica felt something move inside her. Her heart filled with small, foolish hope. But perhaps it was not so foolish after all, for Cedric was studying her with a very odd expression. Indeed, his eyes held something very like that which echoed in her own heart.

Monica glanced over at her son, who was trying not to appear to eavesdrop. "Eustace?" she called.

He rose, ready to do battle for his mother's honor. "Yes, Mother?" He glowered at the squire.

"I promised Mrs. Thornton that I would return this book to her." Monica took a book from the table near her chair. "She lent it to me more than two weeks ago."

"Heavenly's friend in Kensington?" Eustace frowned. "Very well. I will return it tomorrow."

"She is nearly an invalid, Eustace, dependent on others for her well-being. I would prefer that you take it now."

He eyed her incredulously. "But it is past tea time. It will be supper before I can get there — if I remember the way. Cannot this errand wait until —"

"Now," Monica said firmly. "If you please."

Eustace's gaze darted from his mother to Squire Gibbs, who was regarding him quite benignly. Eustace glared at the book in his mother's hand. Then, without a word, he took it and strode from the room.

"I believe that boy is growing up," Cedric said carefully.

"Not a moment too soon," Monica replied. "Would you care for a brandy? Sherry, perhaps?"

"I'm not one for spirits these days."

"You are to be commended for your self-discipline, Mr. Gibbs."

Cedric eyed her thoughtfully. "Mrs. Tanksley?"

"Yes?" To Monica's great embarrassment, the word came out a squeak.

"We have known each other for many years. And yet, I feel as though I am seeing you for the first time. Do you understand what I mean?"

Monica's heart turned a little somersault. "I think s-so," she stammered.

"Then I hope you will understand when I say that I hope Eustace gets quite lost in Kensington." Rising, he reached for her hand.

"Oh, dear," Monica said breathlessly as she realized his intent. "Oh, dear."

"My sentiments exactly," he murmured, and pulled her into his arms.

CHAPTER FOURTEEN

RAGE CAME IN many forms, as Elias well knew. Hot anger could turn a man into an instant fool and blind him to all reason. But sometimes rage sharpened reason, elevated it to the edge of a newly honed stiletto. Zephyr's abandonment on their wedding day had produced something close to that, and he had responded by calmly walking out of St. Paul's with whatever dignity was left to him and abandoning London for Jamaica. It was there, amid the hot sunshine and fertile land, that Elias redoubled his efforts to expand his spice business — unwittingly, with the help of Harriet's dowry. And so it was from rage that, in time, he forged a new life.

But while Elias had gotten over the debacle with Zephyr, he did not think he would soon forget Harriet's stiff, dispassionate reception of him and her lifeless acquiescence of his request to end their arrangement. She would doubtless dispense with the matter by a missive, and that would be that. It was clear she intended never to see him again.

That he would not allow. She was his. He would not lose her.

If it wasn't rage he felt now, it was just as consuming — a wave of emotion blocking all reason. It was the kind of emotion that throughout history had spawned schemes of revenge, murder, abduction.

Sweet, satisfying abduction.

And so he was here, outside this ancient castle in the dark of night, prepared to launch a tactical maneuver. Elias dismounted, careful to stay within the shadow of the castle, though in truth it was nigh impossible to see anything on this moonless night.

But a man who risked nothing, achieved nothing. If she would not come willingly to him, he would take her anyway. He'd even brought a sword. He would fight for her, perhaps to the death.

Good God. He sounded like a Norman invader. What was wrong with him?

As Elias surveyed the endless expanse of stone above him, cold practicality made a mockery of his irrational scheme. Had he been a Norman invader, perhaps he would have stood a chance. As it was, Sidenham's castle must have been impregnable to generations of invaders — and almost certainly to a lone man on horseback with a sword he hadn't used in years. Had he thought to slay dragons?

With a rueful shake of his head, Elias walked toward the same door through which he had entered yesterday, the one in front that led into the Great Hall.

There was much to be said for the direct approach.

Heavenly was worried. Lady Harriet had not left her room for hours, and she'd given her food only an indifferent glance. That was likely the fate of the dinner Heavenly now carried on her tray, as well. Though her mistress had not shared details of her private meeting with the earl yesterday, Heavenly suspected he was the cause of her distress.

Thus, when Heavenly saw Lord Westwood standing in the Great Hall, demanding of a hapless footman that he produce Lady Harriet forthwith, Heavenly strode over to him.

"Why are you here, my lord? Haven't you done enough to her?"

Lord Westwood turned to her. She had forgotten how very tall the man was. Even in the largest room in the castle, his stature was impressive. "Am I to understand that she is not well?" he demanded, concern and something far darker etched on his features. "Has a doctor been summoned?"

"What ails her is not something any quack can mend," Heavenly snapped. "I'm thinking it can be laid at your door. She hasn't been the same since your visit yesterday."

He absorbed that with apparent interest. "I see. Where is she now?"

Heavenly studied him. From the looks of things, Lord Westwood was prepared for anything. He wore a great cloak and a sword, and his demeanor was one of wary readiness. Almost, she believed this man could help her poor dear. Her gaze narrowed. "What is your purpose, my lord?"

"I intend to make off with her."

Heavenly blinked. "What?"

"I cannot say it more plainly." He took a step toward her. "I will not leave without her."

Heavenly eyed him warily. "I'll not be party to anything that hurts her."

"Of course. And now you must either move out of my way, or take me to her forthwith."

With a silent prayer, Heavenly shoved the dinner tray into his hands. "Follow me," she ordered gruffly.

⚬⚬⚬

Harriet did not look up from her window seat when Heavenly brought in the tray. The last thing she wanted was another bowl of Cook's beef knuckle soup, which would have been helped enormously by a pinch of tarragon.

"Close the door, Heavenly," she said crossly, staring out into the gathering fog. "You are letting in the draft."

Harriet felt, rather than heard, the door swing shut. That in itself was unusual, for Heavenly had taken to slamming doors to show her displeasure at Harriet's refusal to unburden herself of her private thoughts. Perhaps this was a different tactic.

"It is no use," Harriet admonished. "I have nothing to say about Lord Westwood. And were you to ask him, I am sure that he would have nothing to say about me."

"Not so," said a masculine voice.

Harriet looked up with a start. He stood in the center of her room — indeed, he very nearly filled it — wearing a cloak and sheathed sword.

It was a moment before she could speak. "Why are you here?" Her heart was racing. "Where is Heavenly?"

"Come," he commanded. "We are leaving."

She took a deep breath, striving for calm. "I have no intention of going anywhere with you, my lord. Indeed, it is quite possible that I loathe you." Harriet willed him to believe her lie. If he did not leave, she feared she would never free herself from the strange power he exerted over her.

That statement did not faze him. Instead, he took a step toward her. "If I thought that were true I would not be here. But it is not, is it?"

Harriet turned away from him. Once more, he had seen through her. Was there no sanctuary from this man? Was there no way to make herself whole again? To be who she was before he entered her life and upended it?

Perhaps he read her mind, for suddenly he upended her world anew — literally lifting her off her feet and carrying her over his shoulder and out of her chamber.

In the end, it had been amazingly easy. Elias carried her down two wide stairways and through the Great Hall without incident. She did not fight him. One or two servants stopped to stare, but they did not intervene. Clearly, Heavenly had matters well in hand. When the footman who had initially confronted Elias watched calmly as he strode off with the duke's daughter, Elias's estimation of Heavenly's skills rose.

Though she offered no resistance, Harriet held herself stiffly as he settled her on the saddle behind him. He took no comfort from the fact that she was forced to hold onto him as they rode down the dark road. Nor did he delude himself that she would acquiesce to his plans.

Truth be told, Elias had no plan beyond having her with him. Knowing the roads would be unlit and rutted, he had taken a room at a nearby inn. It was clean and comfortable enough, and when they arrived the innkeeper promptly provided a meal of mutton pie and pastries with blackberry jam in the private adjoining parlor.

Harriet showed no interest in food or conversation as she sat at the small table across from him. Her features were flat, lifeless. She was unusually pale, but Elias thought that stemmed from a disorder of the spirit rather than any physical ailment. She took but a sip of wine. She seemed determined not to meet his gaze.

The wine bottle bore no label, but the vintage was clearly French, doubtless the product of the smuggling trade that flourished on Cornish shores. Elias eyed her over the rim of his glass. "The French ever understand the grape," he said in a half-hearted attempt at a neutral topic.

She made no response.

"Fruitier than the coastland vintages," he continued stiffly. "Inland, I think. Strong and lusty, with a hint of the oak that aged it."

She put her fork in her plate and her hands in her lap.

"God's blood, Harriet." Elias set his glass on the table with a thump. "I could no longer abide the pretense."

"So you have said." She stared fixedly at the wall behind him.

What had become of the spirited woman he'd come to know? Elias wondered. Why was she denying what they both knew?

"Pretense erodes all possibility of trust," he said. "And trust is imperative between business partners — and lovers."

She flushed. "You seduced me. How is there trust in that?"

"You know that I did not. You came to me."

At last her gaze met his. "You only wanted my shares."

"At first," he agreed.

"You wish to change me." Her tone was accusing. "You loathe my salons."

"I acknowledge that I do not find them entertaining," he conceded.

"They are part of who I am —"

"I think not," Elias said. "You offer your home to malcontents and ne'er-do-wells in order to deflect attention from yourself. 'Tis the perfect mask for one who doubts her worth."

She stared at him. "You know nothing of me!

Why do you come for me in the night with all this talk? What is it you wish? If it is trust, you must know that is impossible."

"Because your husband was a cheat?"

"You know the answer."

Elias rose and came around the table to her. He pulled her to her feet, but she pushed him away.

"You wish to control me, Elias, just like —"

"No," he growled. "Do not compare me with the other men in your life, whether it is your feckless husband or your hermit of a father. I am not like them. Look at me, Harriet, and see the truth."

This time he did not reach for her. This time, he waited.

He watched as her eyes searched his. Would she find in them what she sought? Or would she continue this madness, this willful denial of the thing that was between them?

An eternity passed.

"Perhaps you wish a reason not to fear the consequences of lowering your guard," Elias said quietly. "The truth is, I cannot name one." He paused for a heartbeat. "But if it is any consolation, my own fear is considerable."

He heard her sob. Then she was in his arms, and his world righted itself at last. Elias kissed the top of her head and tightened his arms around her, locking them together, a perfect fit.

And that is when he knew. This thing that had lurked at the edges of his awareness, biding its time. That which had driven him across the country, caused him to brave a medieval fortress and carry her away like some marauding knight. The thing that brought him here, with his arms around a recalcitrant woman he could not live without.

Without a word, he lifted her and carried her to the bed.

❧

Harriet's heart was beating wildly, her body trembling, as he lowered her to the bed. Reaching for him, she did not try to hide her desire. Her arms went around him as he covered her body with his. Her mouth opened to his, burning for him to fill her there — and everywhere. She no longer cared if she disgraced herself with her keening, pleading need. He had done this to her, and there would be no help for it until she was his.

His mouth moved lower, depositing fierce kisses at her throat, marking her. Arching into him, Harriet felt shameless and wanton — and cared not. Need was all. She wanted no slow awakening. She was already there. She wanted him now.

He sensed it. His hands found her breasts through the fabric of her dress, and when the fabric would not yield, Harriet heard a muttered curse — and then a tear. Then his mouth was on her nipples, hot and teasing. She dug her hands into his shoulders and her hips moved upward, against him.

Now his hands were on her ankles, now higher still, ripping at her stockings, caressing her thighs, touching her intimately at last. Now, she begged silently. *Now.*

Stroking her, exploring her, he eased his finger inside her, setting a new rhythm for her desire. But Harriet fought the urge to give in to the gathering forces. She wanted more. She wanted *him.* Frantically she reached for him, fumbling with the fall of his trousers. She heard his sharp intake of breath when at last he was hers, filling her hand. Her legs wrapped around him, bringing him to her center.

Hesitating, he searched her face, but she had no patience for subtlety. Her hand tightened around him.

Suddenly his arms went under her, raising her, and then — *at last* — he was inside her, filling her. She arched upward, urging him deeper still, calling his name. She heard his low, savage growl.

Then he began to move within her, drawing her into his rhythm, driving them on. Her body instantly found the cadence and moved with him. And in the gathering storm nothing existed but the pounding, consuming need between them. No sound penetrated, no thought, only the burning demand for release.

It came for her in the moment she heard him cry out, driving deep into her, burying himself there for all time.

Tears ran down her face, and Harriet knew she would never be the same.

"You!"

Henry stared at the angry woman at the door. He was quite sure he had never laid eyes on her before, though she seemed to recognize him. She was comely enough — something unusual about her eyes — but her glare was sharp enough to kill a man at twenty paces. How fitting that she presided over this frigid old pile of stones. "I am looking for Lord Westwood," he began. "If you will tell me where I might find him —"

"You're the one what brought that note!"

Before Henry could gather his senses, she grabbed his sleeve and jerked him inside. "In London, it was. I recognized you right away. You brought that note round to the kitchen door. The one from that Hunt fellow. You started all the trouble!"

Alarm shot through him. Henry wondered how a wild-eyed harpy in Cornwall came to know of his scheme. "Nonsense, woman," he said imperiously. "I am in Lord Westwood's employ. I have important business for him. Take me to him immediately."

"His lordship ain't available," she snapped. "And I'll not be taking orders from the likes of you."

To his horror, she walked over to a cabinet, pulled out a pistol, and pointed it at him.

"Now," she said, leveling that eerie gaze at him, "suppose you tell me why you wanted Lord Westwood to think my mistress was dallying with Mr. Hunt."

Henry knew a thing or two about guns. The

pistol pointed at his heart had a hair trigger. When she cocked the weapon, he swallowed hard.

Slowly, she smiled — the kind of smile a cat might give a helpless rat with the misfortune to wander into its lair.

CHAPTER FIFTEEN

ELIAS WAS NOT entirely surprised to see the duke. He had gone downstairs in search of a breakfast tray to take to Harriet, who was still sleeping, and saw Sidenham in conversation with the innkeeper. His Grace did not bother to hide his satisfaction as he spied Elias.

"Well met, Westwood," he said.

Elias regarded him calmly. "I suppose you have procured a Special Licence."

"Ah. I give you credit. You had my measure, did you?"

"And it seems you had mine, sir."

The duke grinned. "I wasn't entirely certain at first, but when a man professes he cannot do without a woman — and that woman is my daughter — and when, moreover, they clearly have anticipated their vows several times over, there is really only one solution. You did not think I would allow you to make off with her without benefit of marriage, did you?"

"She will object," Elias said.

"Yes." The duke studied him closely. "But you will not, will you? I can read that in your soul."

Elias arched a brow. "Reading a man's soul is a rare skill."

"Not for a Cornish man," the duke said. "But I digress. I see I have played into your hands as much as you into mine. Indeed, I daresay I have made things easy for you."

"As to that, sir, I would caution against any assumption that the path ahead will be a smooth one."

The duke nodded. "God help you, Westwood, you do know my daughter. Come. Let us get on with it."

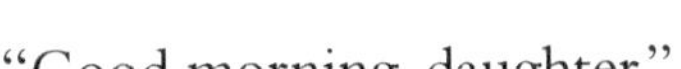

"Good morning, daughter."

Harriet opened her eyes. "Father!" She pulled the bedding up to her neck, and looked wildly around. Elias was nowhere to be seen.

Her father hovered over her. "Are you well, then?"

"Yes, but why are you here?"

"He did not force himself on you?"

Harriet turned scarlet. "No."

"Appears to be a bruise there on your neck," he said, studying her.

"Father, please! Allow me some privacy, so I can dress," Harriet said.

The duke moved toward the door. "I will be in the parlor. And have a care with your toilette, my dear. This is your wedding day."

Harriet stared at him in horror.

A half hour later, she stood before to her father,

her expression grim. "This is not necessary, Father. I am neither a child nor an innocent."

"No, you are a widow," the duke replied. "And while many of the breed comport themselves in a common fashion, I will not tolerate such behavior in my daughter."

She turned to Elias, who stood silently next to her father. "Why do you not say something? He has no right."

"He is your father," Elias said.

"But he is not yours!" she said. "He has no right to force you marry me."

"I am here of my own will," he said quietly.

Confusion swept her. *Marriage.* She knew Elias loathed such a step as much as she did. And yet, he had not objected. Were they to be swept into this union without a word of protest?

"We should not suit, as you well know," she persisted. "We are nothing alike."

Elias regarded her. "As to that —"

Suddenly, her father stepped between them. "The vicar is on his way," he said, and put his hand at her elbow, propelling her into a larger room.

There she was surprised to see Heavenly and another man, although by the looks of things, the state of their relations was not a cordial one.

"I'm not too late, am I, your lordship?" the man asked. Harriet recognized him as the servant who had greeted her so frostily when she went to Elias's house.

"You don't have to marry her, now," he

continued eagerly. "Wilson has bought back the shares she sold!"

"Henry?" Elias frowned. "What is this?"

"Mr. Wilson has laid it all out in these papers," Henry said, holding a sheaf of documents. "He was most anxious that you have the news posthaste." He spared a moment to glare at Heavenly. "The purchasers were all too happy to sell, since you offered more than they paid. Even that fellow Hunt finally gave in. So you see, my lord," he finished happily, "you have the controlling interest. You don't need her anymore."

The shares, Harriet thought weakly. Always the shares. That explained so much. "Then again," she said softly, "why stop with a controlling interest, when you can gain all of them by marrying me?"

"That is not my purpose," Elias said.

"What's this nonsense?" her father demanded.

"Harriet sold some of her shares to pay for various repairs in the village," Elias said. "I instructed my solicitor to try to buy them back."

Harriet felt as if her world had crashed down around her. This man who wanted her to trust him had conspired to get her shares by any means necessary, even going so far as to secretly obtain what she had already sold. Why had she even dared to think otherwise?

"Tell him the rest," she said in a dull voice.

Elias eyed her assessingly before turning to her father. "Before I began that effort, your daughter and I arrived at an agreement by which she would deed to me the remaining shares of the business that came to her as Freddy's widow, provided certain, er, terms were met. It was a business agreement. I have since released her from it."

"Yes," Harriet confirmed. "All between us was business." She tried to banish the awful roaring in her ears, the sound of her fragile hope collapsing.

Elias's dark gaze held hers. "You know that it was not."

Harriet did not see obvious treachery in his eyes, but what did she know of such matters? What did she know of anything? The man who had just made love to her, who had possessed her as none other, had betrayed her, maneuvered himself into a marriage that would give him all of the shares of his business without her cooperation.

"Was any of it real, my lord?" she asked bitterly.

His eyes, dark with some emotion she could not discern, held hers. "You know the answer."

"Why did you not come to me, daughter, if you needed money?" her father demanded.

"I did not want your money." Harriet turned to Elias. "I will freely give you what shares of mine remain. There is no need for a wedding to seal the bargain. None of this is necessary." She yearned for him to take her in his arms, to reassure her that her worst fears had not been realized. But not here, not before her father and the others.

"Your Grace!" called a cheerful female voice. All eyes turned to the doorway, where the innkeeper's wife stood with a small man, nervously adjusting his spectacles. "I have brought the vicar," she announced with a broad smile. "The wedding can begin!"

Her husband sat opposite her in the carriage. They had barely spoken since leaving Cornwall. For three days Harriet and Elias had traveled in silence, neither attempting to bridge the strained gap between them. The inns at which they stopped had not been full; without asking her, he had obtained separate rooms for them.

All Harriet could think of was the extent of his perfidy. She had played into his hands. Now he had her shares, and she had a husband once more. Once again, she was shackled to a man with the power to hurt her.

But perhaps he would soon be off on his travels, seeing to his business. Then she would be free to go on with her life. Everything would be the same except for the minor inconvenience of having a husband somewhere. She would have her stimulating salons in town and her home in the country. She would talk with Cedric about his plans for the mill. They would move forward.

Life would be tolerable. That was what she wished for, was it not?

Harriet tried very hard not to think about the intimacies they had shared, for that made her want to weep in despair. She would not give in to that weakness.

Had he married her for her shares? Harriet did not want to believe that the man who had caressed her so tenderly was capable of such a thing. But to believe otherwise would require a leap of faith.

It would require trust.

And that was something she had never learned.

"Celestial!" Horace peered out the window at the carriages.

"'Tis Lady Harriet!" Celestial beamed. "I will get a supper ready. She will be famished after her long journey."

Horace put a restraining hand on her arm. "But look! there is Lord Westwood. He is with her."

Celestial studied the scene on the drive. Lord Westwood was indeed with her mistress. Both wore grim expressions as they descended from the carriage. Emerging from another carriage were Heavenly and a slightly older man — one of Lord Westwood's servants, perhaps — who looked equally glum.

"Something momentous has occurred," Celestial said. Her gaze narrowed thoughtfully. "She returns from Cornwall without her father but with Lord Westwood — that is three days' drive in a closed carriage. Perhaps Lord Westwood means to marry her after all. Mayhap he applied to her father. Oh, Horace! Perhaps they are already wed!"

"I don't think so." Horace shook his head doubtfully.

Celestial clapped her hands together. "This would be an excellent time to tell them about us. She'll not object that we married without her permission. Neither will Heavenly, what with Lady Harriet embracing happiness and her new love."

"That is not the face of a woman who has been embracing anyone," Horace declared.

Celestial peered at Lady Harriet, who was climbing the front steps slowly, as if the weight of the world sat on her shoulders.

Horace hurried to throw open the door. "My lady! Welcome home."

Celestial could not hear Lady Harriet's response. But her mistress's tone told her that Horace was correct — something was very wrong.

When Lord Westwood's servant carted his trunks into the house behind him, Celestial's eyes widened. So they had married! But no newly married woman looked as downcast as Lady Harriet.

As Celestial hurried to the kitchen, she stole a look at the earl. He was studying Lady Harriet, and Celestial was surprised to see longing in his gaze. He cared for her, then. That was more than her mistress had from Lord Worthington. That man had nearly ruined her for anyone else. She would not easily overcome those scars. Lord Westwood would have his hands full if he hoped to truly win her heart.

Perhaps, thought Celestial, he needed a little help.

CHAPTER SIXTEEN

"MONICA AND CEDRIC?" Harriet shook her head in disbelief.

Eustace, who had just returned from Worthington after ascertaining for himself the state of his mother's welfare, shrugged. "I was leery myself. But Mr. Gibbs seems a changed man. And Mother is happy."

Harriet thought Eustace must be a changed man as well. Gone were the stiff, impossibly high collars he favored earlier. Now his jacket molded to his lanky form with none of the sharp angles and exaggerated padding typical of the dandy set. His straight-legged trousers were far removed from the voluminous Cossacks that Monica had found so unattractive. Eustace now dressed very much like Elias, with understated but impeccable taste.

Harriet did not want to think about her husband. It was enough that he sat across from her night after night, that they ate their meals together as if everything were perfectly normal. They spoke little to one another; indeed, were it not for the presence of Eustace, they might very well sit in utter silence.

She took another spoonful of turtle soup. She could not place the seasonings and made a mental note to ask Celestial about it. The taste was not off-putting, but it did not fit with turtle.

"I hope Cedric understands that he must follow my rules as to the fair use of the mill and distribution of the flour," she told Eustace.

"He does," Eustace assured her. "Mother made certain of that before she agreed to return to Worthington with him. He is very excited about some new grinding stone from the Continent. Says it will produce a better quality flour. That is why they are planning a wedding trip to the Rhine."

Harriet wished her friend all happiness, but she could not help but feel a little abandoned. With Eustace doing so well on his own, Monica would turn her attention to the children who needed her, which was right and necessary. But she likely would not have time to share Harriet's confidences.

Harriet took another sip of soup. "I do believe Celestial has erred in the seasoning." She waited for Elias to comment, for his palate was remarkable, but he had eaten his soup as if nothing were amiss. So intently did Harriet watch him that she almost jumped when his gaze met hers.

"Is something wrong?" he asked.

Yes. I do not wish to be living in this house with you, seeing your face every day, knowing that your chamber is next to mine. I do not wish to think about your kisses and wonder why you do not so much as venture into my room at night. Because even though you betrayed me, I cannot stop thinking about your touch.

But Harriet did not say those things. She merely shook her head.

His eyes searched hers. "Nevertheless, I sense that something is amiss."

Her gaze shot to Eustace, the only other occupant of the dining room. Thank goodness he provided a buffer against the need to answer such probing questions. But even as she formed the thought, Eustace placed his napkin on the table.

"Please excuse me," he said, rising. "I have an engagement."

Harriet eyed Eustace suspiciously, but Elias merely wished him a pleasant evening, then returned his attention to her. "I wish to know what is causing you distress."

Hadn't she forsworn silence? Hadn't her reluctance to speak up during her marriage with Freddy left her all but a ghost in their union? She would not repeat the mistakes of the past. She would not cease to exist. She would not play the silent, obedient wife.

Harriet took a deep breath. "Perhaps it is not a proper topic for dinner conversation, but since we are private..." She faltered as she saw him studying her intently.

"Yes?" he prodded softly.

"I am forced to point out, my lord, that — that our marriage is as much of a sham as our betrothal," Harriet finished.

She thought he flinched at that, but in the next

moment, that intent expression returned to his eyes. "Pray, continue."

"In the week that we have lived in this house together," she said — the words coming all at once now that she had braved them — "we do not converse in any meaningful fashion, nor can we sit in the same room together without there being a strained air between us. Indeed, I find your presence stifling, my lord."

He took a sip of wine. "I would never wish to stifle you, Harriet."

Harriet placed her napkin on the table. "I simply cannot tolerate this atmosphere of...of unnaturalness."

He regarded her thoughtfully. "What would make it more natural?"

Absently, she fanned herself with the edge of the napkin. The dining room was uncommonly warm. "Perhaps it is simply that we are too aware of each other," she said.

"Perhaps. I am very aware of you, certainly."

"Yes, well, perhaps if we try to ignore it —"

"It?"

"The, er, unnaturalness," she said. "Freddy and I had a tolerable arrangement. Indeed, we scarcely noticed if the other was in the house."

"Is that what you wish?"

Harriet shook her head. "I do not want a marriage like I had with Freddy."

"And yet, his shadow is in every room," he said quietly. "It follows us around like an unwelcome guest. When you look at me you see him. Our marriage is freighted with the weight of Freddy's perfidy and your expectation that our union will replicate the dismal experience of marriage to him."

Harriet shook her head. "No."

He took another sip of wine, then set his glass on the table. "Let me be clear, Harriet: I do not want a 'tolerable' arrangement. I want more." He paused. "Much more."

Harriet was not surprised that his patience was near an end. Perhaps now he would seek out other women who could provide him what she could not. But, no — that is what Freddy would have done. Was there truth, then, in what he'd said? That she was hobbling them with the legacy of her first marriage?

Much of the blame for this strained air between them was hers, Harriet knew. She'd been angry that her father forced her into marriage, as if she were a green miss trying to save herself from scandal. She'd been angry at Elias for allowing them to be rushed into a ceremony neither could have wanted. She was angry that those shares had been so important to him that he had married her for them. Her anger had festered and caused a wedge between them. But lately, it had become increasingly harder to maintain her anger, to remind herself of the reasons for it.

In the week since they had wed, Elias had made no demands of her. He had not pressed her for marital intimacies, not engaged her in any meaningful examination of what their marriage was to be. It was as if he held himself back, waiting for something.

And the more he held himself aloof, the more she wanted him, the more thoughts of their intimate moments intruded. Indeed, she could think of little else. Harriet scarcely recognized the wanton woman she had become. This was a strange magic that he had wrought. It hovered in the air between them, lurked around the corners of this house she had shared with Freddy. It tormented her, made her acutely aware of the empty place in her bed at night.

She yearned for him to touch her. Even here in the dining room, on this very table. Could he read her thoughts? Did she wish him to?

Slowly, Harriet raised her gaze to his.

Abruptly, his chair scraped the floor. "Please excuse me," he said politely. "I have something to attend to." With that, her husband of one week rose and left the dining room.

Harriet stared numbly at his empty chair. Without thinking, she speared a piece of turtle meat and put it into her mouth. Again, that strange taste.

Dear Lord. What was happening to her?

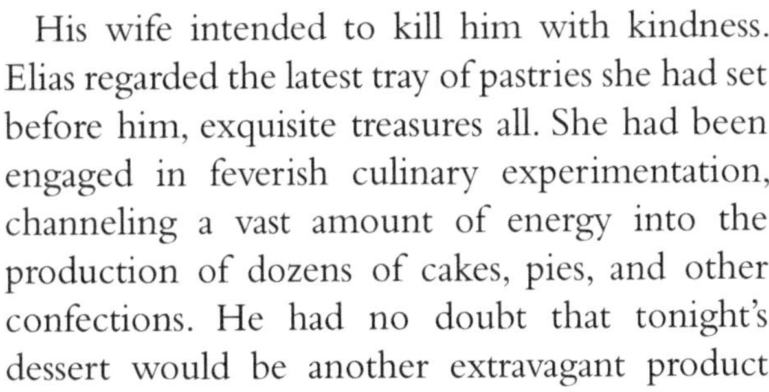

His wife intended to kill him with kindness. Elias regarded the latest tray of pastries she had set before him, exquisite treasures all. She had been engaged in feverish culinary experimentation, channeling a vast amount of energy into the production of dozens of cakes, pies, and other confections. He had no doubt that tonight's dessert would be another extravagant product

— a drunken trifle, perhaps, or the cheesecake she recently adorned with a baroque sculpture of blueberries, kumquats, and marzipan.

If he did not expire from overconsumption, he might die of unrequited lust. No matter what she served him, his appetite would not be satisfied by the most exquisite of Harriet's pastries, only by the woman herself.

That he had even consented to that extemporized wedding ceremony in the ancient little church near the inn was a measure of his need. After the spectacle at St. Paul's, Elias had thought never to set foot in such a structure again. But marrying Harriet in a tiny stone chapel that had served Norman invaders and druids alike seemed fitting, somehow. Certainly, it was nothing like the grand spectacle at St. Paul's.

It surprised him that he'd entered a state which he had so long disparaged. He knew little about marriage or how their life together would be. Yet he would have married her in a barn or even in St. Paul's had she wished it. He would have taken her on any terms, so long as they bound her to him.

But as he had predicted, the path since then had been difficult. Elias thought perhaps her anger had faded, but there were still barriers between them. He sensed she was trying to avoid him, to the point of exhausting herself in the kitchen night after night. Sometimes she stopped long enough in the afternoon to take tea with him. The tea seemed to restore her. After one cup, she usually lost her look of embattled fatigue. After another, she would fan herself and complain about the heat.

Elias yearned to bed his wife, but he was determined not to press her. She would come to him willingly, or not at all. It must be her decision — at least that is what he told himself. Still, it was becoming increasingly more difficult to keep his distance.

Night after night Elias had stared at the door between their rooms, knowing that if he went to her she would allow him to make love to her. But instinct told him that he would never possess her fully unless she came to him. Only then would he know that she was ready to trust him, that her heart was ready to love.

Love was new to him. He had never felt this way, certainly not with Zephyr. He suspected it might take a lifetime to understand it. If only Harriet would grant him that. If only she would not always flee to the kitchen.

"I am almost satisfied with the new sourdough," Harriet said, sinking into a chair. She was followed by Celestial, carrying the tea tray.

Harriet accepted the cup Celestial poured from one of the teapots. "I will not rest until I have it just right. The Egyptians made a wondrous loaf with that flour Lady Hester sent. It is called —"

"Kamut," Elias replied wearily, taking the teacup Celestial gave him.

"Oh." She eyed him uncertainly. "I have mentioned it, then?"

"Several times."

Harriet frowned at her teacup. "What have you

done to the tea, Celestial? I had just gotten used to that new brew, and now you have gone back to the old way."

"The old way?" Celestial's gaze shot from Harriet's cup to Elias's. Quickly, she removed Harriet's cup, poured out another from one of the pots, and offered it to her.

"Much better," Harriet said after a sip.

Elias stared at his own cup, and then put it carefully on the tray. Celestial, meanwhile, slipped from the room. He cleared his throat. "I wish to tell you about a new arrangement I have made for the shares of Westwood Imports."

"They are no longer my concern. You saw to that." She fanned herself. "It is uncommonly warm in here, is it not?"

"I have made them your concern," Elias said. "I have had my solicitor draw up papers dividing the shares equally between us, effective immediately. There are no conditions. You are free to do with them what you will." He hesitated. "Should you wish to buy more cows for your neighbors, however, it would be more sensible to pay for them outright than to sell more shares. It was rather expensive to buy back those you sold."

She stared at him. "I do not understand."

"I have made you an equal owner in Westwood Imports," he said.

"Did my father —?"

"He had nothing to do with it. It was my decision."

She absorbed that information in silence. "Why?" she asked finally.

"Because I wish you to have equal right to all that is mine," he said. "And because I wish there to be trust between us."

"I…had not expected such a thing," she said slowly. "I thought you married me for the shares."

"Had you bothered to ask me whether that was true," Elias said evenly, "I would have told you that it was not." He could feel his temper rising. "You solicitor was a crook, you see."

She looked shocked. "Mr. Stevens?"

"He sold your shares at a higher price than what he gave you as proceeds. He made a handsome profit by pocketing the difference. And, yes, I was determined to regain those shares, but it had nothing to do with marrying you. It was to right a grievous fraud that was done to you and to the business."

She stared at him. "I did not realize —"

Elias rose abruptly. "Yes, it was easier to assume I betrayed you, wasn't it? As I said, Freddy's blasted ghost is everywhere."

She reached for her teacup, but he snatched it from her and strode from the room. Within moments, he found Celestial in the kitchen, along with Horace. He set Harriet's teacup on the worktable with such force that it nearly shattered.

They stared at him.

"You have been putting ginseng into her food," he growled.

Horace gasped. Celestial merely regarded Elias curiously. "How did you know?"

"You gave me her tea by mistake. I recognized it instantly. When she complained of the taste, you poured her a new cup from the pot containing the ginseng. I'll warrant it was also in her turtle soup and any number of other dishes besides."

"It will stimulate —"

"I am well aware of ginseng's reputed properties," he snapped. "I imagine you thought to help her. But I will brook no more interference. Is that clear?"

Warily, Celestial nodded.

—◆—

The next morning, Elias signed the documents implementing the transfer of half of the shares to Harriet. His solicitor had other documents for his attention, including one from an associate in Jamaica.

"Tell him to expect me there by the end of September," Elias said.

Jeremy Wilson looked uncertain. "But you would have to sail next week. And, well...you have been married less than a fortnight."

"Nevertheless, do as I say."

"Yes, my lord." The solicitor busied himself with his papers.

Elias suppressed a sigh. Jeremy was a good man. Doubtless he thought a newly married husband and wife would not wish to be parted so soon. But at this point, Jamaica seemed a godsend. He could not go on like this with Harriet.

The knowledge that he would soon put an ocean between them should have buoyed him, but by the time Elias reached his chamber, he was in a foul mood. "Brandy, Henry," he barked, flopping into a chair.

His batman quickly set a glass at his elbow. Lately, Henry had been eager to please — suspiciously so, given that the man was probably thoroughly miserable in his new surroundings, what with Heavenly and Celestial ruling the roost above and below stairs.

A more meddling group of servants Elias had never seen. It was beyond tolerating that Celestial had tampered with Harriet's food, even though she'd meant well. He would never resort to artifice to arouse his wife. If Harriet did not come to him of her own free will, nothing else mattered.

In frustration, Elias kicked the footstool, sending it toppling onto its side. Henry made a great fuss of righting the thing. Elias wanted nothing more than to be left alone with his thoughts, but here was Henry refilling his glass and standing expectantly until Elias could no longer ignore him.

"What is it, Henry?" he demanded.

Henry took a deep breath. "I wish to make amends."

"Amends?" Elias frowned. "For what?"

"I, er, perhaps overstepped in one area."

"You overstep in every area, Henry. What the devil are you babbling about?"

Henry faced him squarely. "In the matter of that Mr. Hunt."

"Oliver Hunt?" Elias stared at him. "What have you done?"

"Some time ago I wrote a note to him

pretending to be Lady Harriet. I may have said that I — *she* — admired him. The man was most receptive, I'll say that. Even made me wait for a reply to take to her."

Elias stared at him. "You arranged their assignation that night at her salon."

"I thought perhaps he and your ladyship would form a *tendre* so you'd be able to slip the noose. As I said, overstepped."

"God's blood," Elias swore. "Is there to be no end to the meddling?"

"It was just the one letter I wrote," Henry said indignantly. "Was only thinking of you. It was because of that earlier business with Miss Payne. I saw how you suffered. Didn't want you to go through that again. Anyway, I was wrong. Wish to apologize."

Elias sighed heavily. "How long have you been in my employ, Henry?"

"Since before the war," Henry said proudly. "And during. And after."

"We risked our lives together, didn't we?" Elias said. "Even so, Henry, one day you will go too far. Mayhap that time is now."

"But now that the deed is done —"

"The 'deed'?"

"The, er, marriage." Henry reddened. "It's done, so no harm came of things. And I would not like you to be miserable."

Elias regarded him in mock surprise. "Do I understand that you actually wish me happy?"

"I have always wished for your happiness, my

lord," Henry replied stiffly. "I simply never trusted a female to provide it."

Elias pondered that. Until recently, he had felt exactly the same. He sighed. "Sometimes a man has no choice but to hope that she will."

Henry sniffed disdainfully. Elias eyed him curiously. "Have you never met a woman who left you no choice, Henry?"

The batman glowered. "Oh, yes. No choice about anything, even what to think. An incessant meddler, always telling a man his business."

"A quality she shares with her sister." Elias had little difficulty surmising the identity of the female giving Henry such fits. "Interesting eyes, though."

Henry stared at his employer. "Haven't noticed the state of Miss Heavenly's eyes, or anything else about her person."

"No? Perhaps I was mistaken." Elias drained his glass and rose. "Do not stay up for me, Henry. I am going to my club, so as not to notice the state of my wife's eyes, or anything else about her person."

Frowning, Henry watched his employer leave. Lord Westwood was clearly miserable. Lady Harriet was to blame, but Henry had decided not to hold that against her. The important thing was Lord Westwood's happiness. And since he had not been successful winning his wife over, Henry would have to help things along.

It would not be easy. Celestial's ginseng scheme had been well-meaning but flawed, no match for the earl's inestimable nose. His lordship was now wary of interference, so any plan would have to be brilliant.

What Henry knew about females would not have filled Heavenly's darning thimble. But he did know one aphrodisiac so powerful that poets had found in it the stuff of a thousand passions. Henry knew exactly how to make amends.

CHAPTER SEVENTEEN

"WHAT DID YOU wish to serve tonight, ma'am?"

Harriet looked up from her inspection of several tubs of sourdough culture. "I have given it no thought, Celestial. Prepare whatever you wish."

Celestial busied herself with the pantry. "Won't be as good as when you set the menu."

Other than this less-than-subtle reminder that Harriet was not herself, Celestial had been remarkably restrained in her comments. Harriet was grateful for the distraction of the Egyptian sourdough culture, bubbling away in a state of happy ferment. She had used it to mix a new dough and hoped this time the bread would be perfect.

But she was not really thinking about bread. All her thoughts were on Elias. He scarcely looked at her these days, whereas she found herself constantly staring at him, imagining his hands on her, caressing her.

Why had Freddy never touched her like that? She had begun to believe it was not her fault that he had not. After all, Elias desired her.

Did he still?

Why had he not come to her since their wedding?

In her room at night, Harriet stared at the door between their chambers, hearing him move around. She tried to imagine the precise moment in which he removed each piece of clothing. Did he wear a dressing gown, as Freddy had? Or did he sleep naked, stretching his long, muscled frame out on the bed like a lazy Greek god?

Sometimes she pictured herself undressing him, removing his jacket, his waistcoat, his shirt, his breeches, pulling him into the bed so she could make love to him. He would teach her how.

Now, at last, she knew the meaning of desire. She also knew she had never felt its like for Freddy. He had never sparked in her such feverish, uncontrollable passion. She wondered that Elias did not read the naked need on her face every time he looked at her.

How little she had known when she had forced him into that pretend betrothal. She had thought to understand the source of masculine power, to arm herself against it. Instead, that very power had overwhelmed her. The closer she got to it, the more she realized it was unfathomable, frightening, delicious. She no longer wished to shun it. She wanted to experience it in full measure.

What would happen if she went to Elias and confessed the truth — that she yearned for him but feared losing herself, the way she had lost herself with Freddy? Would he laugh in dismissal, as Freddy would have? Would he stare at her in puzzled disdain, the way her father had when she tried to tell him that she wanted more from life than their lonely existence in Cornwall? She was certain he would not. But neither could she imagine going to Elias and baring her soul in that way. No man had ever made her feel so vulnerable, so utterly at sea.

What had he once told her? That it was best to give in to turbulence, to move with it. But she was beset by so many emotions and fears that she felt as unsettled as that bubbling sourdough culture. To give in to them would mean losing all control. What then?

"A bracing cup of tea would be just the thing," she said to Celestial. "I wish you had not run out of that new blend. Can you get more?"

Celestial did not look up from the vegetables she was slicing. "The supplier is very unreliable."

Harriet dumped some flour onto her worktable. "Can you locate a new supplier? I thought it a very special blend."

Celestial put down her knife abruptly. "There is something about that tea you should know."

"Lord Westwood did not care for it, if that is what you mean," Harriet said quickly, "but that is no reason to stop ordering it." She did not really want to talk about the tea, but she could not stop herself. "A husband and wife may have different tastes. I am sure you and Horace do not agree on everything."

"No," Celestial agreed. "We do not."

Harriet turned the dough out onto the

worktable. She had always loved this stage, the pushing and kneading of the dough until it grew smooth and elastic and satisfying under her hands. But today the process did not give her the usual pleasure. Instead, she felt a sudden urge to cry. She bit her lip and gave the dough a particularly rough turn.

"I have always believed in tolerating differences," she said in a wobbly voice.

Celestial eyed her warily.

"I would not wish to impose my tastes on Lord Westwood," Harriet continued. "Toleration is important in all things." With that, she burst into tears.

"Ma'am, what is wrong?" Celestial moved to her side.

Blindly, Harriet reached for a cloth to wipe her eyes. She tried to smile. "What did you wish to tell me about the tea?"

"Nothing." Celestial gave her a hug so fierce it brought new tears to Harriet's eyes.

"Oh, Celestial!" she said tearfully. "I feel like the veriest fool."

"Now, now," Celestial murmured. "You need to get out for a bit, that's all. Horace is driving me to Kensington later to fetch Heavenly from Mrs. Thornton's. Won't you come with us? You might enjoy the drive. And Mrs. Thornton makes a delicious mutton pie."

"I….do not know." In truth, Harriet wanted nothing more at this moment than to leave this house, which was heavy with the tension between her and Elias.

"It's settled then," Celestial said firmly. "Now let's get to this bread. We will take Mrs. Thornton a loaf or two. It will be just the thing."

Harriet eyed the round ball of dough sitting placidly on the table, unoffended by the rough treatment she had administered. Few things in life were more profound than the way dough was transformed by the blows sustained during its short existence. Without such a transformation, there would be no bread. The process of change was good.

Unless one left the dough too long to its own devices. Then it would rise too much, and the loaf would lose its substance. Wiping away her tears, Harriet wondered whether her own nature had undergone a bit too much leavening.

"What is it, Henry?" Deciding not to pass another empty evening at his club in a futile attempt to assuage his restlessness, Elias had immersed himself in the paperwork on his desk. He did not welcome the interruption.

"There is a lady to see you," the batman replied.

Elias frowned. "I am not expecting anyone. Have Horace send the caller away."

"Horace and Celestial drove with Lady Harriet to Kensington to fetch Miss Heavenly."

Elias noted with mild interest Henry's continuing preference for formal address in referring to Heavenly. He was either afraid of the woman, or — but it did not seem likely there was an "or." His batman had a lifelong loathing of female relationships of any significance or duration. Elias returned his attention to the papers on his desk. "Then you must get rid of her," he said dismissively.

"What if I do not wish to leave?" purred a voice.

Startled, Elias looked up. Lady Caroline Forth stood at the threshold of his study, eyeing him in frank anticipation.

"Lady Forth." Elias rose, wondering how the devil Freddy's former mistress had found her way to his study. He turned to Henry, but the man had discreetly slipped away.

Moving gracefully into the room, she removed her cloak, revealing an azure blue gown that had as its most noticeable feature a deep décolletage. Shimmering diamonds adorned what, it must be acknowledged, was a flawless neck.

"I have been waiting for the opportunity to congratulate you on your marriage." She gave him a knowing smile. "When I learned that you were alone tonight, I knew that the timing was perfect."

Elias frowned. "How —"

"Pity that Harriet has left you to your own devices," she went on, pursing her lips in mock dismay. "Men must be carefully tended, especially in the early days of marriage when their needs are so...acute."

Slowly, she peeled off one white glove, then pointed delicately at the decanter on his desk. "May I?"

With a growing unease, Elias reached for a glass

and poured a splash of brandy. Instead of handing it to her, he merely left the glass on the edge of the desk for her to take.

She eyed him in reproach. "You do not join me?"

"I am working."

Choosing not to recognize the hint, Lady Forth took a delicate sip, shifting her shoulders slightly, with the result that her gown exposed rather more of the rise of her breasts than it had previously. To his consternation, she pulled a lacy handkerchief from her décolletage and laid it on his desk — as if it were a gauntlet. The amusement in her gaze barely veiled a deeper, predatory gleam. Indeed, she regarded him as if he were a well-seasoned pheasant she was about to bite into.

Elias did not even try to suppress his displeasure. With Henry conspicuous by his absence, the task of getting rid of her would fall to him. Elias hoped he would not need to physically remove her. Then again, the woman had no talent for subtlety.

"Let us not play games, my lord," she said softly, moving to stand before him, so close that he could have plucked the brandy glass from her hand. "I have thought of you constantly since that night at Lady Symington's. Before that unfortunate interruption, when —"

"Harriet tossed that tree at us," he finished. "Yes, I imagine you would remember that."

She smiled. "Harriet is a dear," she murmured, setting her glass down, "but there are things she does not understand."

Elias could barely stifle an urge to wring the woman's lovely neck. Harriet's intellect easily surpassed anything rattling around in Lady Forth's brainbox.

"Harriet does not understand a man's appetites," she said in a velvety voice, oblivious to his mood. "Can you honestly say that you are happy, my lord?"

To Elias's utter amazement, she caught his hand and boldly brought it to her breast.

"No," he growled, swiftly reclaiming his hand and balling it into a fist at his side.

"I thought not," she purred. "You do not appear to be happy. I can remedy that."

She'd misunderstood, of course. He was emphatically not happy at the moment, but that had everything to do with her brazen appropriation of his study and — from the predatory look in her eye — soon, his person, if he did not quickly rid himself of her.

She nodded sympathetically. "Freddy felt the same. It is fortunate that I am here, Elias. You do not mind that I call you Elias? I feel that we are… close."

He had the idle thought that Caroline Forth was just the sort of female to have appealed to him not so very long ago. But the time when he might have entered into a dalliance with her was long since passed. Only Harriet could assuage his unhappiness. Only Harriet could satisfy him.

"Lady Forth," he began, "I fear your visit is most inconvenient —"

"Caroline," she corrected in a husky voice

and captured his hand once more. This time, she refused to grant him his freedom. Instead, she slid his hand down her torso to her hip, lowered her lashes, and reached up to kiss him full on the mouth.

It was a kiss like those he had shared over the years with other women — flat, uninspiring, meaningless. Nothing like Harriet's kisses.

Now she pressed her body against his, intimately, and locked her arms around his neck. Elias reached behind him and wrenched her hands away. "Good God, woman," he swore. "What the devil are you about?"

"Now *that*, I think, is rather clear," came the brittle voice of his wife.

Over Lady Forth's shoulder, Elias saw Harriet, silhouetted in the doorway like an avenging angel.

In the next instant, she hurled something foul-smelling and sticky at them.

Lady Forth, who had her back to Harriet, turned just in time to have her lovely face, daring azure gown, and heaving bodice covered in thick, stinking muck.

"More effective than a rubber tree," her husband observed, his gaze flicking from Harriet to Caroline and back again.

Though the sourdough culture had spared him, Caroline was virtually covered in it. Harriet wished her aim had been better; she had intended to douse them both. Even now, with Caroline's lovely features obscured by fermenting ooze,

Harriet could not contain her rage. "How dare you?"

"Are you addressing me or Lady Forth?"To her astonishment, his eyes held amusement.

"Both of you," Harriet said evenly. "How dare you make love to that woman in my house!"

"*Our* house," he corrected. "Have you forgotten our marriage?"

"*You* seem to have forgotten it, sir. I should have known that you would be like...like —" Harriet found she could not continue.

"Freddy?" he offered in a dangerous tone.

"Yes!" Harriet's voice broke. "A faithless, feckless frog of a husband!"

A wail had begun to emerge from the figure whose lovely features were obscured by the thick white substance. The sound grew until at last it erupted in a loud, offended shriek. Harriet and Elias did not even look at her.

"A frog," he repeated. "Most unflattering."

"You had no right to bring her here!"

He arched a brow. "Quite right. Doubtless I should have kept her out of sight in our, er, trysting place."

Lady Forth wiped her face with the sleeve of her gown. "I demand a towel — this instant!"

"You had no right to a tryst," Harriet said. "You are my husband!"

"Do you not preach tolerance, madam?" he returned in an acid tone. "Indeed, I thought it a tenet of yours. That is how you buried your pain over Freddy's infidelities, was it not?" He took a step toward her. "But the pain did not go away, did it? Instead, it festered into a wound that could not heal."

"A towel!" Lady Forth shrieked.

"The only tenet I have at the moment is an abhorrence of unfaithful husbands," Harriet retorted. "Please leave. And take your mistress with you."

His jaw hardened. "Lady Forth got herself here. She can see herself home."

Caroline glared at him. "But you sent your carriage for me."

"What?" For the first time, he turned to her.

"Your note was so poetic," she said indignantly. "And you returned the handkerchief I gave you at the ball — the message was clear. But I should have known that you were only trifling with my feelings." Her wailing started anew. "I demand to be taken home!"

Harriet regarded him coldly. "Yes, do take her home, Elias. In your carriage. The one that you sent for her. Pity that the seats will be ruined by the mess." With that, she fled from the room.

Shortly afterward, Harriet heard the sound of carriage wheels on the drive. Elias was driving her home. Doubtless he would stay for hours, helping her cleanse her flawless body. Tears of hot anger spilled onto her cheeks. She could not block the image of what she had seen: his hands on Caroline's person, her lips on his.

Earlier, the drive to Kensington having improved her spirits immeasurably, Harriet had been delighted to learn from Henry that Elias was at home, instead of out at his club. She had thought about their marriage during the drive. He was right: She had burdened them with the legacy of her marriage to Freddy.

Perhaps they could start over, with the barriers gone. Wasn't that what he had said in Cornwall? That he wanted to start anew, with only honesty between them?

They had made a start, she realized. By giving her half of his business, Elias had tried to teach her about trust. Already, she had trusted him with her passion; he'd made her feel treasured, as if her passion were a rare and precious gift. Harriet saw that she had wronged him. He was not like Freddy. Elias would not hurt her. Had she but realized it, he had created a place of safety for her — within his arms.

Hopeful, even ebullient, Harriet had arrived at his study just in time to witness him caressing Caroline's breast and confessing to marital unhappiness.

Blind pain had driven her into the kitchen, where she had grabbed a tub of sourdough culture that had been bubbling away, unaware that it was fated to ruin the gown of one of the loveliest Cyprians in England.

Even now, Harriet still trembled. She dared not let go of her fury for fear that despair would overtake her.

An hour passed. Elias did not return. Not even Heavenly came to her, though the servants must have heard the commotion. She appreciated their discretion. She had no wish to face anyone. At midnight, Harriet heard Eustace come in and retire to his room.

She knew she could not stay here, waiting in vain for the man who had betrayed her, as she had waited so many nights for Freddy. Sleep was useless. At last, Harriet gathered a few things from her wardrobe, then slipped down the hall to Eustace's room. It took several knocks to rouse him, but finally he came to the door.

"Lady Harriet?" He sounded groggy, but his gaze sharpened the moment he saw her face. "What is wrong?"

"I need you, Eustace. You must take me home."

"Home?" He looked confused. "But, you are home."

"To Worthington. Tonight."

He stared at her.

"I cannot stay here," Harriet said. To her dismay, her voice broke. Eustace held the candle up to study her face. "Has he hurt you?" he demanded grimly. "Have I mistaken his character after all?"

"He did not —"

"I will call him out," Eustace vowed, "even if he is your husband."

Touched by his fierce concern, Harriet shook her head. "He has not abused me, Eustace, but I cannot stay here. Please. I need you to —" But she could not continue. Like a frightened child she threw herself into his arms.

"Oh, dear," Eustace murmured in bewilderment. "Oh, dear."

"Henry!" Elias bellowed, though it was past two o'clock in the morning and the house was dark except for the brace of candles in the foyer. It had taken forever to ferret out the truth behind Lady Forth's visit, for she had refused to speak with him until she had bathed and turned herself out in the style to which she was accustomed. He had spent more than two hours at her house, most of them waiting in the parlor for her to come downstairs in a white satin dressing gown that only served to infuriate him further.

His batman emerged from the shadows. "Yes, my lord?"

Elias pulled out a piece of paper and shook it in Henry's face. "You sent a note to Lady Forth in my name!"

"Aye, and that lace handkerchief you got from her the night of Lady Symington's ball." Henry grinned. "Effective, wasn't it?"

Elias regarded him in disbelief. He held the note up to the candlelight and read: "'When as in silks my Caroline goes, how sweetly flows that liquefaction of her clothes.'" He eyed Henry in disgust. "What revolting nonsense is that?"

Henry looked offended. "Herrick, my lord. The ladies love him. But 'tis the part about the kiss — 'Give me a kiss, and to that kiss a score; then to that twenty, add a hundred more' — that moves them beyond reason."

Dumbfounded, Elias stared at him. "Why in God's name did you do it?"

Henry took a step backward. "From what I saw — heard — of tonight's little tiff, my scheme to bring Lady Harriet around worked to perfection."

"Scheme? Explain yourself," Elias commanded.

"Old-fashioned jealousy, my lord — a better aphrodisiac than ginseng. Lady Harriet was as mad as a hornet — she was ready to drown Lady Forth in that stuff. My plan worked like a charm."

Elias took a deep, calming breath. "You sent flowery poetry and my carriage round to Lady Forth so that you could bring her here and make Lady Harriet jealous?"

Henry nodded, pleased at his employer's perceptiveness.

"And this jealousy was supposed to make Lady Harriet an amiable wife —"

"In every sense of the word." Henry shot him a knowing smile before he noticed the murderous rage in Elias's eyes. Instantly, he sobered.

"He should not have done it, your lordship," said a voice from the shadows.

"Not at all," agreed another.

"But he meant well," said a third.

Slowly, Elias turned.

"He only wanted your happiness," Heavenly said. At her side stood Celestial and Horace. "You cannot hold that against him."

"On the contrary," Elias said through gritted teeth. "I warned you, Henry: One day you would go too far."

"I think it worked," Heavenly added, approval plain on her face.

"You do?" Henry beamed.

Heavenly nodded, and her gaze was filled with

new respect for the batman. "First time I have ever known Miss Harriet to become enraged."

"A very good sign," agreed Celestial.

"Normally, the mistress is never overset," Horace said. "Though we never discuss such things, of course," he quickly added, giving his wife a stern look.

Elias stared at them. "I warned you, did I not? You have intruded in my personal life for the last time. The whole lot of you are discharged."

They regarded him solemnly. "Lady Harriet would not like that," Heavenly said.

"Not at all," Celestial added. Henry eyed Elias reproachfully. Even Horace shook his head. "Not the thing, my lord."

Elias did not trust himself to speak. He turned his back on them and started up the stairs to find Harriet. When he was halfway up the staircase, Heavenly called out to him.

"She is not here."

Elias froze. "What?"

"Left two hours ago with young Eustace," Horace confirmed.

"With Eustace?" Elias frowned. "Where the devil did they go?"

"To Worthington," said Henry.

"After what she saw, you could hardly expect her to stay here," Celestial said indignantly.

"What she saw," Elias growled, "was a figment of Henry's misguided, impoverished imagination."

Henry shook his head. "I only copied the poem and sent the carriage, my lord. You were the one who kissed the lady. Not much of a lady, though, now that I think on it."

Heavenly eyed Elias reproachfully. "As if Miss Harriet hadn't put up with enough from Lord Worthington."

Damn if he would explain himself to the servants, Elias thought. Anyway, he hadn't kissed Lady Forth — she'd kissed him. But he was hardly blameless, he realized. He should have tossed her out of his study immediately. Instead, he had let her throw herself at him. Why? Deep down, had he, too, hoped Harriet would discover them together? Had he, too, put a modicum of faith in jealousy?

Perhaps progress had been made after all, he mused. Harriet might have disclaimed malicious intent in toppling the rubber tree, but her purpose tonight in flinging that putrid mess at Lady Forth was clear. She had utterly abandoned tolerance. That was victory in itself.

"Have my carriage brought round," Elias ordered.

"Excellent decision, my lord." With a jaunty salute, Henry hurried off.

"We should come, too," Celestial said.

"Celestial!" Horace admonished.

"She may be right." Heavenly eyed Elias skeptically. "How do we know you won't botch this as well?"

Elias closed his eyes and prayed for patience. "You will remain here," he said evenly. "All of you."

"Yes, my lord," Horace assured him, his glare daring his wife to contradict him.

"I don't know..." Heavenly began.

"Heavenly!" Celestial said sharply. "Horace knows what is best."

The butler beamed.

CHAPTER EIGHTEEN

EUSTACE HAD WANTED to take her to Monica's cottage, but Harriet would not hear of it. She had lived at Worthington Hall for years. She was comfortable here.

Or so she had thought. They had arrived just before three o'clock in the morning, but though she was exhausted, the bed in her room was not as comfortable as she remembered. The house itself seemed empty. The few servants who remained when she removed to London treated her with eager deference, even though her arrival had roused them from their beds. Heavenly would have given her an earful of complaints for interrupting her sleep. Harriet missed her cheering, intrusive familiarity.

Tossing and turning in that lonely bed, Harriet found her thoughts wandering painfully to Elias. She could not bear to think of him sharing the same intimacies with Caroline that had made her own body sing with pleasure. His dalliance had hurt her in a way that Freddy's philandering had not, because she had dared to believe in Elias's promises. *I would never betray you.*

Instead, her worst fears had come true. He had

hurt her beyond all measure. The armor she had sought, that which was to protect her from such pain, had eluded her. Perhaps there was no armor that could shield a heart. But how, she wondered, would she go on from here?

It was not even dawn. She had scarcely slept, but she was tired of lying in an empty bed, envisioning Caroline and Elias together. Abruptly, Harriet sat up. She would not become a helpless, lovesick woman. She had her own life, her own interests. She would carry on.

Dressing quickly, Harriet marched out to the stables. A sleepy stable boy stumbled from the tack room, but she waved him back to his bed. She harnessed her dappled gray to the gig and drove down to the village. It was Sunday, far too early for anyone to be about. She would have the shop to herself.

Making bread always calmed her. A woman at one with her dough had no reason to want for anything else. Bread was satisfying, reliable, faithful. Harriet did not even bother to measure the flour and water; her eyes and hands told her all she needed to know. Soon the dough was ready for kneading. She spread flour over the worktable.

And tried not to cry.

Dough was just flour and water and yeast, after all. It could not fill her heart. Staring at the long oak table she'd been so proud of — but which now seemed merely plain and ordinary — Harriet felt the emptiness of years spent denying her feelings. She had pretended not to care that

Freddy betrayed her. She could never do that with Elias.

Defeat sapped her spirit. The work that had fulfilled her seemed desolate and solitary now. Loaves of bread would not give meaning to her life, despite what her bakery sign said. And although the sky had begun to lighten, Harriet's heart felt as heavy as lead. Dawn would give way to morning, and another day would lie endlessly ahead. Her little bake shop no longer held much appeal.

With a sigh, Harriet pushed a strand of hair back from her face, dipped her hands in flour, and resolutely reached for the dough.

Suddenly, the door swept open. A tall figure ducked under the top of the door frame.

"Elias!" Harriet had forgotten how his size overwhelmed her little shop.

He regarded her silently. And in that long, still moment between them, Harriet felt her world shift anew. "Why…why are you here?" she managed. "What do you want?"

"Whatever you are making," he said softly, and closed the door behind him.

Harriet tried to remember how to breathe. Her entire existence was suddenly contained in that dark gaze. Staring at him — *her husband* — she found it impossible to banish a small, treacherous hope. But he had betrayed her. Had she learned nothing from five years of marriage to Freddy?

In two steps, he was at her side.

Defiantly, Harriet glared at him. "I shall not take you back, my lord." Even as she issued that declaration, her eyes drank in new details: his tousled hair, his rumpled clothes, the circles under his eyes — had the man not slept? Had he come to her straight from Caroline's bed?

"You do not intend to share me with Lady Forth?" He regarded her intently.

"Caroline is welcome to you." Harriet hoped he did not hear the lie in her voice. "I shall not tolerate a husband who plays me false."

A burning intensity flickered in his gaze, but it was soon replaced by a strange, almost preternatural calm. "You have decided to throw the bounder out, then?"

"Yes." Staring into that suddenly tranquil gaze, Harriet thought her heart might break.

He studied her for a long moment. Harriet wanted to look away, but she could not. Almost, she could imagine that he —

"I love you, Harriet."

Harriet stared at him. Had he truly spoken or was that her own brain giving voice to foolish dreams? She willed her wildly beating heart to calm. "You cannot love me, my lord, or you would not have played me false."

"I did not play you false."

Now she did turn away, unwilling to let him see the hope on her face.

"Henry sent a note to Lady Forth in my name," he said quietly. "He sent my carriage for her. He was trying to make you jealous."

Jealous? She had never been subject to that corrosive emotion. The notion was laughable. But the laughter on her lips died as Harriet realized how thoroughly she had deluded herself.

"Encroaching of him, to be sure," he continued, "but our sleeping arrangements have not escaped the servants' notice. He meant well. Henry did not know that you were so exceedingly tolerant as to be immune to jealousy."

He paused for a heartbeat. "I suppose I should thank him for helping me discover that you are not, after all. Tolerant, that is."

"I do not believe you." Harriet stared resolutely at the table — anywhere but at him. "I saw you together."

His fingertip brushed her cheek. "And you are certain of what you saw, are you not? Do you not think I have better taste than to willingly cavort with Caroline Forth in our house — or anywhere?"

Harriet tried to block out the tender note in his voice that made her heart stand still. "I…I do not know."

"And yet, I recall a similar situation, when you and Oliver Hunt —"

"Stop!" she said, covering her ears.

Gently, he pulled her hands away. "Look at me, Harriet, and know the truth."

At last, Harriet did look. She saw the pain in those dark depths, and — wonder of wonders — it mirrored her own.

"I did not kiss her," he said. "Not willingly, anyway. It was she who pressed herself on me. But I was not blameless. I should have tossed her out the moment she presented herself in my study."

His gaze burned into hers. "I love you, Harriet. There is no one else. There never will be."

The well of emotions that had bubbled within her would no longer be contained. With a cry, Harriet launched herself at him, flailing at his chest, unleashing the helpless fury that years of a loveless, faithless marriage and self-delusion had wrought. He did not stop her blows, even when her flour-covered hands ruined his coat.

It was that silent stoicism which undid her. At last, Harriet covered her face and sobbed.

Instantly, his arms went around her. "It is all right, my love," he murmured.

She looked up at him, ashamed of her weakness. "I have never felt this way."

"It is because I hurt you." He kissed her ear. "I am sorry —"

"*Freddy* hurt me," she said fiercely. "You are not Freddy."

He captured her hand and brought it to his lips, then slowly kissed each fingertip. "I have been waiting for what seems a lifetime to hear you say that."

"I should die a thousand times over if you so much as look at Caroline Forth again," she vowed. "I will never, ever share you, Elias. You must not think that I will."

"On that we agree."

But as he bent to claim her mouth, Harriet put a fingertip up to stop him. "What of the things on which we disagree? I do not know if I can be the wife you —"

"You need never be anyone but yourself." His arms slipped around her.

"My salons —"

"I cannot promise to like them," he murmured, nibbling at her ear. "But I will try not to ruin them."

Harriet tried to ignore the warmth licking at her insides. "And the bakery? Do you still regard it as unseemly?"

His gaze flicked over the flour-covered worktable, then back to her. "I believe my attitude toward the bakery is undergoing a radical change."

With that, he put his hands around her waist and lifted her onto the table. Harriet trembled — anticipating his embrace, wanting nothing so much as his all-consuming passion.

But when she reached for him, he did not come to her. Instead, he took a step back, his expression suddenly remote. His arms hung still and lifeless at his sides. They did not reach for her.

Did he have second thoughts? What if he did not wish to be saddled with a woman who held salons with people he loathed? But no — he had said he loved her. He had not stated any conditions or doubts. Why, then, this pulling away? Did he not know that she burned for him? That she could not live without him?

No.

He did not know, Harriet realized. She had never acknowledged what was between them, not even to herself.

Perhaps one day you will come to feel that there are

passions worth fighting for. She had not known at the time what he'd meant.

She knew now. Her heart did not belong in the shadows, hidden from all possibility of pain. She must lay it before him, whatever the risks.

"Elias…" She hesitated.

He stood motionless, physically within her reach, yet somehow far away.

"I have been afraid," she said. "I did not know how to trust anyone —"

"Not anyone," he growled. "*Me.*"

"Yes," she agreed shyly. "You taught me about trust…and other things."

"What things, Harriet?" he said softly, his dark eyes holding hers. "I want to hear them."

Harriet felt her face flame. "I had never been touched like that before, Elias. It frightened me at first, but you gave me courage."

"You found your own courage."

"From you," she said. "I…had erected barriers."

"A veritable fortress," he confirmed. "With iron spikes atop the walls, and a fearsome dragon to guard the gates. I would kill Freddy for that if he were not already dead."

His jaw tightened. "Trust, touch — essential, to be sure. But not enough, Harriet. Not for me." His gaze locked with hers. "I want everything. *All.*"

"You have it," she said simply. "You are my life, Elias."

His fingertip touched her chin, tilting it upward. "Words — I want the words, Harriet. I know you have the courage."

Tears came to her eyes. She did not pretend to misunderstand. "I love you, Elias." Her voice broke. "But I do not know how to go about it, exactly. I fear —"

The rest was lost as his mouth covered hers.

And with that kiss, he took her fear and banished it. He took her need, her longing, her love — and returned it to her tenfold. Harriet could only cling to him in wonder as her heart knew him fully at last. She did not care that they were in her bake shop, or that she was on a flour-covered worktable. There was only this man, gifted with every sensual appetite, looking at her with fire in his eyes.

"There is flour everywhere," he said in a ragged voice. "Should you mind?"

"I am accustomed to flour," Harriet said. "'Tis quite all right."

"Trust me, love," he growled. "It will be better than all right."

"I do, Elias," she whispered. "I do trust you."

The sun rose over the village, shooting joyous rays through the window and bathing them in its blessed light. Harriet and Elias made love on the flour-covered table, and it was better than all right.

EPILOGUE

"**T**OLD YOU EVERYTHING would turn out for the best," Celestial said. "With Miss Harriet's way with food and Lord Westwood's — what is that word you used, Horace?"

"Olfactory," the butler pronounced.

"His olfactory skills," she continued, "their business will be a great success."

Heavenly frowned. "I don't know if I want to travel all that distance. Jamaica is such a far place."

"Nonsense." Celestial pulled a loaf of bread from the oven and turned it out on the table to cool. "You will love it there. With Miss Harriet's baby due soon, they will need you more than ever. Besides — if the duke can make the journey, anyone can."

Heavenly regarded her sister uncertainly. "It would be better if you were going."

"I shall miss you, dear, but in my condition, I cannot travel. Dr. Stinton says I may be carrying twins. Besides, Horace rather likes Worthington. And someone must keep the bakery going until Lady Harriet returns."

"Mrs. Tanks — Gibbs could do so," Heavenly

pointed out. "Now that Eustace and the children are helping with the mill, she has more time."

"Mrs. Gibbs does not understand dough," Celestial replied. "Cheer up, sister. You will have Henry to keep you company."

Blushing, Heavenly looked away. "I cannot imagine traveling such a long distance with that infuriating man."

"Henry's heart is in the right place," Celestial said, "but he has a lifetime of bachelorhood to overcome. I would not be surprised if a long sea voyage is just the thing for that. Take this." Celestial set a small vial on the table.

"Celestial," Horace warned, "you are not to interfere in that man's life."

"What is it?" Heavenly stared at the little bottle.

"Ginseng." Celestial gave her a sly smile.

Heavenly lifted her chin. "If a man doesn't want me on his own, I'm not going to slip something in his ale to change his mind."

"It is not for Henry," Celestial replied. "I have little doubt where his inclinations lie. It is for you."

"What?"

Celestial sighed. "If anyone needs a nudge, 'tis you, sister. He won't approach you on his own; he's too proud — and wary."

Horace nodded. "Man won't venture down an unfamiliar road when it's strewn with thorns that could tear him apart."

"Thorns?" Heavenly drew herself up. "There is nothing thorny about me."

Celestial and Horace exchanged a glance.

Heavenly stared at the little bottle of ginseng. She'd never had much faith in Celestial's quackery, but her sister was right about one thing: Henry had been on her mind. But she also knew he would never approach her.

It would have to be up to her. And she was not one to rely on false courage. Eyeing the bottle disdainfully, Heavenly left it on the table and strode out of the kitchen.

They stared after her. "What do you think will happen?" Horace asked.

"What will," Celestial said. She handed him a piece of the freshly baked bread. "Try Miss Harriet's new sourdough."

Horace took a bite. "Excellent," he acknowledged.

"'Tis better than that, dear." Celestial grinned. "It is perfect."

AUTHOR'S NOTE

STRICTLY SPEAKING, HARRIET did not invent napoleons. (But you knew that.) Some food historians think the pastry was named not for Napoleon Bonaparte but for Italy's famed Neapolitan bakers. The confection itself is indisputably French, however. As far back as 1758, a Frenchman published a recipe for *mille-feuille* — a thousand leaves — a sweet, brittle cake with five or six layers of puff pastry and pastry cream.

Which is exactly how Harriet envisioned them. If you have a mind to try making them, read on.

Recipe

Napoleons

Making puff pastry is labor-intensive. The dough is rolled out, folded around cold butter, then rolled and folded and turned — and that is repeated many times.

But for this recipe, simply buy a box of frozen puff pastry and proceed as follows:

DOUGH:
1 package puff pastry, thawed

PASTRY CREAM:
4 large egg yolks
¼ cup cornstarch
2 cups whole milk
½ cup sugar
2 teaspoons vanilla extract
¼ teaspoon salt
2 tablespoons butter, diced

ICING/GLAZE:
1 cup powdered (confectioners) sugar
2 teaspoons corn syrup
2 tablespoons unsalted butter, melted
2 tablespoons milk, more as needed
1 tablespoon unsweetened cocoa powder

DIRECTIONS:

Prepare pastry cream: Whisk egg yolks and cornstarch together until well-combined. Set aside. In a medium saucepan, heat milk, sugar, vanilla and salt until simmering. Slowly add heated milk mixture to the egg yolks, ½ cup at a time. Whisk constantly so the egg yolks do not curdle. When the milk mixture has been completely incorporated into the egg mixture, return the mixture to the saucepan. Cook over medium heat, whisking, for another 2-3 minutes, or until mixture is thick and bubbly. Remove from heat and whisk in diced butter. Put the pastry cream in a bowl, cover with plastic wrap, and refrigerate for 2 hours, or overnight. (Plastic wrap must touch the surface of the pastry cream so it doesn't form a skin.)

Prepare puff pastry: Cut a piece of parchment paper as large as the baking sheet you will use. Lightly flour the parchment paper. Roll out each sheet of thawed puff pastry until it's about 12 x 12 inches square. Using a pizza wheel, cut the square into three 12 x 4 inch strips. Cut each of those strips into three or four pieces, depending on how big you want your napoleons. (Alternatively, you can bake the 12 x 4 inch strips, then cut into smaller pieces with a serrated knife after baking. Whichever method you use, cut *before* assembling.) Prick the dough all over with a fork. Put the parchment paper and pastry strips onto baking sheets and refrigerate for 30 minutes, or until firm.

Preheat oven to 375°. Take baking sheets with pastry out of refrigerator. Put parchment paper on top of the pastry strips and set another baking sheet on top of that. Bake until pastry begins to turn brown, 10-15 minutes. Remove baking sheet and parchment from top of pastry. Bake, uncovered, until pastry is golden brown, 6-8 minutes more. Set aside to cool. Repeat process with remaining 1 sheet puff pastry.

Prepare glaze: In a medium-sized bowl, whisk together powdered sugar, corn syrup, and melted butter. Add milk, 1 tablespoon at a time, until you reach a consistency that is pourable, but still thick. Transfer ¼ of the glaze to a separate bowl and whisk in cocoa powder to create the chocolate glaze. (You may need to add a bit more milk to the chocolate mixture.) Spoon the chocolate glaze into a piping bag fitted with a small round tip or a freezer bag with the tip cut off.

Assemble: Take one of the cooled pastry strips and flip it over. Spread white glaze over the surface of the strip. Pipe two lines of chocolate glaze lengthwise across the pastry strip. Drag a toothpick horizontally across the chocolate glaze to create a pattern. Alternate the direction you drag the toothpick in each line.

Remove chilled pastry cream from fridge. Spread some evenly over one puff pastry strip. Top with the second puff pastry strip, pressing to adhere. Spread more pastry cream over this strip. Top with the glazed puff pastry strip.

Refrigerate for 1 hour to let it set. Some people then slice and serve, but slicing through these after they are assembled can be challenging. Store in refrigerator in airtight container for up to 3 days. Makes about a dozen.

ABOUT THE AUTHOR

EILEEN PUTMAN'S LOVE of England's Regency period has inspired her research trips to Britain, Ireland, France and other countries — there being no substitute for stepping on the soil that Beau Brummell and his champagne-polished Hessians once trod.

She's also a dedicated baker.

www.eileenputman.com

ABOUT THE LOVE IN DISGUISE SERIES

IN THESE TALES of Regency intrigue, nothing is as it seems: A street wench masquerades as a debutante to fulfill a rake's wager; an actress pretends to be a vengeful lord's mistress to catch a killer. A noble war hero disguises himself as a much older man to woo an on-the-shelf spinster. An independent widow forces her disapproving business partner to pretend to be her fiancé — and teach her about passion.

All are daring masquerades, with love is the prize.

THE BOOKS:

The Perfect Bride

Firmly on the shelf, Amanda Fitzhugh is far too levelheaded to again fall for any man's seductive promises and caresses. She had been down that road before and was lucky to escape with her reputation intact. She's content to chaperon her young cousin's come-out and betrothal to Simon Hannibal Thornton, one of England's most esteemed war heroes, now Lord Sommersby.

But when the iron-willed earl with a haunted castle turns his soldierly skills from winning a bride to conquering her companion, Amanda

discovers her own heart in mortal danger amid the ghosts of passion.

The Dastardly Duke

Tormented by a dark secret, Julian LeFevre, Duke of Claridge, is a notorious and dissolute rake. His half-hearted attempt to reform his character has left him bored to death. To relieve the tedium, he wagers a friend that he can mold any pretty trollop from the London streets into a lady who'll pass muster with society's elite.

But Hannah Gregory is no biddable lump of clay. She has solemn gray eyes, a rebellious streak — and is deaf from a long-ago accident. And although she conceals her real past, she can't conceal her attraction to the scoundrel who offers her a small fortune that could pay for a new medical treatment.

The charade might heal her, but it also might break her heart—if she forgets that this dark and dangerous duke is well past the point of redemption.

A Passionate Performance

Lord Linton, a master of illusion as cunning as he is handsome, is out to capture his father's killer. Taking a page from the bard, he decides the play is the thing to catch the villain.

But when he hires an impoverished actress to masquerade as his mistress, even Linton cannot envision the extraordinary performance that awaits. A little magic and a lot of sparks catch this Regency couple unawares...

Reforming Harriet

Having weathered a philandering husband, Lady Harriet Worthington vows never to wed again. She is happily independent, having inherited her late husband's share of a spice company.

But Elias Westwood, her business partner, is at his wit's end. Lady Harriet has been selling off shares of the company, and he means to win them back.

Elias's extraordinary gifts of smell and taste — so useful in the spice trade — prove his Achilles's heel. He cannot resist her culinary creations — or her feminine charms. When she forces him into a daring masquerade, he certainly never plans on falling in love…

A preview of *The Perfect Bride*,
the first book in the series,
begins on the next page.

THE PERFECT BRIDE

CHAPTER ONE

Spring 1816

"My wig, Jeffers, if you please."

"The grey or the brown, major — er, my lord?"

"I believe I shall require the hoary privileges of age for this particular mission."

Jeffers nodded and carefully removed the grey wig from a stand on the massive oak chest. "Do you wish a mustache as well, my lord?"

There was a brief, contemplative silence from the figure in the large wing chair. "The cursed things are a nuisance," came the response, "but I should not care to chance exposure."

From a drawer, Jeffers removed a matching grey mustache that he proceeded to tame into a neat military style. When he offered it for inspection, his employer frowned.

"Too rigid. Something more casual, perhaps with a bit of a droop to gain the young lady's sympathy. I mean to disarm the target, Jeffers, not frighten her."

The batman smoothed the mustache into a less

prepossessing appendage and was rewarded with a nod from the figure in the chair.

"Perfect."

Jeffers preened under the compliment. The man who had commanded his loyalty and service for half a decade dispensed few enough of those.

"Did you procure the clothing?" his employer demanded in the deep baritone that had compelled instant attention on the battlefield.

Jeffers opened the mahogany wardrobe and removed a pair of trousers, waistcoat, and jacket. The frayed edges of the dimity twill betrayed its years, but the suit was impeccably clean.

With a critical eye, the figure in the chair studied the costume. "Where did you obtain it?"

"From an impoverished bank clerk who was only too happy to have the fifty pounds."

A rare smile spread over uncompromising features that had consigned many a foe to his doom. "I cannot imagine how I devised my disguises without your assistance in the early years of the war."

"It was my good fortune that our paths crossed, sir — my lord," Jeffers insisted, flushing with pleasure.

"Nonsense." Briskly dismissive, his employer dispensed with Jeffers's heartfelt declaration. "You would have bested that French bastard eventually. I merely hastened his demise."

Jeffers kept silent, knowing that above all things, his employer disliked praise. Still, nothing would ever persuade the scrawny batman he could have defeated the Frenchman who weighed nearly twenty stone and who ambushed him that day near Bayonne. Fortunately, the tattered "beggar" who had come along as Jeffers made his last prayers possessed extraordinary fighting skills. The French soldier breathed his last in the pauper's lethal embrace.

A rustling of paper from the wing chair indicated that his employer's attention had moved on to other things. "Three names. That is the best you could do?"

Jeffers bowed. "Your requirements were exceedingly stringent, my lord."

A mercurial gaze held his. "You believe I demand too much from my future bride?"

Jeffers took note of the warning tone. "It is not my position to express such a view."

"But it is your opinion, is it not?"

The batman had long ago learned that a strategic retreat could be more valuable than a frontal assault when dealing with his employer's unyielding nature. Silently he returned the worn suit to the wardrobe, making a great show of arranging the garment so as to avoid wrinkling it. Reaching for a polishing cloth, he donned a preoccupied air as he rubbed the ancient suit of armor that stood next to the wardrobe as if in a constant state of battle readiness.

An impatient sigh filled the chamber. "Your silence does not fool me, man. I know what you think of my methods."

Jeffers stared at the ancient broadsword that hung on the wall along with all manner of fighting implements. "I merely find them...methodical, my lord," he replied carefully.

"Method has served me well enough in the trenches and out of them," came the brisk reply. "I defy you to think of a better way to select a bride."

Jeffers cleared his throat. "Some allow the heart to be their guide," he ventured.

"The same people who marry in haste and repent in leisure, no doubt," scoffed his employer. "I do not think it is the heart that guides them as much as another part of their anatomy."

Jeffers bowed. "As you say, my lord."

"Enough of this idle chitchat."

"How do you mean to begin?"

"As with any mission, Jeffers," came the impatient response. "Reconnoiter and reconnaissance. A wife is no different from an enemy target. Both must be chosen carefully and taken from a position of strength."

"Yes, my lord." As his gaze settled on a particularly lethal-looking cudgel from the twelfth century, Jeffers cringed.

⚬⚬⚬

"What a masterful figure! It is too bad you did not have more of his gumption, Edward."

"You know that Edward has not spoken to us in nearly five hundred years, my dear."

"Hmmph. He always could hold a grudge."

"Be reasonable, Isabella. We had him deposed. And roasted alive."

"I still say five hundred years is too long to nurse a grudge. It gets lonely up here."

A hurt silence followed this remark. "You used to say that I was all you needed, Isabella."

"After five hundred years, even your presence becomes wearing, Mortimer. I need something to occupy my time."

"Time is meaningless when one has eternity to atone for one's sins."

"But do you not see, Mortimer? Time is all we have."

"What are you planning, Isabella?"

"We must do something about our tenant. He is missing the passion to which he is entitled in his lifetime."

"I would prefer not to get involved, if you do not mind."

"But I do mind, Mortimer. Our hearts have always beaten as one, have they not? Or so you always said."

"Yes, Isabella. That is what I have always said."

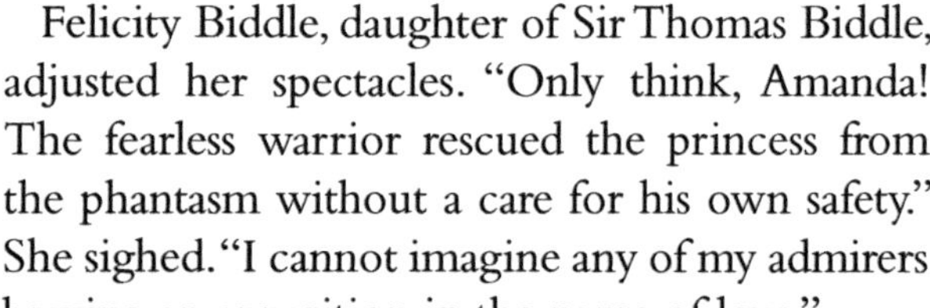

Felicity Biddle, daughter of Sir Thomas Biddle, adjusted her spectacles. "Only think, Amanda! The fearless warrior rescued the princess from the phantasm without a care for his own safety." She sighed. "I cannot imagine any of my admirers braving an apparition in the name of love."

Amanda Fitzhugh regarded her young cousin with a critical eye. "Since phantasms exist only in your exceedingly fertile imagination, it is not

necessary to put any prospective suitor to such a ridiculous test."

Felicity pursed her heart-shaped mouth, which had already provoked several eager young swains into declaring undying love. "You would rob the fairies of their fairy dust, Amanda. Is there not a fanciful bone in your body?"

"No more than there are fairies." Amanda walked over to the hearth in the Biddles' parlor and briskly stirred the fire. "I have lived long enough to understand that fairy tales and dreams derive from wishes, not fact. I am most thankful for the exceedingly practical nature I have developed over the years."

Miss Biddle closed her book, put aside her spectacles, and studied her cousin with brilliant violet eyes that had captivated those same besotted suitors. "You speak as if you are past praying for, when you have but twenty-eight years. You are still a remarkably handsome woman, Amanda. You could have your pick of husbands."

"Only if they are doddering widowers with a clamoring brood to raise." Amanda shot her cousin a wry smile.

"Not so! Why Mr. Merson was most particular in his affections last year, and he is neither doddering nor a widower. I thought him quite appealing."

"He is a reprobate and lecher," Amanda declared bluntly. "You had best clean those spectacles of yours. They must be fogged to see so poorly."

Felicity gave her cousin a reproachful look. Her spectacles were the one aspect of her appearance that she fervently wished to change. Of what use was a pair of exquisite violet eyes if one must hide them behind thick spectacles? She never wore them in public. No lady could captivate a suitor if she could not bat her exceedingly long lashes without the obstruction of thick lenses.

"I only make the point that you would have been wed long ago if you had shown the slightest willingness to entertain offers," Felicity said. And perhaps wore something other than the high-necked frocks that discouraged all but the most determined suitor, she thought.

Amanda bestowed a tolerant smile on her young cousin. "I have no desire to wed, as you know. I could not be happier with my little spinster's cottage by the sea. I shall stand in for your mama this Season, see you happily betrothed, and then return as quickly as I can to Kent."

With a resigned sigh, Felicity shook her head. "I am sorry, Amanda. I have been insensitive. It is all because of that nasty Mr. LeFevre, is it not?"

This untoward statement brought a severe frown from her cousin. "I have long since forgotten about him," Amanda said briskly, "but since you raise the subject, there is no more apt example of how fanciful notions can lead one astray."

Felicity held her breath. Amanda had never spoken at length of the scandalous incident in her past, and she knew she had been wrong to mention it. But Amanda had evidently decided that a purpose was to be served by her cautionary tale, for she fixed Felicity with a stern eye.

"I was no more than a girl when I allowed myself to fall prey to a man I imagined to be the hero of my dreams. Instead, he proved to be a scoundrel of the worst sort, as everyone but me knew to begin with." Her lips thinned. "I wish I had had someone to warn me at the time, but I do not suppose I would have listened, any more than you are listening to me now."

Felicity blushed at her cousin's description of the scandal that had barely been avoided when Amanda had been discovered in the arms of the dastardly Mr. LeFevre on one of the darker paths at Vauxhall, her bodice askew and her skirts in disarray. Felicity could scarcely imagine that the unsentimental Amanda could have been carried away by anything as impractical as passion. Nevertheless, it seems she had.

Fortunately, it was Felicity's father — Amanda's uncle — who found her in the man's embrace, so the discovery went no further. Despite being heir to a dukedom, LeFevre was deemed so beyond redemption as to make a disastrous and totally unsuitable choice for a husband. Thus, Sir Thomas did not press the scoundrel to do the honorable thing and marry his niece. Amanda had abruptly ended what was otherwise a promising Season and beseeched her uncle to take her away to the country. In the eight years since, Amanda had retired to Kent, firmly closed the door on all prospective marriage offers, and become a relentlessly practical woman.

"I respect your opinion," Felicity replied, "but I could not live as you do. There is no harm in seeking a husband who inspires one's fancies."

"As Julian inspired mine," Amanda put in dryly. "Pray, consider the disaster it wrought."

"*Nearly* wrought." Felicity pouted. "And I am not you."

"No," Amanda agreed, laughing. "I am firmly on the shelf."

"By your own choice."

"Nonsense. I know my assets, or rather lack of them." Amanda smiled. "I am a long Meg, whereas you are charmingly petite. My eyes are ordinary brown; yours are violet jewels. My face is plain, and I have neither your delightful curls nor your angelic countenance. Your hair is the color of spun gold. Mine is rather like the dishwater the scullery maid throws out at the end of the day. I do not begrudge you your considerable assets, Felicity. Indeed, they would only prove an inconvenience for one bound to live alone for the rest of her life."

Felicity sighed. Her cousin was determined to don the oppressive mantle of old age long before she reached that deplorable state. Even though Amanda was past her first blushes, she was still quite attractive for a woman of twenty-eight, though her appearance would be much improved if she did not discipline her hair into such a severe knot. And since that long-ago indiscretion, Amanda had conducted herself with such modest propriety and decorum that Felicity's mother, Lady Biddle, suffered no qualms in charging Amanda with the responsibility for Felicity's come-out, although Sir Thomas had stroked his

chin thoughtfully before agreeing to the proposal.

Lady Biddle had brought out Felicity's five elder

sisters with stunning success, as all were married to men of wealth and title. Now, however, the prospect of another London Season seemed to weary her. When she tumbled from her horse and severely sprained her ankle a month before the start of the Season, Lady Biddle immediately — and rather happily, Felicity thought — summoned Amanda to step into the breach.

Delighted to have Amanda's company, Felicity nevertheless worried that her phlegmatic cousin might take her chaperon responsibilities so seriously as to depress the attentions of any true romantic. Amanda eschewed sentiment with such fervor that Felicity shuddered to think of the fate of any suitor who dared quote the poets or offer a fulsome compliment in her presence.

"Cheer up, dear." Amanda regarded her younger cousin affectionately. "I am not a dragon. I promise not to chase away any lovesick gentlemen. Unless," she added with mock severity, "they try to do battle with phantasms."

A vague image of a fearless warrior astride a white horse, churning up the dirt as he raced to Felicity's side, caused the younger woman to sigh wistfully.

Amanda's brow furrowed thoughtfully as, unbidden, an image appeared in her mind as well. It was of Julian LeFevre in all his satanic glory, looking down at her with gleaming midnight eyes that promised a wild paradise of sinful delights.

A shiver rippled through her, though the fire still blazed warmly in the hearth. Thank goodness she no longer believed in fairy tales.

His pitifully thin collar provided scant protection against the rain, but Major Simon Hannibal Thornton had never had the luxury of minding the elements. Downpours that had left his fellow soldiers shaking with cold and cursing the heavens had never affected him. He had simply slid under his clay-smeared blanket, made a pillow out of straw, and slept.

Rain was blessed, life-restoring, and it held off the battle to come. Better to sleep whole and miserable in a quagmire than to rot senseless under the sun in a field of broken bodies. It was what followed the rain one always had to watch out for.

A betrothal would likely follow this rain, a tedious foray into the frivolous world of the Marriage Mart with a woman he had not yet met. She would hold him accountable for her protection and happiness, and he would provide those things for her because that was what was expected.

But facing Napoleon and his entire Imperial Guard paled in comparison to this onerous duty of finding a wife.

Jeffers was partially to blame for his foul mood. The man had outdone himself in procuring a broken-down horse to fit Simon's masquerade. Surely even an earl's impoverished cousin could afford a better mount than this nag. The grey would not make Mayfield by dusk. Simon could not imagine that Sir Thomas would welcome the delay of his dinner.

The real cause of Simon's dour spirits, however, was the fact that his mission had suffered several setbacks.

Lady Serena Fielding had possessed considerable beauty, youth, and the requisite large family. Her reputation was spotless, her dowry considerable, her reading skills superb. But she had proven to be a snob. Though she had treated him with the respect due an earl's emissary, she did not trouble to hide her disdain at his frayed collar. He could have told her that it was not wealth or clothing that made a man, especially on the battlefield, but he elected not to bother. He would not spend the rest of his life with a woman unwilling to welcome a down-on-his-luck soldier for dinner. He crossed the Lady Serena off his list.

The Honorable Harriet Dunham had no such pretensions. She read voraciously and displayed an egalitarian spirit. Her birth and breeding were unexceptional, her dowry superb, and she possessed a sufficient number of siblings to raise no doubts as to the breeding abilities of her family tree. Even at nineteen, her looks had nothing to commend them, but she had a friendly smile and a way of engaging a man in conversation that made the time pass pleasantly.

She had, however, articulated the shocking view that a woman had no obligation to provide her husband with an heir and even hinted that intimate relations ought to be solely a matter of mutual pleasure. Simon did not hold with such radical notions, which he suspected were but an excuse for a roving eye. Nor would he suffer a woman who would shirk her breeding responsibilities.

That left only Miss Felicity Biddle. A baronet's daughter, she was the lowest-ranked candidate on his list, but her father possessed sufficient means as to guarantee a perfectly adequate dowry. Not that Simon needed the money; the earldom had brought him great wealth. But a woman's family ought to contribute to the marriage. It enforced the principles of duty and obligation, which had guided his undertakings on the field of battle and elsewhere.

Youth was on Miss Biddle's side — she was but eighteen. She had five sisters but no brothers, a fact that gave him pause. He wondered whether the Biddle women could only produce girls. That would not do, as he must have an heir. Still, she seemed the most tolerable of the three ladies whose names Jeffers's research had produced. If Miss Biddle were sufficiently biddable, he might take a calculated gamble on her ability to produce a son. When one scattered enough grapeshot, one was certain to hit the target.

Miss Biddle was said to be fond of literature, and although poetry bored him — he favored political treatises and military dispatches for his reading material — Simon was gratified to know that she understood the importance of reading and could see to the education of their children.

Sir Thomas had sent a letter welcoming Lord Sommersby's emissary and inviting him to stay at

Mayfield to discuss the potential suit and business matters that marriage to the earl would involve. The baronet was obviously inclined toward the alliance. If Miss Biddle proved adequate, the courtship could be conducted during the Season and a wedding held immediately after.

Simon's tedious mission would be accomplished with satisfying efficiency.

CHAPTER TWO

AMANDA STARED AT the man Sir Thomas introduced as Major Thornton, secretary and cousin to the Earl of Sommersby. An uncommonly tall figure in a worn and somewhat ill-fitting suit, he surely must be all of fifty, as his hair had gone completely grey and his mustache wore a tired droop. Mr. Thornton's jawline had held surprisingly firm for his years, however, and his keen gaze suggested his wits had lost nothing to age. The eyes themselves ran to neither blue nor green but seemed to change with the light. They radiated a coolly assessing air, and Amanda had the distinct impression that beneath Mr. Thornton's politely respectful exterior lurked a rather arrogant nature.

His proudly erect bearing seemed in keeping with a former military man now in the employ of an acclaimed war hero like the Earl of Sommersby. Were it not for his age, Mr. Thornton might still have been a soldier. His shoulders spanned the breadth of the doorway and appeared quite capable of bearing the entire weight of the door frame, if need be. Never once did he slump to accommodate Sir Thomas's diminutive form;

he was quite at ease towering over his host, as if there was nothing out of the ordinary about his proportions. Amanda wondered why a man of Lord Sommersby's wealth and fame did not pay his employees well enough to procure a decent suit. An imposing form like Mr. Thornton's demanded quality attire.

But of course, Amanda reminded herself, that was not her concern.

Mr. Thornton displayed no embarrassment at his frayed lapel and worn collar. Indeed, there was a subtle confidence about his demeanor, Amanda observed, as the party gathered in the drawing room after a late dinner. Moving with a grace and agility surprising in a man of his size and age, he surveyed the room with hawk-like eyes. And though he was clearly a man of lesser means, there was nothing subservient about his manner. Obviously, Mr. Thornton was a man to be relied upon. Amanda suspected that Lord Sommersby allowed his secretary a great deal of authority.

Lady Biddle's ankle was troubling her, and she retired early. Sir Thomas assisted her up the stairs, charging Felicity and Amanda to get to know Mr. Thornton, as they would be spending no small amount of time in his presence.

Her uncle's cryptic statement confirmed Amanda's suspicion that Sir Thomas favored a match between Felicity and the earl. Over dinner there had been talk of a visit to Sommersby Castle so that Felicity and Lord Sommersby could meet before the whirl of the Season began. That meant the Mayfield party would probably leave within a few days, as it was no inconsiderable distance from eastern Sussex to the western Dorset coast. Amanda never doubted that Mr. Thornton was quite capable of escorting them. The man exuded efficiency and leadership. Indeed, the only awkwardness he displayed came when Felicity, in high spirits over the prospect of meeting such a noted war hero as the earl, began to question him about his employer.

"Is it true that Lord Sommersby's brilliant distraction of French troops on the Peninsula enabled Wellington to win at Salamanca?" Felicity asked, her lovely face becomingly flushed in anticipation of hearing tales of the earl's cleverness.

Mr. Thornton stiffened. "Credit for the Peninsula strategy belongs to Wellington, of course."

Felicity's eyes grew dreamy. "But even Wellington accorded Lord Sommersby a hero, did he not?"

Shifting uncomfortably, Mr. Thornton regarded Felicity as if she had just said something extremely unpleasant. "The true heroes of that mission," he corrected, "were our navy and ships, which held their positions and forced the French to maintain a cordon defense around the entire perimeter of the Peninsula."

Felicity eyed him in confusion. She was not accustomed to being contradicted by any member of the male gender and, in any case, had not truly comprehended Mr. Thornton's explanation.

Amanda wondered why Mr. Thornton was so

reluctant to sing his employer's praises, which had already been trumpeted by Wellington himself and even the Prince. Still, his point was well-taken.

"Mr. Thornton means that the threat of sea landings forced the French to leave no area undefended, greatly diminishing the number of French troops left to fight in reserve," she told her cousin.

Felicity showed no interest in the finer points of military strategy and stifled a yawn. "I believe I will just fetch a shawl from my room," she said, and left.

Mr. Thornton shot Amanda a surprised look.

"You seem to grasp the principles of war, Miss Fitzhugh."

"My father fought on the Peninsula," Amanda said quietly. "I followed the events most avidly."

His eyes searched hers, and Amanda again noted their peculiar, changeable color — now more green than blue. They held a question, but he did not ask it. She readily comprehended the silent query, however, and his reluctance to pry caused him to rise in her estimation.

"He is buried at Busaco," she said.

"I am sorry." Was that compassion in his eyes?

"Thank you," she said. "Some people do not understand why I have so little enthusiasm for the celebrations that have overwhelmed England in recent months. Many families lost loved ones, of course, but I cannot bring myself to celebrate the end of something I wish had never begun."

He eyed her quizzically. "War is nothing to celebrate, to be sure. And yet, a nation must fight."

"Must it?" Amanda challenged. "I cannot see that the sacrifice of so many lives serves any purpose other than to forever separate them from their loved ones."

"Would you have handed the Continent to Napoleon, Miss Fitzhugh?" Beneath his neutral tone, Amanda sensed the accusation.

"It is one thing to defend one's home," she replied, "and quite another to cross the seas to interfere with a tyrant whose overweening confidence would have destroyed him eventually in any case."

This time there was no mistaking the disapproval in his eyes. "Surely you do not mock the sacrifice of thousands, madam." But though his words bore a sting, they were delivered in such an expressionless voice Amanda was seized by an urge to shake that implacable restraint.

"Not at all, sir." For once Amanda was glad of her height, which made it easier to stand up to Mr. Thornton's looming presence. "But I do not believe war serves any end except the causes of those who decree it. And while the soldier whose life is forfeit pays the price, the king and his minions see little change in their comfortable existences."

A silence ensued.

His expression betrayed nothing of the distaste she suspected he must feel. He merely studied her for a long moment. "There are those who would take such talk as treason," he said in such a quiet and unemotional tone that he might have made an idle comment about the weather.

"There are those who dismiss any opposing view as treason," Amanda replied, "though of course you are correct. Were I a man, I might have held forth in the taverns and meeting places and stirred the people with my seditious talk — and no doubt have been clapped in irons long ago. I suppose it is fortunate that I am a woman."

His brows rose. Oddly, they displayed no hint of the grey that had overtaken his hair. Amanda flushed in sudden embarrassment. She had spoken these thoughts to no one. Why had she blurted them out to a man who — given his employer — could have no sympathy for such a position?

But it was not his silent disapproval that made her uneasy. It was the clear gaze that, without seeming to move at all, studied her from head to toe.

If he was taking her measure as a female, he would find her wanting, of course. Surely he would not be so rude as to mention that she was uncommonly tall for a woman or that her features were not small and delicate like Felicity's. His eyes narrowed thoughtfully, and Amanda grew warm under his inspection. For all that he was old enough to be her father, Mr. Thornton did not possess a particularly fatherly air.

Though he made no comment, the prolonged silence between them was commentary enough. Amanda supposed she ought to steer the conversation into more amiable channels.

"I understand that we are to journey to

Sommersby together," she said politely, unable to bring herself to convey much enthusiasm over the prospect.

"It is a pity that Lady Biddle will be unable to come," he replied, accepting her change of subject with an equal lack of fervor, "but Sir Thomas appears to have every faith in your skills as a chaperon."

Despite his polite response, his cool tone suggested that he was wary of the suitability for the task of someone as heretical as Amanda. Amanda decided that anyone unwise enough to cross Mr. Thornton was to be pitied. On the other hand, she thought irritably, who was this tall stranger to judge her convictions?

"That is because I am known to be incorrigibly practical, Mr. Thornton," she replied evenly. "I am not one to be swayed by sentiment, nor do I scruple at plainspeaking. Ideal qualities for a chaperon, do you not agree?"

He did not reply.

"I fear I will not be counted a lively addition to the earl's gathering," she added, unable to keep a cross tone from her voice.

Something volatile flickered in his eyes before vanishing. "On the contrary, Miss Fitzhugh. A practical nature fares best at Sommersby Castle."

"Oh?" Amanda eyed him curiously.

"The castle is very old — rich with history, but plagued by a rather dark reputation. I have spent only a little time there, but —"

"Come, sir. People have reputations. Buildings merely have names," Amanda interjected.

He did not rise to the bait. "I merely suggest that Miss Biddle should be prepared."

"For what, pray? Is the place haunted?"

"Not at all." There was not even a glimmer of humor in his eyes. "But the castle is not in the best condition, and its reputation has made it difficult to secure servants. It seems that over the centuries, the castle's dungeons were responsible for a considerable decrease in the local population. Political disputes, I understand."

Had Mr. Thornton cast some sort of gauntlet before her?

"Fortunately, dark reputations do not frighten me, nor do I believe in ghosts," Amanda replied. "To be sure, Miss Biddle has a rather more fertile imagination, but I will be certain to keep her occupied with other matters. I trust the place is not unsafe?"

"You may count on the earl to see to your safety."

"I do not believe that answered my question, sir." Amanda wondered how she was going to stand two more minutes in this maddening man's company, much less two weeks at Sommersby Castle.

At that moment, Felicity returned with her shawl and insisted on taking the night air, the rain having stopped. Reaching for her own shawl, Amanda buoyed her spirits with the hope that Mr. Thornton would not find it necessary to remain at the castle during the whole of their visit.

Eager to take in the fresh scents of the newly

dampened garden, Felicity moved quickly out onto the terrace ahead of them, leaving Mr. Thornton little choice but to offer his arm to Amanda. Amanda placed her hand lightly on his sleeve, and was surprised at how solid and firm his arm felt. It was rather disconcerting to feel such strength in a man of his years.

"Is something wrong?" he asked.

Belatedly, Amanda realized she was staring at his arm.

"Not at all," she replied quickly. She allowed him to lead her toward the terrace, and his hand briefly touched her back as he propelled her out the door toward Felicity.

In the heavy air, laden with the sweet smells of the garden made more pungent by the recent shower, Amanda was rather acutely aware of his presence. She found herself wondering exactly how many years Mr. Thornton had on his plate and why a man of his age should provoke such a reaction.

Undoubtedly, she had been away from Kent too long.

———∞———

The Perfect Bride is available
in print and in digital for many formats.

Maitland's Rogues Series

Regency historical romances featuring Andrew Maitland's extraordinary group of daring rogues who worked clandestinely for England during the Napoleonic Wars. Hardened and deadly, they have no use for love—until it ensnares them…

King of Hearts
Lord Shallow
Lord Difficult

BOOKS BY EILEEN PUTMAN

HISTORICAL ROMANCE
Maitland's Rogues series:

King of Hearts
Lord Shallow
Lord Difficult

REGENCY ROMANCES
Love in Disguise series:

The Perfect Bride
The Dastardly Duke
A Passionate Performance
Reforming Harriet

https://www.eileenputman.com/